Mistletoe Cake Murder

The All-Day Breakfast Café Series by Lena Gregory

Scone Cold Killer

Murder Made to Order

A Cold Brew Killing

A Waffle Lot of Murder

Whole Latte Murder

Mistletoe Cake Murder

Mistletoe Cake Murder

All-Day Breakfast Café Mystery

Lena Gregory

LYRICAL UNDERGROUND
Kensington Publishing Corp.
www.kensingtonbooks.com

LYRICAL UNDERGROUND BOOKS are published by

Kensington Publishing Corp.
119 West 40th Street
New York, NY 10018

All Kensington titles, imprints, and distributed lines are available at special quantity discounts for bulk purchases for sales promotion, premiums, fund-raising, educational, or institutional use.

Special book excerpts or customized printings can also be created to fit specific needs. For details, write or phone the office of the Kensington Sales Manager: Kensington Publishing Corp., 119 West 40th Street, New York, NY 10018. Attn. Sales Department. Phone: 1-800-221-2647.

Lyrical Underground and Lyrical Underground logo Reg. US Pat. & TM Off.

First Electronic Edition: October 2021
ISBN: 978-1-5161-1047-6 (ebook)

First Print Edition: October 2021
ISBN: 978-1-5161-1050-6

Printed in the United States of America

All-Day Breakfast Café
Cast of Characters

Gia Morelli – Owner, All-Day Breakfast Café.

Thor – Gia's Bernese Mountain Dog.

Klondike – Gia's black and white kitten.

Savannah Mills – Gia's best friend, real estate agent.

Pepper – Savannah's gray and white tabby kitten.

Captain Hunter Quinn (Hunt) – Gia's sort-of boyfriend, Savannah's cousin, Captain, Boggy Creek Police Department.

Leo Dumont – Savannah's fiancé, Hunt's partner.

Harley Anderson – Gia's friend, homeless man.

Earl Dennison – Older man, Gia's first ever customer at the All-Day Breakfast Café.

Cole Barrister – Retired, full-time cook at All-Day Breakfast Café.

Trevor Barnes – Owner Storm Scoopers, ice cream parlor on Main Street.

Brandy – Trevor's German Shepherd.

Zeus and Ares – Trevor's guard dogs, Akitas.

Willow Broussard – All-Day Breakfast Café's full-time waitress.

Skyla Broussard – Willow's mother.

Zoe – Owner of the Doggie Daycare Center.

Donna Mae Parker – Harley's ex-girlfriend, flower shop owner.

Joey Mills – Savannah's youngest brother.

Michael Mills – Savannah's brother, works in construction.

James, Luke, and Ben Mills – Savannah's other brothers.

Cybil Devane – Mysterious older woman who often walks in the woods.

Chapter One

Savannah Mills drummed her glitter-tipped maroon nails against the gear shift of her blue Mustang convertible as she rounded one last curve on the way to Trevor Barnes's mansion, where she and Leo Dumont would be married in a little more than a week.

Few streetlights lined the dark road, casting small pools of light against the slick pavement, compliments of an unusually rainy day in the small town of Boggy Creek, Florida. Gia Morelli would have preferred to head out to the mansion before dark, but they had to wait until after she closed the All-Day Breakfast Café for the day.

Savannah shook her head, tumbling her long blonde hair into her face. She sighed and tucked the strands behind her ear before returning to nail tapping her staccato rhythm.

Gia laid a hand over hers, stilling the steady *rat-a-tat-tat*. "Will you relax. Everything's going to be perfect."

"I know." She glanced at Gia, her bottom lip caught between her teeth.

Gia just lifted a brow.

"All right, all right." Laughing, Savannah returned her attention to the road ahead. She rolled her shoulders, tilted her head from side to side. "Maybe I've been a little stressed lately."

Understatement of the year; better to keep that to herself. "Ya think?"

"Hey," Savannah pointed at her. "A good friend once told me no one likes a smart aleck."

Gia grinned. Nothing like having her own words thrown back at her.

As Savannah pulled into the cul-de-sac where Trevor's mansion stood at the far end, she slowed. Her mouth dropped open. "Oh, wow."

Long strands of evergreen garland, complete with pine cones and ivory bows, had been draped along the stone wall surrounding the grounds. The faux-snow covered garland twinkled with thousands of tiny clear Christmas lights, giving the impression of a winter wonderland, despite the ridiculously hot Florida weather of late. For just a moment, Gia could imagine the rain changing to fluffy white flakes that would bury the estate in rolling hills of snow.

Huge oak trees lined the inside of the wall, their moss draped limbs alight with lanterns that seemed to hover in mid-air, a welcoming invitation to crank up the air conditioning, grab a blanket, and snuggle up with a good book in front of one of the numerous fireplaces Trevor's mansion boasted.

"Wow," Gia repeated, not knowing what else to say.

Savannah stopped in front of the wrought iron gate and pushed a button on the remote Trevor had given her. As the gates slowly opened, she looked at Gia. "Trevor sure did go all-out."

"No kidding." Trevor's mansion and grounds were gorgeous on an average day, which was part of the reason Gia had wanted to hold Savannah's wedding there, but seeing it fully decorated for Christmas left Gia speechless.

"I feel like I'm at the North Pole, heading straight into Santa's castle." Savannah rolled through the gates and closed them behind her. "It's incredible."

"It sure is." The palm trees lining both sides of the driveway were strung with lights. Piles of boxes wrapped in pale pink and ivory paper with silver bows were piled beneath them. The fact that they hadn't turned to mush in the pounding rain told Gia they must be just decorative, made from some material that could withstand the elements, but they sure looked real.

"I can't believe Trevor did all of this for us." With her gaze darting everywhere, Savannah pulled into the circular courtyard and stopped in front of the house.

The gardens were transformed, glittering with lights and an abundance of poinsettias, evergreens, holly and other seasonal flowers that Trevor must have had added for the occasion. Icicle lights cascaded from the mansion's every roofline, peak and window. Warm light spilled out into the darkness from a towering Christmas tree standing sentinel in the center front windows.

"Did you know?" Savannah whispered.

Gia shook her head. Nothing she'd ever seen could have prepared her for the sheer wonder of Trevor's mansion ready to welcome guests for the holiday. Her own experience with Christmas was limited to a small tree she decorated in her room each year while she was growing up, then whatever business parties her ex-husband dragged her to so he could meet with his important clients, clients he'd later steal millions from. She shoved the thoughts away. No way would she allow anything to intrude on this moment. "I knew he was having the mansion decorated for Christmas, but I didn't expect all of this. I thought maybe some lights on the house and a Christmas tree."

Tears shimmered in Savannah's eyes.

"Hey, you okay?" Gia lay a hand on Savannah's shoulder.

She nodded. "I just can't believe he'd do this. How am I ever supposed to repay him for this? I can't even imagine what all of this must have cost."

"Don't worry about it." Trevor had adamantly refused any kind of payment for the use of his mansion as a venue, threating to revoke his offer if they even tried to insult him with payment, and now it seemed he'd gone way over the top with decorating. "Trevor seemed so happy and excited about doing it, so I'd say just be happy and grateful and enjoy it."

The front door opened, and Trevor ran toward them, umbrella held over his head.

Savannah wiped the tears that tipped over her lashes and spilled down her cheeks. She rolled the window down, and rain splashed into the car.

Trevor leaned in and blocked the window with his body and the umbrella.

Thor, Gia's Bernese Mountain Dog, barked in greeting from his spot in the back seat between Klondike and Pepper's carriers.

"Hey, Thor." Trevor reached behind Savannah to give his head a pat, then pointed toward the far end of the cobblestone courtyard. "I put you guys in the same suite you shared last time, and I had the canopy pulled out. I wanted to bring you in the front, so you could behold everything the way your guests will when they arrive, but I figure it's better to keep you dry. I hope that's okay?"

"It's perfect, Trevor, thank you," Savannah said.

He grinned and patted the window frame, then hurried ahead of them to the far side of the courtyard where a canvas canopy covered the entryway and the potty pavilion Thor would use.

Savannah shook her head, a brilliant smile lighting her face as she rolled up the window and followed Trevor. "The man thinks of everything."

"Hmm..." Gia had to admit, that thought was about as surprising as finding out her mild-mannered friend was a millionaire...at least. "Who'd have thought?"

"Not me," Savannah grinned, "that's for sure."

Even the potty pavilion was decorated for the occasion, with festive colored lights strung from every pine tree in the area.

Savannah parked right in front of the now covered archway and hopped out of the car without waiting for Trevor to come around with the umbrella. She ducked underneath and hugged him hard.

Gia climbed out and lifted the seat forward for Thor, who scrambled out and bolted straight for Trevor.

Knowing he would be safe with him, and that the potty pavilion—complete with cabinets, grooming area, and exercise equipment—was surrounded by a low stone wall, Gia leaned into the car to grab Klondike's carrier. "Hey there, sweetie. I'll have you out of here in no time, and you and your buddy can run and get into all the trouble you want."

The little black and white kitten abruptly turned around and flicked her tail against the mesh door of the carrier. Apparently, Gia would not be forgiven so easily for putting her in there.

She sighed and hauled her carrier and Pepper's out of the back seat.

"Here, let me take them." Trevor took one in each hand and gestured with his elbow toward the potty pavilion. "Thor went to take care of business."

Gia peeked in to check on him and laughed. "If by take care of business you mean run straight to the obstacle course on the opposite side of the pavilion to play on the doggie playground, then you're absolutely right."

"What can I say? I like to spoil my dogs." Trevor offered a sheepish smile and swung a lock of too-long-in-the-front brown hair out of his eyes, seemingly embarrassed at his wealth—typical for him. "And, hey, at least it's covered so he won't be soaked and full of mud."

The thought of Thor barreling through the house leaving a trail of sloppy footprints in his wake made her shiver. "That's definitely a plus."

"And he's having fun," Savannah piped in as she popped open the trunk.

"An even bigger plus." Gia started toward the trunk to help her grab their bags.

"Leave that for now." Trevor nodded toward the house. "We'll get it all after the rain stops. Come on; I can't wait to show you your rooms."

Savannah shrugged and slammed the trunk closed, then followed him down the hallway toward the two-bedroom suite she and Gia shared last time they stayed with Trevor, which had been for Savannah's protection.

Gia planned to spend a whole lot more time exploring this time than they had then.

Trevor chatted at warp speed as he strode down the long hallway. "Okay, so, you have a meeting with the caterer for tasting and final approval of the menu promptly at ten tomorrow morning, this way you can both take advantage of Cole, Willow, Earl, and Skyla opening the café tomorrow."

Gia could kiss his cheek. A day to sleep in with no problems nagging at her. Maybe she and Savannah would sit up late and watch an old movie together, share a bucket of popcorn. A small niggle of sadness crept in. Now that Savannah and Leo were getting married, she'd probably be moving out of Gia's spare bedroom. Not that she'd made any effort to find a place yet, so Gia was just assuming. After Savannah was kidnapped last summer while showing a house, Gia didn't want to be the one to bring up the subject. Savannah would talk about her decision when she felt ready.

Hmm...maybe Leo would move in with them? Still, even if he did, things between Savannah and Gia were sure to change. She shook off the thoughts. This was Savannah's time, her moment of happiness. No way would Gia ruin even an instant of it feeling sorry for herself.

"I've already taken care of adding the servers, I hope that's okay. And the florist will be here a little after three to coordinate where you want the flowers, at least the ones that go in the outer rooms and the reception area. You're not allowed to see the actual spot where you'll get married until you're ready to walk down the aisle." Trevor twisted to maneuver the cat carriers up the spiral staircase and onto the loft-style second floor.

Thor bounded after him.

Savannah and Gia followed on their heels.

"You've already spoken with the DJ, so he's set to go." When Trevor reached a set of French doors to their suite, he stopped and set the carriers down, then started ticking items off on his fingers. "You have a week and two days until the wedding, and you're both working until the day before, so I want to make sure you have plenty of time to relax."

Though Gia would have loved to close the café for the week, she just couldn't afford to, so she settled on closing Friday for the wedding and Saturday for Christmas. Even though she had been in Florida last Christmas, and had been welcomed at Savannah's house, everything had been too new for her to fully immerse herself in the celebration. This would be her first true Christmas with her new family, and Trevor had graciously offered to host it since everyone they loved would already be there for the wedding.

Trevor's voice dragged her back to the conversation. "That's why I stacked most of your appointments tomorrow, so you'll have time to rest afterward. Then, on Friday mid-morning, I have people coming to do mani-pedis and massages for the two of you and the bridesmaids."

Savannah laughed out loud.

"What?" Bright red patches crept up Trevor's cheeks. "Was that not right?"

"Are you kidding me?" Savannah flung her arms around his neck, hugged him tight, and planted a big kiss on his cheek. "It's perfect."

Trevor's face reddened to the point of almost purple, and Gia wasn't quite sure if it was from embarrassment or if Savannah was cutting off the circulation to his head. Thankfully, she released him before he passed out from either.

"Good, because the hair stylist will be here first thing Friday morning. Sorry I couldn't get it later in the day, but with Friday being Christmas Eve and all, it was the latest I could get him to come. It doesn't matter anyway, though, because the photographer will be here at eight a.m., so she can document every single minute of your special day."

Gia's mouth dropped open, and she quickly snapped it closed. No need to further embarrass Trevor after he'd not only taken care of every detail of the wedding, but also set up last minute appointments to go over everything and ensure it would all be perfect the day of.

Trevor finally stopped talking and took a breath, then glanced back and forth between them. "What? Did I forget something?"

Who'd have thought Trevor, her good-natured, easy-going, kind-of-goofy, totally clumsy friend would turn out to be an organizational genius? Then again, she'd never have expected the owner of Storm Scoopers, the ice cream parlor down the road from her All-Day Breakfast Café, would turn out to be the wealthy owner of a mansion and grounds the size of a city block back in Manhattan either. Seemed Mr. Barnes was full of surprises.

"It's perfect, Trevor, thank you." Gia hugged him, careful to do so a little less enthusiastically than Savannah had.

"Now that the details have all been discussed..." A smile spread across his face from ear to ear, and he shoved the French doors open and stepped back with a flourish. "Behold!"

A giant evergreen sat against the far wall between two windows, all aglitter in pink and silver, with a bride and groom locked in an embrace to top it off. A wreath hung above the fireplace, the mantle draped in garland and lights.

Gia's breath shot from her lungs.

"What?" Trevor asked. "Too much?"

"Not at all. It couldn't be more perfect." Tears shimmered, deepening the blue of Savannah's eyes.

Trevor squeezed her hand. "Good, because I went all out in the honeymoon suite too."

"The honey...?"

"Yup. You said you guys didn't want to leave on your honeymoon until the day after Christmas, so I set up a special suite for you and Leo to spend your wedding night and Christmas night."

Savannah just stood, hand in his, staring at him, tears spilling over and down her cheeks. That was a first, not that Gia could blame her, but in all the years she'd known Savannah, she'd never once seen her speechless.

Trevor rubbed a hand up and down her arm. "Thank you both for trusting me with this. I really enjoyed doing it, more than I can ever tell you, and I wanted to make it perfect."

"You definitely did, Trevor." Savannah sniffed. "I don't know how I can ever thank you."

"Are you kidding me? No thanks needed. I love planning events, but in case you haven't noticed, even though I have a number of friends, I'm a little socially awkward and uncomfortable outside of my immediate friendship zone. This was like a dream come true. I got to plan not only one, but three events, and I don't have to be the center of attention at any. You actually did me a favor."

"What do you mean three?" Though Gia and Savannah had helped plan the parts of the wedding that weren't meant to be a surprise right along with Trevor, she wasn't aware of any other events.

"The wedding, the rehearsal dinner, which is going to be awesome, and Christmas dinner. Thanks to you two, I will spend Christmas surrounded by my Boggy Creek family, something I'd never have done otherwise."

Gia gripped his free hand. When they'd discussed making Savannah's wedding as perfect as possible for her, especially when she was still somewhat fragile after everything she'd been through over the summer, Gia had never expected anything like this. "Thank you so much, Trevor."

"There's really no need to thank me." He turned to look her in the eye. "When I needed a friend, you were there for me. Now, it's my turn to be there for you and Savannah. Savannah needs to be surrounded by family in a place she feels safe, and you need a proper Christmas with family, something you said you've never had before. Now, we all have what we need."

Gia lay her head against his shoulder. If they could just get through the next week without anything going wrong, life would be just about perfect.

Chapter Two

Savannah pulled against the curb in front of the caterer, rolled down the windows, and turned off the car. "Trevor said promptly at ten, and that's not for about fifteen minutes yet. Do you want to go over the menu one last time?"

"Sure thing." They'd already reviewed the menu a dozen or so times, and that was just this morning, but it seemed to make Savannah feel calmer, so Gia agreed. "You do know you don't really need another tasting, right?"

Savannah nodded as she dug through her oversized gold tote bag. "But Trevor said Alyssa and Carlos had a few other couples coming in for tastings today, and they were making the food anyway, so we could give it all another try before making our final decision."

"Leo didn't want to come?"

Savannah peered up from her bag long enough to roll her eyes. "I'm lucky I got him to go with me the first time. Leo just wants to show up the day of and get married. If it was up to him, we'd have eloped and gotten married on a beach somewhere long before now."

A pang of regret that it wasn't up to him shot through Gia, immediately followed by a wave of guilt. This wedding was everything Savannah wanted...and more, but the stress it was causing her had Gia worried. It also had her wondering if there was more to her heightened anxiety of late, since Trevor had taken care of the bulk of the details. "So, did you decide on a chicken dish?"

"Well, I managed to eliminate one, but I'm still stuck between two."

Gia leaned over the center console to study the list Savannah finally pulled out of her bottomless bag. "Which two?"

"The Bruschetta Chicken, which I think will go really well with the pasta dish, or the Chicken Cordon Bleu, which…well…mmm."

"I agree, the Bruschetta Chicken will go great with the pasta. Plus, it's lighter, and you really do have a lot of food already." But she wasn't wrong, the Chicken Cordon Bleu was delicious. "You know, Trevor's having Carlos cook for the rehearsal dinner too, maybe you could do the Chicken Cordon Bleu for that."

"You know what?" She made a note on the page. "That's a great idea."

Gia sat back in her seat. "Good, we can let them know today, and that will be one less call Trevor has to make."

Savannah tapped her pen against her lips. "I almost feel bad doing that."

"Why?"

"I think Trevor might be disappointed."

"Hmm… You could be right." If not for how much Trevor loved owning his ice cream parlor and interacting with his customers, a lifelong dream come true for him, Gia would think he'd missed his calling as a wedding planner. "Maybe you'd better let him call."

"How about I give them a head's up that we're considering it but let Trevor make the official call."

"Sounds like a plan. Last I heard, he was supposed to go bungee jumping with Alyssa and Carlos tomorrow; he can tell them then." The thought of standing atop a platform, tethered by nothing but a rubber band wrapped around her ankle, and jumping off sent a wave of nausea crashing through her. "I don't know how Trevor does the things he does. Not that he's a thrill seeker, exactly, but he sure does love his outdoor activities. And he's good at all of them."

"I know, right?" Savannah agreed. "Especially when he's so clumsy he falls over his own feet just trying to walk."

Gia laughed. Savannah's assessment was spot on.

"Okay." Savannah tapped the pen against the list to point out each food item they'd already chosen. "We have to keep a seafood dish, since we're getting married on Christmas Eve, and some of our guests prefer to eat fish."

"Yes, and—"

The sound of a door slamming cut Gia off as a man let it drop behind him and strode from Rinaldi's Catering, then headed down the sidewalk straight toward them.

"Will you wait up, Isaac?" A plain looking woman, with mousy brown hair and red-rimmed eyes the color of mud hurried after him. "I don't understand why you have to do this?"

Isaac, who closely resembled the woman, though younger, stopped short, and the woman almost plowed into him. He whirled on her, and she stumbled back. "Why did you even want me here, Mom? It's not like Jeremy and I get along, or even like each other at all. Did you really expect this to go any differently?"

The woman folded her arms across her chest, her chin jutted forward defiantly. "I just don't understand why the two of you can't be nice to each other for one day to make it special for me."

"Because the man is a gold digger, only after you for your money. Dad would turn over in his grave if he knew you were going to marry that guy." Isaac threw his hands in the air and spun away from his mother.

"Isaac wait, please." She grabbed his arm.

His shoulders slumped as he sighed and turned back to her. "What?"

"You're wrong about him."

"No, I am not wrong about him. I already told you I caught him in a bar with another woman, Mom. Men who are engaged to women they love don't cheat on them."

"He wasn't cheating. I already told you he explained everything."

"Yeah, okay." Isaac scoffed and rolled his muddy brown eyes. "He was meeting with the caterer in a dark corner of a bar three towns over, with his arm slung around her shoulders and nibbling on her ear, to go over the menu."

"Will you quiet down? I already told you I talked to him about that. You just got the wrong impression. Now don't go causing trouble." The woman shot a glance over her shoulder before returning her attention to her son. "Please, come back inside. It's time to taste the cake."

He shook his head, then relented. "Fine, but only if you promise to nix the dishes he chose just because they're the most expensive items on the menu."

The woman nodded eagerly. "Sure, fine, I can do that."

"Whatever…" He started back toward the café at his mother's side, a huge rift—apparently both physical and emotional—between them. Gia couldn't hear any more of the conversation as they entered the shop and the door closed behind them.

Savannah glanced at Gia, then at the clock. "What do you think we should do?"

"I'm not sure. Trevor said promptly at ten, which it just about is." Gia squirmed in the soft leather seat. "But I don't want to intrude."

"Maybe we should wait a couple of minutes, give them a little time to get their acts together, then go on in," Savannah suggested.

"That works." Gia stared at the closed door. "Do you think the guy was talking about Alyssa Rinaldi?"

Savannah shrugged. "I don't know. It sure sounded like it, but his mom seemed to think he was way off base. I don't know the Rinaldis well, but the few times we've met with them, they seemed like a solid couple."

"Just to be on the safe side, better not repeat any of that to Trevor." The last thing she wanted to do was cause a problem between the couple a week before Christmas based on something that could be a complete misunderstanding. Hopefully, anyone else who might have overheard the conversation would feel the same.

"True. No sense spreading rumors that could ruin someone's reputation."

"Or cause a divorce." Gia pointed toward the list. "Now, what were you saying?"

"Oh, right, um… seafood."

Isaac ran back outside, unlocked a car out front, and leaned in the passenger side door. He straightened a moment later, pressed a phone against his ear, and talked to someone in a hushed voice Gia couldn't make out despite a concerted effort to eavesdrop. When he was done, he shoved the phone into his jeans pocket and looked around before hurrying back inside.

"He seems calmer." Savannah stuffed the list into her bag. "Think it's okay to go in now?"

"I don't see why not. It is a public place, after all, and we do have an appointment." But that didn't change the warning churning in her gut. She didn't have a good feeling about intruding on what was clearly some kind of family battle, especially if their caterer was somehow involved.

Savannah stared at the closed door, her lips pursed. "I feel so bad for her."

"Who? Alyssa?"

"No." Savannah gestured toward Rinaldi's. "The bride."

"Oh, yeah. I agree." Her son clearly had no use for his mother's choice of new husband. Gia only hoped his assessment was wrong, and the man wasn't marrying her for her money.

"Planning this wedding, even with the tremendous amount of work Trevor's done on it, even with your help and Leo's occasional input, has been stressful enough. Just hoping everything goes smoothly, and nothing gets forgotten or messed up somehow." Gia didn't bother adding she'd been more anxious in a general sense ever since being kidnapped.

"I can't even imagine what it would be like planning to marry someone my family hated."

"Well, that's definitely not something you have to worry about. Everyone I know loves Leo. And the man has been head-over-heels in love with you for like ever, even waited for you when you went to New York to pursue your dreams," Gia said.

"That's true all right." A smile shot across her face, and her eyes filled with joy. "I sure did find a good man."

Gia squeezed her hand. "You sure did. And if anyone I know deserves him, it's you."

Savannah took the key from the ignition, dropped the ring into her bag, and opened her door, then paused, still contemplating the front door the two had disappeared into. "I wonder what I would have done, though, if anyone in my family had hated him."

Gia grabbed her bag and rested her hand on the door handle but didn't open it. "I don't know what you'd have done, but I know what I did. I married Bradley when you despised him. And instead of beating me up over it, you gave me the space to make my own mistakes, then picked me up and helped me put my life back together without so much as an 'I told you so' when things went wrong."

"Of course, I did, Gia. That's what friends do."

Love raced through her. Savannah's outlook on life was so simple. She never even stopped to realize how much she touched people, made their lives better, just by being her. "Well, let's hope it's what sons do too."

They got out of the car and headed toward the shop, but Savannah paused. She dug through her bag and finally pulled out the key ring, which apparently had been swallowed up amid all the clutter she carried around, and locked the car door. She glanced at Gia, then resumed her trek toward the caterer's shop.

Before the kidnapping, Savannah would never in a million years have locked the car door, a point of contention between her and her cousin, Gia's boyfriend, Hunter Quinn. She never used to put up the convertible top when she went in to a local business, instead dropping the keys into the center console and going on her way.

"It's fine, Gia." Savannah must have sensed Gia's thoughts, a far too common occurrence that sometimes bordered on creepy. "I'm good, really. I promise. Now, let's go get this done. I want to actually get to the relaxing part sometime before the wedding."

Gia held the shop door for Savannah, then followed her in. Bells on the door handle jingled, announcing their arrival. The aroma of good food cooking, Christmas music playing softly in the background, and the cozy atmosphere exuded by the small front greeting area welcomed them. A smile tugged at Gia when her gaze fell on the Christmas tree in the corner, decorated with a variety of kitchen items.

While Savannah waited at the counter for Alyssa Rinaldi, Gia browsed the decorations. A set of mixing spoons tied together with a red bow hung on one wall. An elf wearing a red apron that said "A balanced diet is a Christmas cookie in each hand" hung from another. Gia grinned; who wouldn't agree with that sentiment?

She turned toward Savannah to point out the fun decorations. Maybe they could stop at the Christmas Shoppe, find some similar items, and put up a small tree in the front corner of the café. She'd only have to move one table to make room.

"Hmm…" Savannah frowned.

"What's wrong?"

She crooked a finger for Gia to come closer, then whispered, "Alyssa never takes this long to greet a customer, even at her busiest. Do you think that group is still arguing?"

Gia strained for any hint of sound. Other than the music playing, the shop was unusually quiet, especially during a tasting, when you'd expect a high level of excitement. When they came in for Savannah's tasting, all of them had been laughing, talking, enjoying the good food and sharing the joy of the coming festivities. "I don't know. I don't want to interrupt if she's with a customer. Let's give her another minute, and then I'll poke my head in back and see if Carlos is here."

Savannah shrugged and turned a thick book that lay open on the counter.

No doubt if Alyssa didn't show up soon, Savannah would have a whole new list of foods compiled. Waiting might not be the best idea.

"Hey, Gia, look at this."

Of course—Gia resisted an eye roll—just as she'd expected.

Savannah pointed to a picture of a three-tiered cake, a cascade of what looked like mistletoe pouring from the top and wrapping around one side of the cake then pooling beneath it on the tray. "This is amazing. Do you think it's real mistletoe?"

"Sorry, but real mistletoe is poisonous. So, unless you want all of your guests to end up in the hospital, we have to do it with icing and sugar." Alyssa Rinaldi entered from the kitchen and placed two small dishes on the counter. Each held a small square of cake with a plastic fork beside it. She grinned. "I had a feeling this cake might be more to your liking, that's why I left the book open. Go ahead, taste."

Savannah took a bite and moaned. "Oh, man, this is amazing."

"I just finished serving a sample to the group that's in there now." She hooked a thumb toward the dining room where a set of burgundy drapes had been pulled closed, cutting off any view into the room. "So I saved some for you."

When they'd gone there for their first tasting, Alyssa had left the curtains open. Gia had to wonder if the bickering had caused her to pull them closed. Since she didn't know Alyssa that well, and couldn't think of a tactful way to ask, she let it drop and took a bite of the cake. "Oh, mmm…this is so good. And it's beautiful. Can you eat the mistletoe part?"

"Sure thing." Alyssa pointed to a mistletoe leaf and a small clump of berries sitting in the icing. "All created from candy and fondant icing. Every part of the cake is edible, though some people don't care for the taste of fondant. Don't worry, though, the rest of the icing is buttercream."

Savannah finished off her piece and winced. "Would it be too late to change my mind?"

"Hmm…I don't know. It is kind of last minute." Alyssa winked at Gia. "Good thing I already penciled it in for you. I had a feeling—"

A woman's scream from the dining room cut her off mid-sentence.

Chapter Three

Gia whirled toward the dining room. A scream like that could only mean trouble.

Alyssa huffed and waved a hand to stop her. "Don't even bother. Those people have done nothing but argue with and scream at one another since they got here. The whole bunch of them. Whatever their latest problem is, they can work it out among themselves. I'm tired of playing referee, and I'm quite tempted, at this point, to just tell them to go somewhere else."

"How many of them are there?" Savannah asked.

"Only four—the bride, Robyn, her fiancé, Jeremy, her son, Isaac, and her maid of honor, Mallory—but it seems like a lot more. Thankfully, one of them didn't show up. Although, who knows? Maybe he would have been the voice of reason." Alyssa's jaw clenched, deep lines bracketing her mouth. "None of them can agree on a single thing, except that everything I've offered is not good enough."

A pang of sympathy shot through Gia. Thankfully, the All-Day Breakfast Café didn't often have difficult customers, but when they did…well, certain people just had a way of sapping every last ounce of your energy. At least when she'd worked for the deli in New York, she'd been able to pass those customers off to the owner. Here, she was the owner, so she had no choice but to plaster on a smile and make the best of it, which is what she was betting Alyssa would ultimately do with this group, when she was done venting.

With a quick glance toward the curtains, Alyssa sighed. "I just feel bad for Robyn, the bride."

"I know what you mean," Savannah said. "We saw her and her son arguing out front a few minutes ago. It doesn't seem like she's getting any joy out of her wedding."

Gia patted her arm. While she felt bad for Robyn, her first concern had to be Savannah, and she wasn't about to let anything interfere with her happiness.

"So, then..." Gia tapped the picture of the cake and grinned. "The mistletoe cake it is?"

A second scream erupted from the dining room, followed by a loud crash. A man's voice demanding someone call 911 propelled Gia through the curtains into the dining room.

Robyn lay on the floor, a chair tipped on its side next to her.

Her son, Isaac, and two other people, one man Gia assumed was Robyn's fiancé, Jeremy, and one woman—presumably Robyn's maid of honor, Mallory, and probably the one who'd screamed—stood staring at her. No one made any attempt to move toward the woman, nor did anyone pull out a phone to call for help.

Gia dropped to her knees beside Robyn and felt for a pulse. Nothing. There had to be something, because the first aid course she once took seemed like a distant memory when confronted with an actual emergency. It would be so much better for Robyn to have someone who actually knew what they were doing.

She closed her eyes, trying to block out the heightened sounds surrounding her, a clock ticking, traffic passing on the road out front, the heavy breathing of a room full of people who appeared to be in a collective state of shock, Savannah's strained voice as she called for an ambulance. Gia pressed her fingers against Robyn's neck, concentrated on feeling for the flutter that would indicate even the slightest hint of life. Still nothing. She held a shaky hand beneath Robyn's nose. She was no longer breathing. "Does anyone know CPR?"

Savannah was still on the phone, rambling off the address. She hit the speaker button, knelt beside Gia, tossed the phone on the floor beside her, and started chest compressions.

This woman was dying, and apparently none of her companions were going to step up to help. Gia fought off panic. She replayed the instructor's voice in her mind, imagined the dummy they'd used in front of her. Okay, she could do this. She pinched the woman's nose and tilted her head back as Savannah counted off compressions. When she paused, Gia leaned over to give the woman a breath, then froze. She'd almost forgotten to check her airway. "Does anyone know if she choked on something?"

Two "no's" and a head shake were all she got.

She checked the woman's airway and when it seemed clear started breathing for her, keeping watch to be sure her chest rose. When it did, she fell into an easy rhythm with Savannah. After each breath, she paused for Savannah to do compressions, and glanced around the room, expecting someone, anyone, to step in and try to do something to help.

Alyssa bent over Savannah, chewing on a thumbnail, her gaze riveted on Robyn.

Alyssa's husband, Carlos, who was also her cook, stood against the wall behind her, arms folded across his barrel chest, a stern scowl marring his usually jovial features.

Isaac, who'd argued with his mother only moments before, glared daggers across the room at a tall man with shaggy dark hair and eyes so dark they were almost black.

The man didn't meet his gaze. Instead, he inched closer to Alyssa and laid a hand on her back. Maybe Gia had been wrong about him being Robyn's fiancé, though he was the only other man present.

Savannah paused.

Gia quickly gave the woman a breath. *Come on, now, Robyn. Breathe. Please.*

Carlos took two steps toward his wife, his jaw clenched tight.

At the sound of sirens, Alyssa shrugged off the man's hand and hurried through the curtains to the front of the shop.

Carlos met Gia's gaze, then elbowed the man aside, none too gently, and tied the curtains back behind his wife to allow the paramedics room to get a stretcher through.

Gia concentrated, careful to keep time with Savannah, pausing now and then to see if the woman had started to breathe on her own. She hadn't. To check for a pulse. There was none.

Tears blurred her vision, then tipped over and rolled down her cheeks. They were losing her. In her mind, Gia begged the paramedics to hurry, because the woman had no chance if they didn't get there soon.

Savannah paused and wiped tears from her face with the back of her wrist. Pain twisted her features as she caught Gia's gaze.

They had to continue. Gia remembered that much from her course; once you stared CPR, you had to keep it up until help arrived. No way would she give up if there was any chance they could save Robyn.

"Don't stop," Gia huffed, winded from her efforts.

"I won't." Savannah shook her arms out and returned to doing compressions when Gia knelt back.

The other woman in the room, Mallory, a curvy blonde with big green eyes, wrapped her arms around herself and rocked back and forth sobbing softly. "Come on, Robyn. Don't die. Please, don't die."

Gia echoed the thought, silently urging Robyn to breathe, to fight, to live.

"I've got her now." One of the paramedics nudged Gia aside and took over. His partner, a woman Gia recognized from the café, took over for Savannah.

Gia scrambled out of the way and held out a hand to help Savannah to her feet, then whispered, "Do you think she'll make it?"

When Savannah stood, she smoothed her long hair back and kept her gaze glued to Robyn. "I don't know. I hope so, though. What do you think happened?"

Though Gia had noticed the people in the room while she and Savannah tried to save their friend, she hadn't noticed anything about her surroundings but the chair that had fallen beside the victim. She took a moment to survey the room as the two paramedics worked.

Plates of cake and cups of tea or coffee sat at each of four place settings. A fifth place setting sat unused on the round table. Three chairs were pushed back from the table, one still lay on the floor, and one stood in its place against the table in front of the unused place setting. Nothing seemed out of place, and Robyn didn't have any injuries that Gia could see. Maybe the poor woman's heart couldn't take the stress and had just given out.

The paramedics loaded Robyn onto a stretcher and started toward the door.

Gia fell into step beside them and lay a hand on the female paramedic's arm, then pitched her voice low. "Do you think she'll be okay?"

Without breaking stride, the woman held her gaze for a moment then gave a quick glance around the room. She patted Gia's hand, which still rested on her arm, and hurried out.

A couple of uniformed officers had already started asking questions, and Alyssa waved her arms animatedly as she explained the order of events.

Gia found Savannah sitting on a chair in a quiet corner of the small greeting area. "You okay?"

She nodded. "I hope she makes it, though. I feel so bad for her."

"I know; me too."

Detective Leo Dumont, Savannah's fiancé, strode through the door. "Hey, Gia."

"Hi, Leo." Gia kept an eye on the door. Her boyfriend, Captain Hunter Quinn, wouldn't be far behind.

Leo kissed the top of Savannah's head. "You okay, babe?"

She smiled up at him and briefly gripped his hand. "I am."

He studied her another moment as if to be sure she was being completely honest, especially with herself, then nodded. "What happened?"

While Savannah explained, Gia looked around for Hunt. As expected, she found him out front talking to the paramedics as they loaded Robyn into the ambulance. She watched him for a moment, his thick, dark hair beginning to curl over his collar, and her heart stuttered. Her relationship with Hunt had been slow starting. Between his promotion to captain soon after they met, and her trying to build her new business, they hadn't had much time to spend together. And many of the evenings they did share ended with both of them falling asleep on her couch minutes into whatever movie they'd decided to watch. But somewhere along the line, they'd fallen into a level of comfort with one another, not the sparks that could sometimes herald the start of a new relationship, but an easy friendship that was beginning to evolve into something more. A solid foundation maybe? At least for Gia.

Hunt wasn't big on sharing his feelings.

He looked over and caught sight of her, then frowned.

Unless he found her with his cousin at a crime scene, then he was all too willing to share exactly how he felt, loudly.

She smiled and waved.

He just shook his head and started toward her.

"Why aren't you arresting him?" A man's voice demanded.

Gia whirled toward the dining room.

Isaac stood in the curtained doorway, toe-to-toe with Regina Kenney, a uniformed police officer and another of Savannah's cousins. He gestured toward the dark-haired man who'd stood a little too close to Alyssa while Gia and Savannah had tried to revive Robyn. "I already told you her fiancé, Jeremy Nolan, killed her."

Jeremy reached around Regina to shove Isaac's shoulder. "You'd better shut your mouth, boy, and watch where you're hurling accusations."

Staying between the two men, Regina held up her hands. "Enough, both of you."

Gia gave Regina credit. The way those two were glaring at each other, practically foaming at the mouth, it was not a position she'd want to be in. Truthfully, if it were up to her, she'd probably just step back out of the way and let them go at it.

Hunt gave her arm a quick squeeze as he strode past Gia and approached Isaac.

Isaac's face turned beet red, his hands balled tightly at his sides. "That monster killed my mother, just like he planned to do all along. He never loved her; he only loved the money she inherited when my father died."

Savannah slid a hand into Gia's as Leo hurried to help diffuse the situation. "She didn't make it?"

The ambulance had just pulled away, and Gia's attention was fully focused on Hunt since he stood talking to the paramedic. Surely, he'd have reacted, and the ambulance wouldn't have left with the lights and sirens going, if Robyn had died. And he hadn't taken any phone calls or spoken to anyone on his radio since the ambulance left. "I don't know. If she did pass away, I don't see how anyone could possibly know yet."

"You spoiled little turd. What's a matter? Afraid Mommy's money's gonna go to me now instead of you? Afraid you might have to go get a real job?" Jeremy taunted. "Afraid—"

Isaac took a swing, precisely aimed between Hunt and Regina, and landed a solid blow to Jeremy's jaw.

He staggered back, but Leo caught him before he could go down.

Hunt hooked one of Isaac's arms and wrestled him against the wall, keeping him pinned there while Regina pulled out handcuffs.

"Me?" Isaac used his shoulder to shove against Hunt's hold. "You're arresting me? You have got to be kidding. That man is a murderer!"

"I need you to calm down, sir." Hunt nodded toward Regina. "I assure you I will listen to anything you want to tell me, but only if you calm down."

Regina took hold of one of Isaac's hands. "Turn around, please."

"He killed my mother." He glared at Jeremy, then pointed to Alyssa. "And the way I figure it, she's his next target. He'll off the old man and woo her into marrying him, then steal everything."

"Oh, please." Jeremy used the back of his wrist to wipe a trickle of blood from the corner of his mouth. "Give me a break and shut up before I sue you for slander, or defamation of character, or just kick your—"

"That's enough!" Hunt pinned Isaac back against the wall. "Turn around. Now."

Leo guided Jeremy into a far corner of the room. Probably for the best to get a little distance between the two before Isaac lost it completely.

"I know I'm right; I saw them together," Isaac whined once more, then relented and turned to face the wall.

Alyssa's cheeks flared bright red, and she turned and fled the room.

A husky man in jeans and a T-shirt hurried through the front door and stopped in his tracks.

Jeremy's gaze focused on him. "Where have you been, Ethan? You were supposed to be here an hour ago."

"Uh…" Ethan looked around, taking in the entire situation, then scratched his head. "I got held up. I'm sorry. I take it things didn't go well?"

"And you!" Isaac screamed, his rage rekindled by the addition of the newcomer.

Thankfully, Regina had cuffed Isaac already, and she and Hunt each had ahold of one of his arms as he lunged toward the man, his face nearly purple. "This guy was here an hour ago. I saw him walking out when I pulled up out front. Where did you disappear to, huh, buddy?"

Ethan frowned and looked over his shoulder, then returned his gaze to Isaac. "I don't know what you're talking about. I just got here. There was an accident on the highway, and I got caught up in traffic. What is going on?"

"I'll tell you what's going on," Isaac screamed. "This monster killed my mother, probably with your help."

"Liar!" Jeremy took a step toward Isaac, but Leo and another officer were on him before he could take a second. They grabbed his arms and dragged him into the dining room.

"Wait." Ethan hurried after them. "Robyn's dead?"

Silence echoed through the shop as everyone looked around.

Hunt shrugged. "As far as I know, the victim is on her way to the hospital. Alive. Whatever happened here, no one has succeeded in murdering anyone. Yet."

Jeremy's eyes went wide.

Isaac slumped against the wall, every drop of color draining from his face.

Mallory, who'd remained in the dining room when Robyn was taken out, gasped and dropped onto a chair.

Ethan staggered backward, and Gia had to jump out of the way to keep him from plowing her over.

Her heart broke for Robyn. These were her closest family members and friends, those who should have loved her and cared for her above all else, and they'd already accepted her death, before she was even gone.

Chapter Four

Gia paused on the walkway in front of the All-Day Breakfast Café, only for a moment since she was already running more than two hours late thanks to the incident at Rinaldi's. She'd trimmed the front windows and surrounded the doorway with garland. Although the lights didn't illuminate much in the daylight, the red ribbon she'd weaved through brightened up the entranceway.

Savannah opened the front door, then glanced back at Gia. "Is everything okay?"

How could she explain the rush of emotions she felt staring at her café, the thing she'd worked so hard for, devoted so much of herself to? If anyone would understand, Savannah would, but still Gia couldn't summon the words to express her feelings. "Yeah, I'm okay."

Savannah smiled. "Well, come on then. I'm sure Cole and Willow are ready for a reprieve after handling both the breakfast and the lunch rush by themselves."

Gia and Savannah had been scheduled to assist through the lunch rush, then take care of the late afternoon lull and dinner hour themselves. Thankfully, Cole, a good friend who'd retired and now spent most of his time working at Gia's, had agreed to man the grill a bit longer, and Willow, a young girl who'd been Gia's waitress since she opened, had offered to handle the lunch rush on her own until they could get there. "They're both probably exhausted by now."

She'd been spending too much time out of the café lately. First, while doing the Haunted Town Festival this fall, then from there, she jumped right into Savannah's wedding preparations. As much as she loved sharing so much time with Savannah, it was time for her to get back to working the café. She'd built a regular breakfast and lunch crowd and become one of Boggy Creek's hottest gossip spots, mostly thanks to the Bailey twins, Esmeralda and Estelle. The two elderly women made a habit of planting themselves at a table smack in the center of the café every time something gossip-worthy happened in town, either to gather or dole out information. It didn't matter which; the end results were the same. People congregated where the Bailey sisters did to share the latest Boggy Creek buzz.

Willow set a dish in front of a loan diner with a book open on his table, then turned and caught sight of Gia and Savannah. "Oh, hey. How's everything?"

Since Gia had called to let them know what was going on, Willow and Cole already knew about Robyn's misfortune.

"Unfortunately, I don't know any more than I did when I first called." By the time Leo had taken statements from her and Savannah and let them leave, Regina had already loaded Isaac into her patrol car and taken off with him. She hadn't spoken to Hunt, who was still in the process of interviewing the other participants when Gia had left.

Savannah took Gia's bag on her way by and went to stow them in Gia's office and get ready to take over for Willow.

Gia hurried behind the counter for a much-needed dose of caffeine. "Have the Bailey sisters been in yet?"

Willow slid the tray she'd been holding onto a pile at the end of the counter to be washed, then grabbed a bus pan to clear the few tables people had just vacated. "Seriously? I literally hung up the phone with you, turned around, and there they were, standing in the doorway waiting to be seated."

Like clockwork. Gia smiled at the thought, happy she'd reached the point where she could anticipate when certain customers would show up. She poured a cup of coffee for herself and one for Savannah, then lifted the pot toward Willow, who shook her head. "Did the sisters have any useful information?"

"Nah, nothing you didn't tell me already. At least, not that I heard, but things got busy right after they came in, so I can't say for certain." She finished clearing the closest table, then stretched her back before lifting the bus pan to move on. "Doesn't matter, though; when they paid, they promised they'd be back later, so I'm pretty sure they'll pop in again if anything new happens."

So was Gia.

"Rumors are flying fast and furious, though, about the woman's fiancé and the caterer having an affair. I tried my best to quash them when I could, since you said when you called that the accusation came from the woman's son and could be untrue."

"Thanks, I appreciate that." Willow had already heard that news by the time Gia had called to say she'd be late. Having grown up in a big city like New York, Gia was often awed by the speed with which news in Boggy Creek could travel. "The last thing I want is a woman's reputation being ruined by gossip spreading in my café."

Savannah returned, her long blonde hair wrapped neatly in a bun, dark blue apron tied around her waist, and grabbed the bin from Willow. "I've got this. You go ahead and get out of here."

"Thanks. I have a few tests I still have to take before the end of the semester, so I'm headed home to study." She took off her apron and wadded it into a ball, then tossed it into the hamper in back and grabbed the backpack full of books she always carried just in case she got some downtime to study. "I'll see you guys tomorrow morning, but if you get busy, you can always give me a call, and I'll come back."

Savannah grinned. "No hot date tonight?"

"Ha!" She laughed. "More like no hot date ever. Not all of us are lucky enough to snare Mr. Right."

Wasn't that the truth. Gia's mind conjured a vision of Hunt, his shaggy dark hair curling below his collar, five o'clock shadow when he didn't have time to shave, ready grin when he saw her, even under the most demanding circumstances. And the scowl he often wore when he found her and Savannah had gotten into one sort of predicament or another. Her heart warmed, and a smile tugged at her.

"See you guys." Willow pushed through the front door with a wave, then paused and held it open for Alyssa on her way out.

"Alyssa, hi." Shaking off any further thoughts of Hunt, Gia rushed to greet her. "How are you? Is everything okay?"

Alyssa caught her bottom lip between her teeth, and tears shimmered amid her thick lashes. The long dark hair she usually wore up in a hair net while working, cascaded around her hunched shoulder, accentuating her slim build and giving her a vulnerable appearance.

Savannah stowed the bus pan beneath the counter and hurried to her side, laying a gentle hand on her arm. "Do you want to sit down? Have something to eat or drink?"

"Thank you." Alyssa gestured toward the counter. "I wouldn't mind sitting for a few minutes, if you don't mind. And a latte would be wonderful."

Gia led her toward a stool at the counter. "I just added holiday lattes to the menu, if you'd like to try one. I have eggnog, gingerbread, or peppermint mocha."

"Peppermint mocha sounds great, thank you." She hooked her purse strap over a stool back and pulled the stool out from the counter.

"Would you excuse me for just one minute, Alyssa?" As much as Gia wanted to spend a few minutes with Alyssa, she couldn't do so without at least talking to Cole first, not after she was already more than two hours late.

"Of course." Alyssa slumped onto the stool, propped her elbows on the counter, and cradled her head in her hands.

Gia hurried toward the kitchen while Savannah made Alyssa's latte. Hopefully, Cole would understand if she took a few more minutes, though Gia was starting to feel like she was taking advantage. Maybe for Christmas she'd give him a raise. Willow and Savannah too. The café was doing better now; what better way to celebrate than to share with the people who'd helped her achieve that goal? "Hey, Cole."

He looked up from where he was chopping peppers at the center island. A pile of onions and another of potatoes sat on the counter nearby. "Oh, hey there. I was just getting started on some of the prep work for tomorrow while things are slow. I figured I'd cut this stuff up now, and maybe you guys can get out of here early tonight."

Gia kissed his cheek. "Have I told you lately how much I appreciate you?"

He grinned. "Only about a hundred times."

"Well, I'm telling you again." He'd already cleaned up from the lunch rush, and other than a small pile of pots in the drying rack waiting to be put away, there wasn't much for her to do. "Did you have a busy lunch?"

"Not at first, but then news of the incident at Carlos and Alyssa's place broke, and the Bailey sisters came in." He scowled and shook his head. "I really don't get it. Those two are like rock stars; as soon as they show up somewhere, all of their groupies pour in behind them."

"That's no lie." She laughed. His comparison wasn't far off. "Listen, I hate to ask you this, but would you mind giving me a few more minutes? Alyssa just came in, and I wanted to talk to her."

His expression sobered. "Of course. Go, please. I was going to finish this up anyway, so not a big deal. If an order comes in; I'll just take care of it."

"Thanks, Cole."

"Any time, dear."

She started toward the door, but when Cole called her name, she stopped and looked back.

"Alyssa's a good woman, but Carlos can be a bit...possessive, I guess is a good word for it, and short tempered too." He paused, giving Gia time to absorb whatever he was trying to imply. "Make sure she's really okay before you send her home."

"Sure thing, Cole, thanks." Though she wanted to know a lot more about whatever Cole was hinting at, she didn't want to miss speaking to Alyssa, so she left him in favor of returning to the dining room as questions ricocheted through her mind. Hopefully, Cole would have time to elaborate once Alyssa left.

Savannah set Alyssa's latte in front of her, then put Gia's coffee in front of the stool next to Alyssa and remained standing on the opposite side of the counter. She glanced around the empty dining room before leaning forward on the counter and returning her attention to Alyssa.

Unsure if Savannah was scanning to see if anything in the dining room needed her attention or just giving Alyssa time to compose herself, Gia took a seat and sipped her coffee but remained silent.

Alyssa sniffed, grabbed a napkin from the holder on the counter, and dabbed her eyes. She took a deep, shuddering breath. Her hands trembled as she began to shred the napkin. "I just wanted to come and apologize for this morning and let you know the police have shut down the shop while they investigate what happened to Robyn. I realize your wedding is barely a week away, and I completely understand if you want to look for another caterer. I will refund your deposit immediately."

"Alyssa, sweetie…" Savannah laid a hand over Alyssa's, stilling them. "None of this is your fault, and you have nothing to apologize for. I expect the detectives will have you back open in no time, just as soon as they sort out whatever mess was going on there this morning."

Alyssa's gaze, filled with hope, shot to Savannah. "Do you really think they'll let me open again soon?"

"I don't see why not. I happen to know the lead detective and the captain both have a vested interest in getting this investigation done quickly. Trust me; they'll move faster'n a hot knife through butter to get you back open again." She winked and stepped back. "Besides, it's not like you had anything to do with any of those people, so it shouldn't take long to eliminate any suspicions anyone might have about you and Carlos."

Alyssa chewed on her bottom lip again and dropped her gaze to the growing pile of napkin slivers. "Have you heard from Leo?"

"Not since I left your shop. Why? Did something happen?"

"Not that I've heard." With her napkin completely torn apart, Alyssa lifted her latte and took a sip. "I was just wondering if you knew how Robyn was doing?"

"I'm sorry, I haven't heard anything." Savannah swallowed hard.

"I'm sure rumors would be flying by now if she didn't make it." Gia rubbed a hand up and down Alyssa's arm, wanting to offer comfort, especially if her husband was giving her a hard time about anything, but not really knowing what to say. She didn't dare question her relationship with Carlos, not without knowing more than the few words Cole had uttered before she ran out of the kitchen. And she certainly couldn't ask if Savannah's assessment that Alyssa had no personal relationship with any of the players, most notably, Robyn's fiancé, Jeremy, was true. Despite the fact that rumors of her involvement with him were running rampant, Gia didn't know her well enough to dig into something so private. Besides, the way Isaac carried on about her and Jeremy, there was a good chance those rumors had been overheard that very morning and had begun to circulate already. "Nothing you can do now but say a prayer and hope for the best. We don't even know for sure any foul play was involved."

Alyssa sniffed and nodded. "You're right, of course."

"Robyn might well have had a heart attack or something." Unless you asked Isaac, which no one had, though that didn't stop him from voicing his opinion that Jeremy killed her as loudly and as often as possible.

Savannah snorted. "I wouldn't even be surprised, considering the stress that poor woman must have been under trying to plan a wedding with everyone bickering like a bunch of children. Especially when it seemed her son hated her fiancé so fiercely. When Gia and I heard the two of them arguing out front, it didn't seem Isaac would even give the guy half a chance."

"How well do you know Jeremy?" Oops. Darn. The question blurted out before Gia could censor it. She'd meant it innocently enough, but considering the rumors, maybe a little insulting.

Red patches blossomed on Alyssa's cheeks, and tears shimmered in her eyes.

"I'm sorry, I didn't mean to imply...I mean...uh...I wasn't...It's just that Isaac—"

"No, no." Alyssa waved a dismissive hand, but her gaze shifted, and she carefully avoided eye contact with Gia. "It's fine. The question just caught me off guard is all. Jeremy did a lot of the preliminary work for the wedding. I met with him several times before I even spoke to Robyn. He seems like a nice man."

No doubt she had more of an opinion than she was admitting to, but Gia had already overstepped, so she changed the subject. "What about Isaac? How long have you known him?"

"Besides yesterday, I only met him one other time." She shrugged and took a sip of her latte, then massaged her temples between a thumb and forefinger. With a sigh, she finally met Gia's gaze. "Jeremy and I met to discuss the menu and what other options I could offer for servers and table settings…you know, the usual stuff. I was visiting my sister a few towns over that day, and Jeremy happened to be close by on business, so it turned out to be more convenient to meet up at a restaurant out there. Since we were looking through pictures, it was easier for both of us to sit on the same side of the booth. Isaac happened to walk in and see us together and confronted Jeremy. He said some very unkind things, threatened to tell Robyn something was going on between us, and stormed out."

Since Alyssa had broached the subject, Gia asked softly, "Was anything going on?"

Tears tipped over and rolled down Alyssa's cheeks. She averted her gaze and grabbed another napkin. "No. Isaac got the wrong impression. Unfortunately, that didn't stop him from spreading his wild accusations all over the place. When Carlos heard the rumors…Well, let's just say it didn't go over too well."

"Did he believe them?" Gia's heart broke for her, especially if she'd been dragged into a family feud and had her marriage affected by something she played no role in.

"I don't actually know what he believes." She stood and slung her bag over her shoulder. "Anyway, I have to go. I have calls to make, appointments to reschedule. Thank you for understanding and thank you for the latte. It was delicious. I'm sorry I couldn't drink more. My stomach's been in knots since this morning. How much do I owe you?"

"Don't worry about it. It's on the house." Gia couldn't think of anything else to say. She wanted to let Alyssa know she was there if she needed a friend, but at the same time, she didn't know her that well, and the woman had divulged more information than she seemed comfortable with already. "I'm sure everything will work out, Alyssa. Hopefully, Robyn will be okay and whatever happened to her will turn out to have been from natural causes. Isaac seems to have a habit of jumping to conclusions, so maybe that's what happened this morning too."

A smile wavered for the first time since she came in. "Thank you, Gia. You're right. We'll just have to wait and see."

Unless of course Isaac was right on either or both counts. That could be a game changer.

Chapter Five

With Alyssa gone, Gia left Savannah to deal with the few customers who'd trickled in and went back to relieve Cole on the grill.

He'd just finished cutting the vegetables and was covering the stainless-steel bins. He glanced over his shoulder when Gia entered. "How's Alyssa?"

"She seems okay." Or about as good as could be expected under the circumstances.

"Glad to hear it."

"Could I ask you something, though?" She ripped a piece of saran wrap from the roll and handed it to Cole.

He used it to cover the last bowl, then started transferring them to the commercial sized refrigerator. "Sure thing."

Gia held the door open for him. Watching what Alyssa was going through brought back memories of her own past, her own struggle to keep her business going after the scandal involving her ex's death had shut her down. Having lived through a far too public divorce amid a court battle and death threats, then moving twelve hundred miles away to Boggy Creek—only to have her every move put on display again after Bradley's murder—Gia understood all too well, the pain of having your life turned inside out for all the world to see. "What did you mean before about Carlos being possessive?"

He finished loading the bowls into the fridge and washed his hands, then dried them on a towel and perched on the edge of a stool at the center island. He gestured for her to sit across from him.

Knowing Savannah would be putting up orders any minute, she leaned against the counter instead. No sense getting too comfortable.

"I heard a rumor this morning that Alyssa was having an affair with the woman who collapsed's fiancé." He held up a finger. "It's just a rumor mind you; I'm not sayin' it's true."

"Of course." But how had Cole managed to hear that when he was stuck in front of the grill all day?

He grinned, reached across the island, and tapped her temple. "I can actually see the gears spinning."

Gia laughed. One of these days she'd learn to keep her thoughts from being displayed so clearly in her expressions.

"Earl stopped in earlier. He came back to say hello right after news of the incident at Alyssa's broke. Seems one of his sons went to school with Alyssa, stayed friendly even after high school, until she married Carlos and he put the kibosh on any friendships she had with men."

"Hmm…" Gia could certainly relate. Her ex-husband had been the same way, all while working his way through a long list of mistresses Gia had been blind to. Sadly, that wasn't the worst of what he'd done. Her heart went out to Alyssa.

"Supposedly, Carlos wasn't very supportive when Alyssa wanted to open her own catering company, didn't like the idea. Until he decided to quit his job and go to work with her as her cook. Then, he warmed up to the idea right quick." He shrugged. "According to Earl anyway."

Sure, he did. Then he'd be able to keep an eye on her all day long. "What else did Earl say?"

"Just that Alyssa didn't deserve this. Seems his son cared a little more for her than he'd let on all those years ago, but by the time he worked up the courage to admit it, she'd already gotten serious with Carlos." Cole pushed his stool back and stood. "Oh, and he mentioned the fact that Carlos made a habit of having a chat with any men he saw as a threat to his marriage. Whether or not that threat was real or imagined apparently didn't matter."

Gia couldn't help but laugh. Earl's information this time rivaled the Bailey sisters, and it seemed he had shared every bit of dirt he had. "Thanks, Cole. Maybe I'll give her a day to get through whatever business arrangements she needs to make with having to close down for the investigation and then reach out to see how she's doing."

"Earl was hoping you'd say that. He also said to tell you he's sorry he missed you this morning. Honestly, I think that's why he stopped back in later. Seems he's developed a bit of a soft spot for you."

Heat flared in Gia's cheeks.

"Oh, not in a weird way. If it's possible for a man to be maternal, Earl is." A wide grin spread across his face. "As evidenced by the pack of children and grandchildren he's always doting on. I just meant, I think he's sort of unofficially adopted you."

Warmth spread through her at the thought. Gia had been so young when her mother passed away, she could barely remember her. The memories she did have, she clung to for dear life. Maybe her father had been devastated by her mother's death, or maybe he'd always been indifferent and cold as ice. She'd never know, because he barely acknowledged her throughout her childhood and had thrown her out the day she graduated high school. Their relationship never afforded an opportunity for personal questions. The thought of a father like Earl, a man who cherished his children above all else, had tears prickling the backs of her lids.

"Sorry." Savannah rushed in and stuck three tickets above the grill. "Break's over, lady and gent."

Cole gave Gia's arm a squeeze and dropped a kiss on her head. "I'll see you in the morning."

"Sure thing, thanks, Cole."

"Uh, huh."

"Hey, Savannah, wait," Gia called before Savannah could sprint back out the door. "Anything going on out there?"

"Nah, nothing. But we're starting to pick up a bit, so maybe we'll have a nice dinner rush."

If that was the case, Gia hoped it was the great food and cozy atmosphere attracting the crowd.

With Savannah manning the dining room, doing what she loved and did best, interacting with people, Gia looked over the three tickets. Breakfast pies, easy enough. They were already pre-made, so she sliced two meat lover pies and popped them in the microwave. She pulled enough vegetables for two southwestern omelets, sliced several pieces of pre-cooked sausage from the bin on the back of the grill, and tossed it all into a small drizzle of oil to the far side of the grill.

With that warming, she ladled batter into the waffle iron, grabbed the berries from the fridge and the confectioners' sugar from the shelf above the counter. As she worked, comforted by the familiar routine, the scents of home surrounding her, her mind drifted back to Alyssa. Surely, Hunt and Leo would complete the investigation quickly, especially if Robyn made a full recovery and it turned out whatever had happened to her had been nothing more than a force of nature. As much as Gia liked Alyssa and felt bad for her, fact was, Savannah was getting married in just over a week. The rehearsal dinner, which they planned to have Alyssa cater as well, was a week from right this minute. If Hunt and Leo didn't clear her soon, they were going to have to get someone else.

"Earth to Gia."

"Oh." She flinched, startled by Savannah's voice right behind her. "Sorry."

Savannah laughed and grabbed the breakfast pie slices from the microwave. "You seem like you're a million miles away."

She shook off her concerns. "Sorry, I guess my thoughts wandered."

Savannah's grin lit her eyes as she slid the slices onto plates and left with them.

Gia would keep her thoughts to herself, for now, at least. She didn't want to say anything to dull Savannah's good spirits. There'd be plenty of time to panic later if things didn't work out and they had to find a caterer at the last minute. At worst, Gia would do it herself. She had no doubt Cole would pitch in, as would Earl and his kids. Trevor, too. Although, she realized she didn't have a clue if he could cook. No matter; she could always give him things to do.

The knot in her stomach began to uncoil. Though the idea didn't always come to her right away, it eventually did occur to her that she wasn't on her own any more. She had a family now. And together, they could work through anything.

She finished the southwestern omelets, ladled homemade salsa over the top, added home fries to both plates and set them on the cut-out to the dining room so Savannah could get them without having to come back to the kitchen.

Then, she turned her attention to the waffles. She loaded a pile onto each of three plates, sprinkled confectioners' sugar over them, and poured a generous serving of mixed berries over the top. After adding a cup of cream to each plate, she put all three on the cut-out and rang the bell.

Though several more tables had been seated, Savannah was nowhere to be seen.

Most customers were looking over their menus, though a few started to look around, their menus closed on the table in front of them. Since no orders were up, and the omelets were still sitting on the cut-out, Gia grabbed a tray and loaded the omelets and waffles onto it. She'd serve them up quick, then take orders if Savannah needed a hand.

She lifted the tray and turned.

Savannah stood in the doorway, her eyes red, tears shimmering.

Gia stopped short and lowered the tray onto the island. "What's wrong? Are you okay?"

Savannah nodded and lowered her gaze to the phone clutched in her hands. "Leo just called."

Uh oh.

"Robyn Hackman didn't make it."

"Oh, Savannah, I'm so sorry. Are you okay?"

"He and Hunt are on their way. They need us to take a few minutes to answer their questions. I figured you could work the grill while they question you, but I called Willow and asked her to come back so I could talk." She sniffed. "She's on her way."

Gia just nodded. "Did he say what happened?"

She blew out a breath but didn't look up. "They think she was poisoned."

"Poisoned?"

Her gaze finally met Gia's. "Something in the cake."

The same cake Savannah had eaten a full slice of. Gia forced her heart back down her throat into her chest. "That's not possible. You ate the cake, and you're fine. You do feel okay, right?"

Gia only took a small bite, but Savannah ate a whole piece. Surely, she would have had some kind of reaction by now if she'd been poisoned. No?

"To tell you the truth, I feel a little queasy at the moment."

Chapter Six

"All right. Okay." Gia pulled out a stool and guided Savannah to sit. "Take a few deep breaths. It's probably just anxiety making you feel sick, but maybe I should take you to the hospital just in case."

"No. No, please. I definitely don't want to go to the hospital. After last summer, I'd be happy never to set foot in another hospital." Savannah nodded and sat. "I'm okay. I don't think I'm sick or anything. It was just a lot to take in, you know?"

"I do, but if you start to feel even the slightest bit off, let me know."

Savannah nodded. "I will, but I'm really okay."

Gia ran through the timeline in her head as she grabbed a water bottle and set it in front of Savannah. Could you dilute poison with water? Probably not, but she needed something to do. "You only left the kitchen a few minutes ago, then got the call from Leo and had time to get in touch with Willow, so Leo couldn't possibly have told you much."

She wiped her eyes. "No, you're right, he didn't. Just that she didn't make it and they suspected there was poison in the cake."

"Okay, so they just suspect it. They don't know for sure." No sense panicking just yet. There would be plenty of time to panic when they actually knew what was going on. Considering how fast Robyn fell ill after eating the cake, Savannah would be showing symptoms already if she'd been poisoned. "Besides, even if it was poisoned, maybe it was just Robyn's slice. I'm sure you're fine."

Savannah sucked in a shaky breath and nodded, cradling her forehead in her hand. "You're right of course. I just let my imagination run away with me for a minute."

"You just sit, drink some of that water. I'm going to get these dishes out to the customers." As much as she hated to leave Savannah, she couldn't leave the dining room with no one working. And even if she closed, there were still customers eating and waiting for their food.

"No, no. I'm okay now." She offered a quick laugh. "I just overreacted for a minute. I've got this."

"Are you sure?" With the dining room filling up and Hunt on his way to ask questions, she had to either get moving or close.

"I'm positive." Savannah hefted the tray onto her shoulder and headed out. Gia watched her through the cutout.

Though she'd taken the news hard, she seemed to pull herself together as she moved smoothly through the room, apologizing for the delay, serving plates, and taking orders. Within minutes she posted several orders above the grill. Gia got started on them. She still couldn't wrap her head around the fact Robyn hadn't made it. She'd really hoped she would. And poisoned. It was sad enough that she'd passed away just when she should have been moving on to an exciting new chapter in her life. But to think someone had murdered her. The scent of the food sizzling on the grill sat heavy in her gut, turning her stomach.

"Hey, you." Hunt kissed the side of her head and snatched a piece of bacon. "Did Savannah tell you what's going on?"

"A little. I don't think she knew much. Have you and Leo eaten?"

He leaned a hip against the center island and took out his pad. Apparently, it was going to be work before pleasure. "Haven't had anything since the stale cereal I ate for breakfast. Dry, since my milk was spoiled."

"What would you like?" She scanned the tickets and gathered what she needed for two steak and egg orders. Since she'd changed the steak to a thin sliced London broil, she'd noticed an increase in sales.

"I don't have time to eat right now." He tilted his head from side to side, stretching his neck. "We've got to take yours and Savannah's statements and get back to the caterers."

She grabbed a meat lovers breakfast pie from the fridge and cut two large slices, popped one into each microwave, then paused and studied him for a moment.

A five o'clock shadow Gia found beyond sexy stubbled his face. His dark eyes captured her gaze, sending a rush of heat through her cheeks and straight down to her heart.

She ignored the flush. No sense letting him know the effect he still had on her. Though they'd fallen into a comfortable routine, often spending what little free time they had together, usually having dinner or watching a movie at her house so Thor and Klondike wouldn't be left alone, they hadn't shared an actual date since…Huh, she couldn't remember when.

"Gia?" Hunt frowned.

"What? Oh, sorry. I guess I got sidetracked." A quick survey of the grill told her at least she hadn't burnt anything while she'd zoned out. "So, uh…was the cake really poisoned?"

"We're still waiting on results, but it looks that way. The doctors believe she ingested atropa belladonna." Hunt dropped onto the stool that Savannah had recently vacated and tapped his pen against his leg as he studied something on his pad.

"Atropa belladonna?" She'd heard the name belladonna before but couldn't place it. "What's that?"

"A poisonous plant. Also known as deadly nightshade."

Still didn't ring a bell. She'd have to look it up later. "And you think it was in the cake?"

"The cake is at the lab now, and tests are being run, but that's what we suspect."

Fear prickled the back of her neck. Maybe she should have insisted on taking Savannah to the hospital. "Did Savannah tell you she ate a piece of the cake?"

He nodded. "Belladonna is a fast-acting poison. If she'd ingested enough of it to be harmful, she'd be sick by now. And there is an antidote; it was just too late to administer it to Robyn."

She swallowed the lump clogging her throat. Would Robyn have made it if Gia had acted sooner, if she hadn't hesitated after the first scream?

"Right now, that's our theory. According to Alyssa and Carlos Rinaldi, all of the decorations on the cake should have been edible, made from some kind of icing and sugar."

"Yes, she told us the same thing, everything was edible."

"Well, Mallory Levine, the other woman who was present at the tasting and Robyn's maid of honor, is adamant there were real leaves and berries on the cake."

Gia tried to remember her slice of cake. She hadn't really been as interested in the cake as she had in Savannah's reaction to the cake. "I don't remember any real leaves or berries on my slice. Or Savannah's. The mistletoe in the picture and what was on the small slices we ate were beautiful, but you could tell they weren't real."

He looked up from his notes. "Any chance they could have been mistaken for the real thing?"

She shook her head and slid three plates onto the cutout for Savannah or Willow to serve. "No, I don't see how. What about Mallory? Did she eat any?"

"Nah." He flipped a page. "Robyn finished her own slice, and Mallory wasn't eating hers, so she pushed it over to Robyn. Said she was a big stress eater."

No surprise she'd eaten two slices of cake then, considering the amount of tension she must have been under. The microwave dinged, and Gia handed Hunt a plate with one of the breakfast pie slices. She set the other slice aside for Leo.

"Thanks." He grabbed a fork and a napkin, then poured himself a cup of coffee before sitting back down and digging in. "Do you remember hearing a scream?"

"Yes." Caught up on orders, Gia washed her hands, grabbed a diet soda from the fridge, and took the stool across from him.

"What can you tell me about it?"

Gia shrugged, not sure what exactly he was trying to figure out. "I heard a scream. I'm pretty sure it was a woman. I assumed it was the other woman in the room, Mallory."

"What made you think that?" He took another bite, giving her time to think.

Why had she been so sure it was Mallory and not Robyn? Actually, she hadn't been. "I didn't know who it was at first. I think I just figured it was Mallory after I ran into the dining room and found Robyn unconscious."

He pulled his notebook closer, flipped a page, and ran the back of his fork down a few lines. "According to Mallory, Robyn ate the cake and then moments later started screaming."

Guilt once again dug its claws into her. "That was Robyn screaming?"

"Yeah, that was confirmed by everyone."

Her stomach turned over. Even though she was terrified of his answer, she had to ask, had to know. "So if I'd gone back to her right away, she might have been saved?"

He paused mid bite and lowered his fork to the plate. When he reached out to her, she placed her hand, which had gone ice cold, in his. "I doubt that few minutes would have made a difference, Gia. She was gone by the time they got her to the hospital. If you hadn't tried to save her, she'd have been gone sooner. Sometimes all you can do is give someone the chance, and you did that. Actually, there was a roomful of people there, and you and Savannah were the only two who made any attempt to save her or summon help."

She nodded, holding her gaze steady on the counter to keep any of the threatening tears from falling, though she had no doubt she'd rehash the moment Robyn had screamed over and over again in her mind, and what ifs would surely chase her through her quiet moments for quite some time.

He tilted his head to look up into her eyes "You okay?"

She nodded again. The best she could do for Robyn now was give Hunt whatever information she could to help him solve her murder. "Yeah, I am. I just feel bad that I didn't go to her sooner."

"I understand that. I'm curious, though, why didn't you go back when you heard the scream?" He set his plate aside and sipped his coffee. "That was great, definitely hit the spot, thank you."

"Any time." She stood and put his dish in the sink with a few others, then started cleaning up. Doing something helped her think. She'd heard the woman's scream, and had started to go back, but Alyssa had reached out and stopped her. "Alyss...uh..."

Uh oh. That might not bode well for the other woman.

"It's all right, Gia. Just tell me what happened."

There was no way Alyssa could have had anything to do with Robyn's murder. She'd been with Gia and Savannah when it happened. "Alyssa had just brought out two slices of cake for Savannah and me to try. She said she'd just served it to Robyn's group. A couple of minutes later, we heard a scream. When I started to go back to see what was going on, Alyssa stopped me, said they'd been screaming like that since they got there, fighting with one another over everything."

Hunt nodded absently as he scribbled notes in his notebook. When he was done, he flipped the page. "That's what Alyssa told me too. What happened after that?"

"There was another scream and someone yelled to call nine-one-one, so we—Savannah, Alyssa, and me—all ran into the dining room and found Robyn on the floor." She shook her head. "I think that's when I first assumed it was the other woman who'd screamed."

"Do you know who yelled to call nine-one-one?"

She'd heard Isaac speak when he argued with his mother outside the caterer, but she couldn't recall his voice, couldn't be sure one way or the other if he'd been the one to issue the demand. "No, it was a man's voice, so either Isaac or Jeremy, but that's all I can tell you. I'm pretty sure it wasn't Carlos, since he came into the dining room after we were already there."

"Okay. Anything else?"

She tried to recall all of her observations while she and Savannah were trying to save Robyn, but the only thing that stuck out in her mind as unusual was Jeremy's proximity to Alyssa. And, of course, the fact that no one tried to help, but they could have been in shock, and everyone reacted differently to stress. Had it been a spider coming toward Gia, her irrational phobia probably would have made her freeze. Perhaps that's what had happened. It wasn't up to her to judge.

"Gia?"

Oh, right, he'd asked her if she'd noticed anything else unusual. Though Jeremy's hand on Alyssa's back could definitely seem inappropriate, it also might have been completely innocent. Perhaps he'd lost his balance or was simply trying to see past her to where his fiancé lay on the floor. Or maybe he was offering comfort he thought Alyssa might need. It was possible Gia was making more of the gesture than necessary, maybe because of the rumors that were flying. Honestly, though, how many times had Trevor touched Gia or Savannah, always in a completely platonic, friendly way? He was just an affectionate person. Probably better not to mention anything since she couldn't be sure.

"Whatever you're thinking that has you so frazzled, do share." Hunt lifted a brow and stared at her. Either he knew her too well for her to keep secrets from him, or his detective skills were that spot on. Probably the former.

"I'm not really sure of anything, but at one point, Jeremy put his hand on Alyssa's back, and the gesture seemed...I don't know...somehow inappropriate...too...um...familiar, maybe? Kind of intimate. But I could be thinking that only because Isaac was carrying on about the two of them."

"Fair enough." Hunt flipped his notebook closed without writing anything down. He stood and stuffed it back into his pocket.

Gia took a quick peek through the cutout into the dining room where Willow was taking an order. Savannah must have taken Leo to Gia's office to answer his questions. She turned to tell Hunt she was going to take Leo his dinner before the orders picked up again and ran right into his chest.

His dark eyes fixed on hers. He slid his hand along her cheek, then tucked a strand of hair that had come loose from her bun behind her ear. His fingers lingered, caressing her neck, before sliding around to cradle her head as he kissed her.

Her insides melted as she kissed him back.

"Okay, enough of that now." Savannah whistled from the doorway.

They jumped apart.

Savannah grinned. "There's a time and a place, y'all. And this here ain't it."

Heat burned in Gia's cheeks.

Hunt just laughed.

Wanting to get off the subject quickly, Gia grabbed Leo's dinner and set it on the counter for him, then gestured for him to sit down and eat.

"Yeah, well, now's definitely not the time." He took a forkful of the breakfast pie but didn't bother to sit. "A nine-one-one call just came in, and we've got to go."

Hunt frowned. "What's up?"

"Seems Jeremey Nolan and his friend, Ethan Cater, walked into a bar…"

It sounded like the set up to a bad joke, and Gia held her breath waiting for the punchline. She had a feeling it wasn't going to be funny.

"Isaac was there drowning his sorrows, and there was an all-out brawl between the three." He took another quick bite.

Hunt sighed and gave Gia a quick peck on the cheek. "Don't wait up."

Chapter Seven

By the time Gia finished cleaning up and picked up Thor from daycare, it was fully dark. Despite the crushing desire to go home to her own house, light a few candles, and take a nice long bath with Thor sitting beside the tub, she turned onto Trevor's street, then paused in front of the driveway and used the remote to open the wrought iron gates. "You know, with everything going on, I almost forgot Christmas is just over a week away. I still can't get used to wearing capris and short sleeves in December."

Savannah, who'd slouched quietly in her seat the entire way to Trevor's, smiled. "You'll get used to it one of these days."

"I still haven't decided what to get Hunt." Whom she still hadn't heard from since he left with Leo earlier. She studied Savannah in the glow of the Christmas lights lining Trevor's driveway. "Any brilliant ideas you're willing to share?"

"Sorry, hon, I got nothin'. Hunt's pretty much impossible to buy for."

"That's not much help." She parked in the courtyard and turned off the engine, then sat and admired the decorations. "What are you getting Leo?"

"We decided not to buy each other gifts this year so we'd be able to go on a nice honeymoon."

"Hmm…" That might be an idea. She'd been thinking a lot lately that she and Hunt never got to do much together. Between both of them having demanding careers that didn't give them much time off, and being exhausted at the end of the day, then spending their days off doing all the things they didn't have time for while working, there wasn't much time left for fun. And often when one of them did manage to get a free day, the other had to work. "How do you think Hunt would feel about going away for a few days?"

She sat up straighter. "I think that's a great idea. Where would you go? The Keys, maybe?"

"Ha ha." She didn't dare go to the Keys after Savannah repeatedly begging Gia to go with her and Gia repeatedly screwing up their plans. Of course, Savannah was going with Leo for her honeymoon, so maybe…

"No, I'm serious." Turning in the seat to face Gia, Savannah tucked one leg beneath her, a sure sign she was settling in for a conversation. "Hunt would enjoy it. You can go snorkeling, parasailing, paddle boarding, maybe take some haunted tours."

"I don't know, I was thinking more along the lines of laying on the beach somewhere with a pina colada." Maybe dipping her feet in the water now and then when it got too hot.

"I guess that's good too." Savannah shrugged and reached for the door handle.

"Then again…" Maybe Savannah was right. She and Hunt could just sit together at home. If they were going to take a few days off, may as well make them exciting. "We haven't been on a date in forever, so maybe it would be nice to go somewhere and actually go out and spend some time doing things together."

Savannah bounced in the seat and clapped her hands together. "Great, I have all the brochures with me, so we can look through them when we go inside."

Accepting it was going to be a long night of sorting through brochures filled with pristine beaches, palm trees, and smiling vacationers, Gia climbed out of the car. She could think of worse ways to spend the night. Besides, Savannah would be married in a week, and their nights together would come to an end. It would be foolish not to take advantage while she could. "I can't wait. Want to make popcorn?"

"Sounds like a plan." Savannah climbed out of the car and paused in the courtyard. "I think he added more."

Gia opened the back door for Thor. "What are you talking about?"

Savannah pointed to the garden where a small Christmas village now sat.

Miniature ice skaters glided on a frozen pond ringed with snow covered stones, shoppers bundled in coats and scarfs balanced parcels in gloved hands, and a church, complete with a bell swinging in its steeple, boasted a beautiful nativity scene amid a patch of snow out front. Strands of festive colored lights hung from the line of stores lining the courtyard.

Gia's breath rushed out. "It's incredible."

Savannah hooked an arm through hers. "It is, isn't it."

For just a moment, as she stood staring at the winter scene, a cool breeze washed over Gia, bringing with it the aura of the season. "Come on, let's go make that popcorn."

"You think Trevor has a sewing kit somewhere in there?" Savannah gestured toward the mansion.

"I'm sure he does, why?"

"We're making popcorn anyway; why don't we string some for the tree?"

"Sounds like the perfect night." If they could just forget about murder and the uncertainty of Savannah's wedding plans, even just for a little while.

They stopped at the potty pavilion for Thor, then headed inside. "I just want to stop off at my room real quick before we make the popcorn, if you don't mind. All I want to do is put on my comfy pjs."

"Mmm…that sounds so good." Savannah stopped in front of the French doors, stretched her arms over her head, and leaned from side to side.

Gia pushed open the door to their suite.

Klondike and Pepper froze, took one look at Gia from amid a chaotic array of evergreen, lights, tinsel, and ribbon and darted for the other room, leaving the Christmas tree lying on its side in front of the fireplace.

"Klondike! Pepper!" Gia surveyed the damage.

"What have you two gotten up to?" Savannah fought a grin.

A smile tugged at Gia. "I guess the popcorn will have to wait until we get this mess cleaned up."

Savannah bent and grabbed hold of the tree. "You keep it from sliding, and I'll stand it back up, then we can assess the damage."

After they righted the tree, they spent some time rearranging the ornaments that had been knocked askew, lined the lights back up, and straightened the bows. Gia grabbed a chair and climbed up to put the tree top back in place. Thankfully there were only two casualties, one pink and one ivory and gold ball. A quick trip to the pantry for a dustpan and broom took care of the glass and evergreen needles that had scattered all over the floor. "How long do you think before they come back out?"

Savannah waved her off. "Oh, please, as soon as they hear their food cans pop open, they'll come running."

Since Klondike was Gia's first experience with a kitten, she'd have to take Savannah's word for it. "You're sure?"

"Trust me on this."

Of course, Savannah was right. A little while later, when she popped the top open on a can, Pepper and Klondike skidded around the corner and into the kitchen at lightning speed.

Gia scooped Klondike in her arms and nuzzled her head. "You, little missy, need to behave."

Klondike purred and snuggled back. How could Gia possibly stay angry at her?

Not to be left out, Thor nudged her hand. When she didn't immediately respond, he nudged her again with his nose, harder.

"Don't worry, silly." Gia set Klondike down to eat and weaved her fingers into Thor's thick fur. "Mama's got plenty of love for you too. Come on, it's time to make popcorn."

Half an hour later, with the tree none the worse for wear, and all of the animals fed and taken care of, Gia and Savannah sat cross-legged on the Persian rug in their comfiest pajamas, a fire crackling in the large stone fireplace behind them, and a gigantic bowl of popcorn between them. They'd been fortunate enough to find a small sewing kit in the kitchen junk drawer, as well as cranberries to add a little color to their strands.

Thor snuggled against Gia's leg, while Klondike and Pepper slept tangled together a few feet away. Seemed knocking over the Christmas tree was exhausting work.

Savannah set her phone aside, her Christmas playlist softly playing in the background.

Hunt wasn't the only one Gia still had to shop for. While she'd already gotten Christmas gifts for Savannah and Leo, which had been easy with the wedding coming up, she hadn't decided on something special for their wedding. She'd give them a card with the money she'd saved for the occasion, but she still wanted to do something extra special for her best friend, a friend who'd stood beside her through everything and helped her achieve her dreams. How could she do the same for Savannah? Her thoughts drifted through a myriad of ideas, all of which she dismissed as not perfect.

A soft knock on the door interrupted.

"Come in," Savannah yelled.

Trevor cracked the door and poked his head in. "Am I interrupting?"

"Not at all." Gia patted the rug between her and Savannah. "Come sit."

Savannah shifted over to give him room, then threaded a needle and handed it to him.

He took it and looked down at it. "What do I do with this?"

Gia laughed. "Haven't you ever strung popcorn before?"

"Actually, no." He didn't elaborate, just took a piece from the bowl, studied Savannah's perfect technique for a moment, and gave it a try. The popcorn crumbled, and he blew out a breath.

Savannah patiently showed him how to place the needle directly in the center to keep the popcorn from breaking. "Give it a try."

With *Winter Wonderland* playing behind them, the three sat together making piles of popcorn strands for their tree. Though Gia had made her own popcorn strings when she was a kid, she'd always done so alone, cooped up in her room, sitting on her bed beside the tiny tree on her nightstand. Tears pricked the backs of her lids, not tears of sadness for the child who'd grown up so alone, but tears of joy for the adult who'd found a family in Boggy Creek.

"Come on, let's see how they look." Savannah jumped up and grabbed a strand. The warmth of the fire reddened her cheeks, and a soft glow lit her features. It was the best she'd looked in quite a while.

Together, they started to wrap the strands around the tree.

"Hey, Trevor," Savanah called. "Have you spoken to Carlos or Alyssa?"

He tied off the end of the string and handed her his strand. "Carlos came into Storm Scoopers earlier for his typical banana split stress reliever, and I took a few minutes to talk to him at a booth in the back. He's pretty torn up over the whole thing."

"I can't blame him." Gia knew all too well what it was like to have someone murdered at your place of business. "First the murder and then having the police shut them down to investigate."

After handing Savannah enough to wrap around the back of the tree, Trevor propped his hands on his hips and stood back to admire their work. "I actually don't think it's that as much as the rumors."

"About Alyssa and Jeremy?" She wouldn't blame him for being torn up over that, but hopefully he'd dismiss them as idle gossip.

"Yeah." He nodded, then reached out and draped one of the strings up a branch. "I never really viewed Carlos as possessive, but I saw a different side of him today."

Gia might not know Alyssa well enough to ask blunt questions, but she did know Trevor well enough. "From what I've heard, Carlos didn't permit Alyssa to maintain friendships with men. If that's true, why would he have tolerated your friendship with her?"

"I don't know." Trevor started to back up just as Thor stood. Unable to stop his momentum, Trevor fell over backwards and plopped back down on the floor.

"Oh, no." Gia reached for him. "Trevor. Are you okay?"

"I'm fine." He laughed. "Not the worst spill I've ever taken."

"Still, you went down pretty hard."

"I'm fine. Come on and sit with me, Thor." He swung around to sit facing the fire, stretched his legs out in front of him, and watched Savannah work. "If the rumors, which I've been hearing all day too, are actually true, I'd guess because the three of us always did things together. It's not like we hung out every day or anything, but when we did, we had a good time. All of us enjoyed the same things, and I never called Alyssa directly. I always spoke to Carlos to make the plans. Besides, lately Zoe's been joining us too."

"Really?" Gia grinned.

Thor lay beside him, his head on Trevor's lap, peering up from beneath his lashes at Gia.

She petted his head.

Zoe had been taking care of Thor at her Doggie Daycare Center since Gia first brought him home, and she was a sweetheart. Gia was thrilled the two of them were spending time together.

Bright red patches flared on his cheeks. "Well, she takes such good care of Brandy and all, and she's a really nice person, and we got to talking one day when I was picking Brandy up, and it turns out she likes a lot of the same things I do. It's not always easy to find someone who enjoys the same sense of adventure as me."

When he finally paused to take a breath, Gia bent and patted his shoulder. "I think it's awesome the two of you are hanging out. And you're right, finding someone who enjoys kayaking might not be so difficult, but finding someone who wants to dive off high things attached to a rubber band is probably a bit more challenging."

Trevor laughed. "Hey, what can I say? I live for the thrill."

Gia just shook her head. At this point, she knew Trevor well enough that his incredible organizational skills surprised her way more than his thrill-seeking did. "So, what else did Carlos have to say?"

Trevor shrugged and turned his gaze to the flickering flames. "He asked me if I thought there was any truth to the rumors."

"And do you?"

"I told him I didn't..." Shadows cast from the flames flickered and danced across his scowl.

"But?"

"Hey, give me another strand of the popcorn, will you?" Savannah held out a hand, her focus fully on Trevor as she waited for him to answer.

Gia handed her another and held the end while she started to wind it around the tree.

"To be honest, I'm not really sure. I don't know why, and it's not that I believe everything I hear, and I certainly never witnessed her flirting or acting inappropriately, but every time I try to dismiss the gossip, I'm left with the tiniest bit of doubt." He shook his head. "Anyway, I'd never repeat it anywhere but here with the two of you, but I wouldn't say it's entirely out of the question. She did enjoy a good thrill, and the excitement of doing something wrong without getting caught definitely seemed to be a draw for her. She suggested more than once sneaking into the air obstacle course after hours and trying it in the dark. So, who knows if the idea of cheating might appeal? Though, of the two, I'd say Mallory was the more likely to have been fooling around with someone on his way down the aisle."

"Mallory Levine? Robyn's maid of honor?"

"Oh, yeah." Trevor turned to face them, folding his legs and resting his elbows on his knees. "It wouldn't be the first time she went after a man who was already spoken for. Nor would it be the first time an evening ended with her in a cat fight with a jealous woman. She seemed to enjoy flirting with men who had dates, then smiling and walking away, leaving the men flustered and uncomfortable and their significant others furious."

"Hmm..." Savannah frowned. "How do you know Mallory?"

"Just from around. She'd sometimes end up in the same place as us or even join us on occasion. She never came on to me or anything," he added quickly. "Of course, I only started seeing Zoe recently and haven't run into her since, so maybe that's why. Her interest in men she'd known for years suddenly piqued when they showed up with a date on their arms."

"Do you know if she ever went after Jeremy?" It didn't seem Robyn would have asked her to stand up for her if she had. Unless she knew it was all in good fun on Mallory's part. Then, maybe she'd have tolerated it.

"I have no idea. I don't know him, and I've never seen them together." He shrugged and waved it off. "Anyway, she lives kind of out by you, Gia, on five acres a couple miles past your development. She's a real estate agent and sells a lot of properties in your area."

"Hmm." Savannah frowned. "I'm surprised I've never met her. I know most of the agents in town."

Before taking a leave of absence to work with Gia at the All-Day Breakfast Café, Savannah worked as a real estate agent in a local office. After her kidnapping, she decided not to go back to work, said the thought of going into a house with a stranger was just too upsetting.

"She works for an agency in the next town over and doesn't spend much time in Boggy Creek." He scratched Thor's head.

Thor propped his chin back on Trevor's leg and turned his big brown eyes lovingly up at him.

"Jingle Bells" came on, and Savannah turned up the volume. She bopped and twirled, dancing around the tree as she wound strands of popcorn and cranberries.

Despite the talk of Robyn's murder and the players surrounding it, the night was just about perfect. Not only was Gia having a great time with her friends, but the beginnings of an idea for Savannah and Leo's wedding gift had begun to niggle at her. And if it played out like she hoped, she'd get a chance to talk to Mallory Levine herself. If she was close enough for Robyn to have asked her to be her maid of honor, she should have an opinion on what was going on among the bunch of them. Not that she was planning on interfering in Hunt's investigation, but she sure was curious.

Chapter Eight

Gia slid a plate filled with three scrambled eggs, bacon, sausage, and home fries onto the counter in front of Earl Dennison. The older man had been her first customer when she opened and had since become a close friend. Cole's words from the previous day came back to her and filled her with joy. Earl had become more than a friend. She smiled as she added a plate with two biscuits, a bowl of gravy and one of grits. "You know you're going to clog your arteries with all of this, right?"

Earl laughed, as he always did when she admonished him. His wife, Heddie, had always told him the same thing before she passed away, and he'd taken to eating his breakfast out. "You sound like one of my kids now."

"Well…" Gia refilled his coffee cup. "Did you ever consider maybe they're right?"

He raised a brow. "Not a once."

She laughed as she refilled her own coffee cup and grabbed a can of Diet Pepsi from the fridge beneath the counter and set it in front of Savannah. Satisfied everything was ready for her to unlock the doors and open up for the day, Gia settled onto the stool between Earl and Savannah. She'd come to enjoy the moments spent with Earl, Savannah and sometimes Cole or Willow, before she opened the café each morning. It had become routine, like spending time lingering over breakfast with family before the rigors of the day demanded her attention.

"Oh, Gia," Savannah slid one long maroon nail beneath the tab of her soda and popped it open. "Did you ever get a chance to look up belladonna poisoning last night?"

"No, I didn't. By the time we got home and finished hanging out and doing the tree, I forgot." But there was a another, more immediate situation she needed to discuss with Savannah, and now was as good a time as any. Probably the only quiet time they'd get before tonight. "You know, Savannah, I've been thinking…"

"Uh oh." She grinned as she scrolled through something on her phone. "Hey! What happened to no one likes a smart aleck?"

Savannah just laughed.

Gia braced herself. She had to somehow steer the conversation where she needed it to go without Savannah figuring out what was on her mind. And since Savannah pretty much knew what was on Gia's mind before it came out her mouth, and sometimes even before she thought it, that would be no easy task. It would have been easier if Savannah hadn't been privy to the conversation with Trevor about Mallory, but she had been present, so there was a better than average chance her mind would follow the same path Gia's had as soon as she started asking questions. "Have you given any thought to where you and Leo are going to live once you're married?"

Savannah lifted her gaze from the phone to stare at Gia. "I have, but every time I think about it, I change the subject on myself."

"I mean, you are both more than welcome to stay with me, if you want to?" She slid her crossed fingers behind her back. She really hoped they'd decide to stay with her. She'd gotten used to Savannah living in her spare bedroom.

"I know, and thank you, Gia, that means a lot." She shrugged and went back to staring at her phone. "But we do need a home of our own. Unfortunately, the thought of looking at houses always sends a wave of anxiety crashing through me."

Savannah had always loved showing houses, finding that just perfect home for each couple she worked with, until she'd been drugged and kidnapped from a mansion she was showing. After that, going into empty houses with strangers no longer appealed. Gia took the easy dismissal for what it was, apprehension she wasn't quite ready to deal with.

"Well, I just wanted to let you know that you are also welcome to the apartment over the café if you want to stay there until you guys find something instead of staying at my house." Other than Gia staying over now and then when she worked late, no one had used the apartment since her last tenant didn't work out.

"Really?" Savannah shot to her feet and flung her arms around Gia's neck. "I hadn't thought of that. Thank you."

"You bet." Now for the tricky part. "I know it won't be permanent, but at least it's somewhere to get started and have some privacy until you find something."

"It's awesome. I can't wait to tell Leo. Of course, we'll pay you a fair amount of rent—"

Gia held up a hand. "You can just stop right there. You'll pay me no rent, and you'll save all of your money for a down payment on the house of your dreams."

"Gia—"

"Speaking of the house of your dreams," Earl interrupted. "Where do you think you'll end up buying? Somewhere in town or out by your dad or Gia, maybe?"

Gia shot him a silent thank you look. She'd shared her plan to speak to Mallory about a house out by her while Savannah was in the back room, and he'd intervened at the perfect opportunity. Not that Savannah seemed to be paying enough attention to catch on anyway, since she was once again fully engrossed in whatever she was reading on her phone.

"I don't know. I was kind of thinking of finding something out by Gia's. It's quiet, peaceful, has plenty of land for as many dogs as I want, and would be a nice place to raise a family."

Gia choked on her coffee and sputtered. "Family?"

"Uh huh."

She grabbed a napkin and patted her mouth. "Like in kids?"

Earl laughed out loud. He set his fork on his plate. "Yes, Gia, that's what she means by a family. And for the record, I think you're right, Savannah, it would be the perfect neighborhood to raise kids."

Since Savannah came from a large family, it wasn't surprising she'd want kids, but Gia hadn't really thought about it. Kids. Huh. She warmed to the idea. Savannah would make an amazing mother. Now Gia had all the information she needed, and thanks to Savannah's distraction with her phone and Gia being caught off guard with the whole kids thing, she hadn't tipped her hand. "Well, I'd love to be an aunt."

"Yup."

"Okay, enough is enough." The distraction had served its purpose, but now Gia's curiosity was piqued. She tapped Savannah's phone screen. "What has you so enthralled with that phone?"

"What? Oh…" She finally looked up with a sheepish grin. "Sorry. I was just reading about belladonna."

"The poison?"

"Uh huh." She cleared her throat and read from the phone. "Atropa Belladonna, also known as deadly nightshade, gets its name from Atropos, one of the Three Fates in Greek Mythology. Legend has it, Atropos has your life in her hands as she snips the final thread of your life's tapestry after her sisters have spun and measured it. And then you die. And the term belladonna comes from the Italian for 'pretty lady' because women during the Renaissance used the juice of the berries in eyedrops to dilate their pupils and make them more seductive."

"Hmm…" While Gia found the history interesting, she was more focused on who could have gotten it and used it to poison Robyn.

"It seems odd they'd use such a toxic substance for things like cosmetics, medicine, and even at one point, love potions," Savannah continued.

"Do you think that has anything to do with why Robyn was killed?" Try as she might, Gia couldn't think of a motive to give someone belladonna, other than to kill her. And if someone had given it to her as a love potion, then who? Surely, not her fiancé, as Isaac claimed repeatedly.

Savannah shrugged and dropped her phone into the bag hung on the back of her stool. "Probably not, unless it was her fiancé, Jeremy, who gave her the potion to make her fall in love with him. Then again, why would he need to do that? Surely, she wouldn't have been marrying him if she didn't love him."

Unless she had an ulterior motive. Savannah always assumed the best in people, always saw everything in innocent terms. Unfortunately, not everyone was as innocent as she was.

"Anyway…" Savannah gestured to the front door, where the Bailey sisters, Esmeralda and Estelle, stood staring in the window, then rounded the counter, stuck her bag beneath the register, and grabbed two menus. "Time to go to work."

Gia unlocked the door and greeted Boggy Creek's two unofficial gossip mongers. "Good morning, ladies."

"Gia." Estelle nodded.

"Good morning, dear." Esmeralda didn't wait for Gia to seat her, just made a beeline for the table in the exact center of the café, where the two would be sure to hear everything that went on. Not that there was much at the moment, since no one other than the Baileys had come in yet. Which meant they had news they were willing to share.

"How have you both been? I haven't seen you since…" Gia riffled through her memory for the last time the Bailey sisters had been in. Oh… right…last weekend, just hours after Maureen and Clifford Harris had an all out blow up in the middle of the bowling alley after Maureen's mother showed up unannounced and declared she was moving in. "Last weekend."

"Oh, right, yes." Esmeralda patted her perfectly coiffed blue updo. "I heard Clifford's still sleeping on the couch."

"Well, where else would he sleep, dear?" Estelle winked at Gia. "Maureen's mother took the bed. Poor Maureen is stuck sleeping with her youngest."

Gia made a mental note never to let these two know anything personal about her. She had no idea where they got their information—she had visions of them sitting in front of a control panel to rival NASA's with TV screens showing every house in town bugged—but the pair were a menace.

"Anyway..." Estelle waved a hand in the air to dismiss the old news in favor of something new. "Did you hear Isaac Hackman got arrested?"

Gia hadn't heard, as her few conversations with Hunt since he'd left with Leo the day before hadn't included the case. Which had been a nice change.

"Again." Esmeralda added knowingly.

Gia's interest perked up at the sudden shift in the conversation. "You know Isaac? He's been arrested before?"

"Oh, please. That man has been arrested more times than I can count." Estelle looked to her sister for confirmation.

With a nod, Esmeralda took up where Estelle left off. "Usually for fighting with someone or another. Isaac spends too much time in bars, squandering his mama's inheritance, and he is not a pleasant drunk. More often than not, a night out for Isaac ends in a confrontation."

Gia ignored the comments. As much as she enjoyed chatting with the Bailey twins, she knew all too well what it was like to be on the wrong end of their rumors. "Did you know Robyn?"

They both nodded, and their eerily similar expressions turned somber as if on cue.

Savannah poured the sisters coffee, then returned to the front door to seat a young couple dressed in business suits. Gia didn't have much time before she'd need to head back to the kitchen.

"Robyn was a sweet girl. And her husband treated her like gold before he was taken from her in a car accident." Both sisters made the sign of the cross, and Estelle said, "Bless his soul."

"And hers," Esmeralda added. "After the accident she withdrew, stayed to herself for several months."

Estelle harumphed. "Not long enough to be appropriate, if you ask me."

Esmeralda only nodded at the interruption and continued. "Spoiled that no good son of hers something awful."

"Then one day, she just snapped out of it..." Estelle's snap caught the attention of a few customers who turned to look. "Next thing you know, that man was on her arm everywhere she went."

"Man? You mean Jeremy?" Gia watched Savannah move through the room, pouring coffee and orange juice, taking orders. It was time to wrap this up and get in the kitchen.

"Yes, that's the one." Estelle fished her glasses out of her bag and perched them on the edge of her nose.

All right, one more question. "Did he and Isaac get along at first?"

"Oh, goodness, no. Like oil and water…" Estelle started.

"Went at it from the day she brought him home, those two, with absolutely no regard for how it upset her so." Esmeralda lifted her menu and began to peruse her choices, signaling the end of their conversation. It was time for the sisters to listen for new dirt and for Gia to get to work.

She stopped briefly to say hello to a group of college students who were friends with Willow and sometimes came in early to study for exams. With the semester ending, she figured they were either cramming or celebrating.

She then left them to Savannah, said good-bye to Earl, with a quick whispered thank you for his help with Savannah, and went in the back to cook. She'd already preheated the grill, so she washed her hands, donned gloves, and waited for Savannah to put up the first order.

While she waited, her thoughts wandered to Mallory, and her excitement grew. Would she be working this soon after her friend died? Maybe not. But if her office handled a lot of the sales up by Gia's development, she didn't necessarily have to speak to Mallory. Maybe someone else in the office could help her. It didn't matter, since she wasn't investigating, but she had to admit to a certain amount of curiosity about the woman.

Anyway, when Gia had been ready to flee New York, between her divorce, her ex's trial, and the constant stream of death threats, she hadn't had much time to make it down to Florida. Savannah had handled finding the building for the café and setting most of it up. While Gia would have been perfectly content to live in the small, one-bedroom apartment upstairs, Savannah had insisted she needed a home.

So she'd hunted for something affordable with the scant amount of savings Gia had left. She'd sent Gia pictures of the three-bedroom Spanish style ranch, its cream-colored stucco walls contrasting beautifully with the scalloped terra cotta roof tiles. The house was surrounded by woods that brought to mind what the world must have been like before the intrusion of skyscrapers and city blocks, more peaceful than anywhere she'd ever known. Gia had fallen in love instantly.

Of course, she hadn't known about the critters then. But that was beside the point. She'd managed a sort of peace with them as well. She'd learned to use bear-resistant garbage pails—who even knew that was a thing?—kept a careful eye out for snakes as she walked the property, and had even come to terms with using the butterfly net Savannah gave her to catch the occasional lizard that found its way into the house and release him outside. But when it came to spiders the size of her hand, all bets were off. She still screamed and ran every time one skittered across the wall, its hairy legs tap, tap, tapping as it ran. Savannah and Hunt had both tried to tell her the spiders were more scared of her than she was of them. They were so wrong.

"Hey, Gia."

She screeched and whirled toward the sound of Savannah's voice.

"You okay?" Savannah lifted at brow at her, the same expression Hunt often used, and stuck the first two tickets above the grill.

"Oh, yeah, sorry." Her heart pounded wildly, and she pressed a hand against her chest. "You caught me off-guard."

"Mm…hmmm." Savannah scanned the floor. "You had that horrified look on your face, the one usually reserved for when you find spiders or other scary critters."

"No, no critters. Not this time." Gia laughed out loud, glad to see she and Savannah were back on the same page again. "Thanks, Savannah."

"For what?" She tilted her head, her brows drawn together as she stared at Gia like she might have lost her mind.

"Just for being you and for always being by my side. I'm going to miss you." Tears she wouldn't let fall prickled the backs of her lids. She blinked them away.

"Don't worry. You'll still see plenty of me. Probably so much you'll get tired of me."

"Never happen."

Savannah smiled as she whirled toward the door and went to visit with the customers she so adored.

Gia grabbed a bowl and started cracking eggs to scramble for several omelets. Time to get to work. At least until Cole arrived and she could slip away to her office to call the real estate office.

Chapter Nine

The weekend flew by in a haze of wedding preparations, last minute Christmas shopping, wrapping paper and ribbons. Because it had been Savannah's last weekend as a single woman, she and Gia had spent it together, preparing for the holidays, enjoying time curled up on the couch watching old movies with a bucket of popcorn between them and Thor, Klondike, and Pepper snuggled up against them. They reminisced about the past, with more emphasis on the good times than the bad.

Plus, the café had been packed. With everyone running around doing last minute holiday shopping and preparations, and news of Robyn's murder spreading like wildfire, the café had maintained a steady stream of customers. Not that Gia was unhappy about that, but she was looking forward to a couple days off this coming weekend. She switched on her windshield wipers and shifted in her seat to pay better attention to the curving stretch of road bordered on both sides by towering pine trees that had probably been seedlings when dinosaurs still roamed the land. If dinosaurs had populated Florida, which she had no clue about. When the GPS warned her to make a right turn in two miles, she eased off the gas.

Monday morning brought gray skies and a cool drizzle, unusual weather of late. While Gia might have missed fall, winter was a different story. Christmas shopping in capris and short sleeves might take some getting used to, but it was a whole lot better than hurrying from place to place on icy sidewalks, her breath coming in frigid gasps that froze her lungs, wearing a bulky winter coat that stretched across her back every time she shifted her packages. She braced herself for the familiar wave of homesickness that usually accompanied such thoughts, but it didn't come. She smiled.

Reality intruded as she hit her turn signal, even though there were no cars around for miles, to make the turn into the parking lot at the real estate office where Mallory Levine worked. As much as she hated to admit it, they were going to have to look for another caterer. Now, how to break it to Savannah, since she had her heart set on Carlos and Alyssa. Not to mention the logistics of finding someone four days before a Christmas Eve wedding. She sighed and shifted into park. It looked like they'd have to do it themselves. Unless...

If Gia was catering a large event in less than a week, she'd have started the bulk of the shopping and ordering already, leaving only perishables for the last minute. If Alyssa had done the same, she'd be stuck with all of that food if she wasn't able to cater the wedding and Christmas dinner. And there was no reason she couldn't cook; it's not like either she or Carlos had been arrested or anything, just closed down while detectives investigated and looked for clues in the shop. So, technically, there was no reason they couldn't do their jobs from anywhere other than their shop. And Gia had already planned to close the All-Day Breakfast Café for the day. Maybe Alyssa could work from there. She jotted *call Alyssa* on the ever growing to do list stuck to her dashboard before climbing out of the car.

She thought about taking her umbrella out of the back seat, then dismissed it. The slow drizzle would hardly soak her in the few feet she had to run to the front door. Although she was surprised Mallory was back at work already, Gia was glad to have gotten the appointment with her. When she'd gotten a few free minutes Friday and called, Mallory was cool and professional, obviously not realizing Gia had been at Rinaldi's when Robyn died. Or if she did realize it, she hadn't mentioned it. She simply took Gia's information, spoke to her about what she was looking for, and told her she'd have a number of houses lined up to show her on Monday morning.

A thrill coursed through her. She'd missed out on this when buying her own house. A niggle of doubt crept in. Maybe Savannah would want to look for something herself. Or with Leo. Gia shook off the apprehension. All she was doing was narrowing down Savannah's options for her. Savannah would still have the final say, and they'd go together with Leo and maybe Hunt so she'd feel comfortable.

A bell rang when she pulled the door open, announcing her arrival.

A woman with her hair pulled back in a severe bun and glasses perched on the end of her slightly crooked nose looked up when she walked in. "Can I help you?"

Did everyone in this office have that cool, reserved tone? She much preferred Savannah's perky, welcoming style. "Good morning. I'm Gia Morelli. I have an appointment with Mallory Levine this morning."

"Oh, yes. Have a seat, and she'll be right with you."

"Thank you." Gia glanced around the sleek, contemporary office, then took a seat in one of the black-cushioned stainless-steel-framed chairs. She picked up a tattered copy of an architectural magazine from the glass table and flipped through the pages. When nothing caught her interest, she returned the magazine to its precise position in the fan of magazines spread across the table and scanned the waiting area. Generic landscapes dotted the walls, all of which could have been of local areas. One particular painting, a group of monkeys skittering across a tangle of mangrove roots, pricked the desire to go kayaking with Trevor again. After the wedding she'd have to see when he would be free and make time to do so.

"Good morning, Ms. Morelli." Mallory, dressed in a slim black skirt with a pink blouse, crossed the waiting area and extended a hand.

"Gia, please." Gia stood and took her hand. "It's nice to meet you."

Mallory's grip on her hand tightened, and her eyes narrowed. "Hey, I know you."

"You do?" Should she admit to knowing who Mallory was when she made the appointment or play dumb? Too coincidental. She had to fess up.

"You were there when Robyn died."

"Yes, I was. I'm so sorry about your friend."

"Thank you." She finally released Gia's hand and stepped back. Her facial expression remained completely neutral, and her thick black eyeliner and what had to be false lashes appeared freshly applied, not so much as one smudge. "What do you want?"

"I…uh…" The unexpected hostility threw Gia off. What was she supposed to say to that? "I spoke to you on Friday about finding a house out in Rolling Pines for my best friend who's getting married this weekend. Trevor Barnes mentioned you handle a lot of sales out here."

"Trevor, huh?" She narrowed her gaze on Gia. "Isn't that the guy who owns the ice cream place in town?"

"Yes."

"Hmm…"

A phone rang, and Mallory looked over her shoulder toward a cubicle then back at Gia. "Why would your friend want to live way out here?"

The thought that this might have been a mistake eeked its way into Gia's mind, and she had to resist the urge to squirm beneath Mallory's pointed gaze. "I live in Rolling Pines, and Savannah's been living with me. She loves it out here, and I thought I'd help her out by narrowing down her choices since she has so much else to do getting ready for the wedding."

"Mmm…hm. Okay, well, I've lined up six houses to take a look at. You're in luck, there's a lot for sale out here right now." She turned and started toward a cubicle on the far side of the office.

Gia looked around, unsure what she was supposed to do, and then followed. If nothing else, she'd get a look at Mallory's personal space.

She didn't know what she'd expected to see, but what she did see was literally nothing. No personal items, no photos of family or friends, not even a hastily scrawled note on the calendar or a post it anywhere in sight, only an unmarked folder, a cup with two pens, and a phone. Mallory grabbed the file folder off the desk, her purse from the bottom drawer, and a set of keys from the desk. "You can follow me."

"That's fine." She'd hoped they'd drive together so she could get a chance to ask about Robyn, but even if they did, there was no way she was prying any information out of this woman. She may as well take her own car so she could get back to the café as quickly as possible when they were done and before Savannah started asking questions about where she was.

Mallory stopped short, and Gia almost plowed into her back.

She skidded to a stop then stepped around Mallory just as Hunt opened the door and walked in.

If he was surprised to see her, he didn't let on. Then again, Hunt had mastered the poker face. He kissed her temple. "Hey, Gia. Imagine running into you out here."

She resisted starting off with *I can explain,* a phrase she used all too often when running into Hunt in unexpected places. "Hey, yourself. I'm just heading out with Mallory to look at houses for Savannah and Leo."

His eyebrows shot up, and a slow smile spread across his face. "What a great idea."

She didn't have to explain the reason she was doing the legwork; Hunt would understand, and it was none of Mallory's business. "Thank you. It's kind of a wedding surprise, though, so can you not say anything to her or Leo?"

"No problem."

"Thanks." Speaking of surprises, she still had to work out Hunt's vacation gift. Savannah was right, a trip to the Keys to do some fun things together would be a wonderful break. Who knew? Maybe the two of them could even find somewhere to go kayaking down there.

"Do you have a quick couple of minutes, Ms. Levine?"

Gia stepped aside to give Hunt and Mallory some semblance of privacy, though everyone in the small office would clearly hear what was being said.

"Good morning, Captain. Call me Mallory, please." Mallory's smile lit her green eyes, and she flipped her wavy blonde hair behind her shoulder with a seductive swing of her head. Her voice had gone down an octave, from smooth and professional to a sultry purr. "What can I do for you this morning?"

"I'm sorry to bother you at work, Ms. Levine, but I had a few questions I wanted to follow up on." Hunt pulled the notepad from his pocket and flipped it open.

"Of course, anything to help you find Robyn's killer." Mallory leaned back against the nearest desk, crossing her legs at the ankles. Her skirt fell open at the slit exposing a good length of bare, perfectly tanned thigh. She folded one arm across herself, boosting her cleavage, then ran one hand delicately down the collar of her button-down shirt, moving lazily past the first two open buttons.

Whoa! Gia bristled. Was this even the same woman who'd greeted her so coldly?

Hunt didn't even look up from his notepad, and Gia couldn't help a small surge of satisfaction, petty though it might be.

When he did finally look up, he got right down to business. "Ms. Levine—"

"Mallory, please."

"Sure. I'm just trying to go over the timeline of events again." He tapped his pen against the notepad. "You said you were late arriving at Rinaldi's for the tasting."

"Yes." She didn't elaborate, simply batted her fake lashes and waited him out, cool as could be.

"What time would you say you got there?"

Even her shrug was sexy. "I didn't look at the clock, maybe fifteen minutes before Robyn...well, you know..."

"And you parked out front?"

"Yes. And ran across the street and in the front door."

"And who was in the room when you arrived?"

"No one, actually. For a minute I thought I was too late and they'd already finished, but then Jeremy walked in and said Isaac and Robyn were out front. Arguing. Again." She rolled her eyes.

Wait a minute. Fifteen minutes before Robyn's demise, Gia had been sitting out front with Savannah, and Robyn and Isaac had been arguing on the sidewalk. She'd seen them walk out of the café, so Mallory would have had to walk in while they were on the sidewalk. Even though the two walked down the sidewalk a ways, Gia still had a clear view of the front door. She hadn't seen Mallory walk in. She was pretty sure no one had walked in. But could she be positive? Hopefully, there were surveillance cameras somewhere along the street, because she was pretty sure Mallory just told a whopper of a lie.

Hunt lowered the pad. "But you didn't see them on the sidewalk out front when you walked past?"

Ha! He's gottcha there.

"No, I was in such a rush because I knew Robyn was going to be disappointed. I'm the one who usually ran interference between Jeremy and Isaac." She sighed dramatically.

"And you didn't hear them arguing?"

"I'm sorry. I told you everything I know, and I'm trying to keep myself together so I can do my job." Tears welled in Mallory's eyes, shimmering just short of falling over and making her eye makeup run. She peered at Hunt from beneath lowered lashes. "But if you'd like, you can stop by my house later after I get off."

"I'm sorry, ma'am. I just have one more question, and I'll let you get back to what you were doing."

She sniffed daintily. "Of course, thank you."

"At any point before Robyn fell, did you see Ethan Carter?"

Mallory heaved in a deep breath and let it out with a shudder. "No, I'm sorry, but I didn't. As far as I know, he only got there after the fact."

"When he didn't show, did anyone try to call him to see if he was running late?"

"Not that I know of."

"What about you? Did Robyn try to call you to find out why you weren't there yet?"

Her eyes widened, only for an instant before switching to a sultry pout. "Why, Captain, you said only one more question."

"You're right, I did." He tucked the pad back into his pocket and nodded toward Gia. "I can get that information from the cell phone records. Thank you for your time, Ms. Levine. I'll be in touch."

"Any time, Captain." She swiped beneath one eye and managed to catch a tear without smudging anything.

Her gaze lingered on Hunt as he walked out, and Gia's insides boiled. It wasn't like she hadn't seen Hunt and Gia together. She'd seen him walk in and kiss Gia. Okay, only on the temple. But still.

When Hunt climbed into his Jeep, Mallory turned toward Gia, her eyes completely dry. "All right, let's go get this done."

Chapter Ten

Gia followed Mallory toward the fifth house of the morning, with no more hope of finding just the right house for Savannah than she had of getting Mallory to open up and part with any information. Of course, she hadn't really tried, since she'd been too annoyed with her for flirting with Hunt. She shook off the thought. It didn't matter; finding the perfect home for Savannah did.

They'd already looked at a log cabin and a pretty A-frame, but they were both in disrepair and would need a tremendous amount of work. She didn't think Savannah or Leo would want to put that much work or money into their new home, but she'd keep them in mind. They could always live in the apartment until the work was completed if they wanted to. And the property surrounding both houses was beautiful. With a little TLC, both houses could be amazing. The other two houses Mallory showed her were large contemporary homes and quite a bit over budget. She just couldn't picture Savannah in either of them. She needed something cozy and homey, something that would suit her personality.

Gia turned onto a quiet dead-end street just two blocks over from her own home. Not that her neighborhood was laid out in the grid pattern she associated with blocks in New York, but she couldn't help but think of it that way.

The location would be perfect for sure, close enough to walk back and forth if they wanted to brave the bears, snakes and alligators. Gia shivered as she pulled over to the side of the road and stopped when Mallory did. She climbed out of the car and stood on the front lawn of a beautiful pale yellow cottage with a blue metal roof and a white wrap around porch. A swing hung from the ceiling, paddle fans gently rotating above it. A stone path led from the concrete driveway to the front porch steps, and flowers spilled over from flower boxes beneath every window.

Hibiscus plants in an array of colors, one of Savannah's favorite flowers, ran along the front of the porch railing, bordering a garden split by the walkway.

"Wow." Gia sucked in a shaky breath. "It's perfect."

Mallory smiled at her side, the first seemingly genuine reaction Gia had seen from her. "It is, isn't it."

"Is the inside as nice as this?"

"Come on, I'll show you." Mallory led the way to the front door and used a key code to unlock it. "The price on this was just reduced, and the owners are in a hurry to sell since they've already moved back to Colorado, so it will go fast. If you think your friends will like it, they should get an offer in right away."

Gia didn't think it was a sales pitch; she expected this house would go fast. Savannah had once told her houses in Rolling Pines that were in good condition usually sold quickly. It was not only a great neighborhood, if you didn't mind living a bit off the beaten path, but the houses were fairly inexpensive compared to others closer to town. Of course, she'd been trying to sell Gia on her house at the time, and resale value and turnaround time were two factors to consider. "I'll tell you what, if the inside is as perfect as the outside, I'll call and have her meet us out here now if you have time to wait."

"Sure thing." She pushed open the door and stepped back for Gia to enter. "I can wait."

When Gia stepped in the front door, she had a clear view straight through the open floor plan to the back of the house, and a tropical oasis. Sliding glass doors at the far side of the great room led to a screened free form swimming pool surrounded by palm trees and flowers in terra cotta pots. A small waterfall cascaded over stacked stones between a thick array of tropical looking flowers planted on either side. Her mouth fell open, and she glanced at Mallory.

Her smile was smug. "Would you like to finish touring the house or just call your friend now?"

"Why in the world didn't you show me this one first?" The view from the great room, which stretched from the front of the house to the back, was breathtaking. A breakfast bar separated the great room from the kitchen, the open floorplan allowing for viewing of the lanai and pool from pretty much everywhere in the downstairs.

She shrugged. "If I showed you this one and you didn't like it, we'd have had to backtrack to look at the others."

You'd have to be crazy not to love this house. "I'll call Hunt now and see if he can pick up Leo and Savannah and bring them out here."

"You do that." Mallory pulled a compact from her purse and checked her face in the mirror, then pulled out a tube of lipstick.

Gia tempered her annoyance and stepped outside to call Hunt. She walked back toward the road, leaned her back against the side of her car, and surveyed the house. She could see Savannah living here. And it would be worth dealing with Mallory's flirting if it meant Savannah would have the house of her dreams. As long as Hunt stayed as indifferent as he had earlier.

A sudden thought struck Gia. She had no doubt Hunt wouldn't show any interest in Mallory, or any other woman, and the certainty staggered her. After the situation with her ex, Gia would have never expected to trust another man, and yet, here she was. She trusted Hunt completely. Hmm... who'd have thought?

Hunt answered on the third ring. "Hey there, Gia. What's up?"

She pulled her mind back to the matter at hand. "Can you get away for about an hour?"

"Uh...hang on." He held the phone aside and said something to someone, but she couldn't hear what. "Yeah, I can get away. Is everything okay?"

"Yes, more than okay, actually. I found it, Hunt, the perfect house." An image of Savannah running after a pack full of puppies on the expansive front lawn came to mind. Puppies Gia could handle, kids...well, she wasn't quite there yet, even in her imagination. "Can you track down Leo and bring him and Savannah out to Rolling Pines?"

"Isn't Savannah working?"

"Willow's there. She can cover for an hour."

"All right." He rolled the chair back from his desk and it creaked as he stood. "Leo shouldn't be too hard to track down since he's sitting across from me. With his feet on my desk."

She rattled off the address. Even though Mallory remained inside the house with the front door closed, Gia lowered her voice. "And, Hunt, I couldn't help but overhear your conversation with Mallory earlier."

"Uh huh. Why am I not surprised?"

She chose to ignore that, since they both knew she'd have overheard that conversation if it had taken place three rooms away. It was just part of her inquisitive nature, no matter that Hunt called in nosy. "Savannah and I were sitting out in front of Rinaldi's when Isaac stormed out and

Robyn followed, and I never saw Mallory pull up out front or go inside. It's possible I could have missed her, but the scene between Robyn and her son was pretty intense. Hard to believe she could have missed it if she was right there on the sidewalk."

"Yeah, well, unfortunately there's a lot of hard to believe discrepancies in the timeline, not only for Mallory but for the others as well. Seems to be a lot of confusion about who was where when." He told Leo to grab his stuff, they were heading out. "I'm on my way. And Gia?"

"Yup."

"Stay out of trouble until I get there."

"Don't I always?"

He groaned and disconnected the call.

She laughed as she stuck her phone in her pocket. She was pretty sure by "Stay out of trouble" Hunt didn't mean she shouldn't ask questions. Surely, that was okay. Now that Mallory was hyped up that she might make a sale, maybe she'd loosen up a bit and let something slip. She opened the front door and stepped back inside.

Mallory stood at the back door, looking out over the pool, phone against her ear. She glanced over her shoulder when Gia entered, said, "She's back. I gotta go," and disconnected the call.

She was too far away for Gia to see the screen. "They're on their way. You're sure you don't mind waiting?"

"No, it's fine." She held up the phone and rocked it back and forth. "I just rescheduled my next appointment."

Far be it from Gia to make a judgement from the five words she'd overheard, but if the cool professionalism she'd first greeted Gia with was indicative of her normal behavior, there was no way that call had been business. Though, in all fairness, Mallory hadn't said it was a business appointment. For all Gia knew, she could just as well have rescheduled a lunch date with a friend or an appointment with her hairdresser. "I don't want to hold you up from meeting with any other clients, unless you meant to show them this house. Then by all means, I totally want to interfere."

Mallory smiled and waved off the comment. "It's fine."

"It will take them about twenty or so minutes to get out here. Do you want to sit outside?"

"Sure." She returned her phone to her bag. "We can wait on the porch so you see them pull up."

Gia followed Mallory outside, and when Mallory leaned against the porch railing facing the swing, Gia took a seat and gave a gentle push with her foot against the floor so she'd swing lazily back and forth. And suddenly the image of Savannah rocking a baby on this same swing wasn't so far-fetched.

Mallory tilted her head and studied Gia. "You and your friend must be very close for you to go through so much trouble for her."

"Believe me, it's no trouble. Savannah and I are like sisters." She didn't usually share personal information with strangers, especially those she was convinced were lying to the police, but she never minded sharing how much she cared for Savannah. "Savannah has stood by me through some of the most difficult times in my life, and there's nothing I wouldn't do for her."

"It must be nice to have a friend that close."

"I imagine you and Robyn were that close, no? Considering you were her maid of honor."

Mallory shifted her gaze to a spray of palm leaves at the far end of the porch. "No. We weren't that close."

Taken aback by her brutal honesty about her relationship with a woman who'd just been murdered, Gia wasn't sure how to respond.

Mallory saved her the trouble of saying anything when she turned back to look at Gia and continued. "Robyn was married to my brother, Max. She and I weren't close, but then again, Robyn wasn't really close with anyone."

Since Gia didn't know what to say to that, she let it go. "I'm sorry about your brother. She must have been devastated when he passed away."

"When Max had his heart attack—"

Wait! What? Heart attack? She was positive the Esmeralda and Estelle had said he died in a car accident. How could the Bailey sisters have gotten that so wrong? Not that they were always completely accurate, but it was usually their interpretation that was off. Their facts tended to be spot on. "I'm sorry, I thought your brother was killed in a car accident?"

"His heart gave out before his car went into the tree." She waved it off as if that didn't matter. Perhaps it didn't. "Anyway, Robyn became even more withdrawn than usual after his death. I don't know if she spoiled Isaac or if she just didn't care what he did, but he turned into a spoiled, obnoxious brat."

"Oh." Taken aback by her blunt assessment, Gia didn't know what else to say. "How old was he when Max was killed?"

She rolled her eyes. "Twenty-four."

"Oh," Gia said again, for lack of any other ideas for a response. She'd assumed he was a child when his father was killed from the way everyone spoke about him. "How old is he now?"

"Twenty-five."

"Max was only killed a year ago?" She wasn't quite sure why, but she'd gotten the impression it had been longer. Maybe because Robyn was remarrying already?

"Yup, and a few months after Max died, Jeremy started hanging around Robyn. Him and his no-good sidekick, Ethan." She opened her mouth to continue but then clenched her jaw closed tight.

Gia needed to keep her talking. If she clammed up, she might not start talking again. According to the Bailey sisters, Robyn didn't go out much after her husband's death, which would have made it more difficult to meet new people. "Where did Robyn meet them?"

Mallory unclenched her jaw, looked down, and massaged her temples. Gia didn't think she'd answer, but after a moment, she lowered her hands and looked up. "Jeremy and Ethan started hanging out with Max not long before he died. A few months, maybe."

"So they were friends?"

"I guess you could say that, though I never cared for either of them. I never trusted them. And Max acted weird around them, nervous or something, like he didn't trust them either, you know?" When she scowled, her perfectly sculpted brows drew together in what appeared to Gia to be a practiced expression.

Gia could relate to not trusting people well enough, but why befriend people you didn't trust? Why bring them into your home?

"Anyway," Mallory shook her head, "I don't know what the deal was. For as long as I can remember, Max always spent most of his time with family, then all of a sudden, he started hanging out with those two constantly like they were a bunch of teenagers. And then he was gone."

A flicker of pain crossed her face before she once again schooled her features, and Gia had a feeling she'd just seen the first glimpse of genuine emotion regarding her brother and Robyn since meeting her.

"I truly am sorry for your loss." She started to reach for her, then thought better of the idea. Mallory didn't seem the type to share her emotions. Better to just give her a moment to collect herself. "What about Isaac? Where was he through all of this?"

"He didn't get along with Jeremy even when Max was alive. And I don't just mean they didn't get along; I mean Isaac hated him."

"Do you know why?"

"No idea." Mallory glanced at her watch. "If you'll excuse me, I have a few calls to make while we wait."

"Of course."

Mallory started away, and Gia called out to her. "I'm just curious, and please feel free to tell me it's none of my business," because it most definitely was not, "but how did you end up as Robyn's maid of honor if you felt that way about Jeremy?"

"Because Robyn asked." She studied Gia, then shrugged. "Probably because I was the only one who seemed to be able to quell any arguments between Isaac and Jeremy. And I accepted because it was my in to get closer to her and Jeremy. Because I don't believe for one minute that Jeremy and Robyn got together and fell in love after Max died. Sorry, but I'm just not buying it. I was determined to find out what happened to my brother, and now one of the only people who might have had that answer is gone. Awfully convenient, don't you think?"

Chapter Eleven

Gia pushed her foot against the deck, rocking the swing. An unusual cool breeze ruffled her hair off her face, and Gia was reminded winter was about to begin. She envisioned a beautifully decorated Christmas tree sitting in the front bay window of the house, and a zing of nerves sizzled through her. What if Savannah didn't like the house? What if she was too nervous to go inside? What if she felt like Gia was throwing her out?

With another rock of the swing, she dismissed all of the what-ifs. Savannah told her she wanted a place of her own, and she'd be fine to go inside with both Hunt and Leo there. And, as far as the house went, what was not to like?

Mallory retreated to the side yard somewhere to make her calls, out of earshot of Gia's eavesdropping.

Not for lack of trying on her part.

Hunt's olive-green Jeep pulled over on the edge of the front lawn. and Savannah hopped out of the back seat.

Gia hurried across the lawn and yelled, "Surprise!"

Savannah stopped short. Her gaze landed on the "For Sale" sign on the front lawn, and her mouth fell open.

Gia gestured toward the house. "Do you love it?"

Leo got out from the passenger side and rounded the front of the car, then stood beside Savannah and hooked an arm around her shoulders.

"Oh my." Tears shimmered in Savannah's eyes and she shook her head. "Gia, I don't know what to say."

"Please, start with you love it and it's perfect." She held her breath and waited for Savannah to answer.

"I love it, and it's perfect!" She squealed and gripped Gia's hand.

"Come on, wait until you see the inside." When Gia started toward the front door, Savannah's grip on her hand tightened, and she hesitated. Only for a moment, until she glanced behind her at Hunt and Leo. Gia ignored the pause and moved forward slowly with Savannah's hand held tight in hers. "You're going to love it. Now, when you walk in the front door, I just want you to stop and look. Okay?"

"Sure." Savannah shrugged, her attention consumed first by the garden and then the wide wrap around porch. "Oh, look at all the hibiscus plants."

"I knew you'd love those." Gia pushed the front door open then stepped back for Savannah and Leo to walk in together.

One step in, they both stopped and stared through the great room to the pool.

Savannah shot Gia a wide grin.

Yes! She gave a mental fist pump.

"So, do your friends love it as much as you do?" Mallory folded her arms across her chest and leaned a hip against the railing. She peered from beneath her lashes at Hunt, then glanced at Gia and straightened up.

Hmm…interesting. Were they friends of a sort now? Did Mallory consider Hunt off limits because Gia had listened while she talked? Come to think of it; why did she open up so freely to Gia? Could it possibly have something to do with the fact that her boyfriend was the police captain in charge of Robyn's case?

Was Mallory doing the same thing to Gia that she'd done to Robyn when she positioned herself as her maid of honor? Using her? Gia hated feeling that way, hated being suspicious when Mallory might well have just needed someone to talk to. She smiled at Mallory. Whatever the reason, it couldn't hurt to let her know she appreciated her laying off the flirtatious routine. "I'm pretty sure they love it, then again, they haven't stopped oohing and aahing long enough to actually tell me."

She laughed as she followed Savannah and Leo into the house.

Hunt took Gia's hand and kissed her temple. "You did good. I can see them living here."

Warmth spread through her as they stepped inside and stopped in the doorway. She gripped his arm with her free hand and laid her head against his shoulder. "Me too. It's perfect, isn't it?"

"Wow. I'll say it's perfect. Look at that pool area. I can already smell the steaks grilling out there." His stomach growled, and he pressed a hand against it and grinned.

"And you haven't even seen the back yard yet." Mallory set her purse on the breakfast bar and her phone beside it, then pointed toward the window over the kitchen sink, which overlooked another acre of property, surrounded on three sides by towering pine trees and giant moss-covered oaks.

"Incredible." Gia set her bag beside Mallory's. If all went as well as she hoped once Savannah and Leo returned from touring the rest of the house, they might be there for a while. She moved to stand beside Mallory at the window.

A swing, made from a plank with two ropes knotted through it, hung from one branch of a huge oak, swaying gently in the soft breeze. For Gia, it was the perfect touch to make the house feel like a home.

"Did you see the bedrooms? And the master bath?" Savannah rushed into the kitchen and threw her arms around Gia's neck. "I don't know how I can ever thank you for this, Gia."

Gia hugged her back, thrilled to be a part of making Savannah's dreams come true while selfishly keeping her nearby. She stepped back and laughed, then wiped a stray tear that had tipped over and tracked down her cheek. "Actually, I wanted to give you and Leo space to look around together first, so I haven't seen the rest of the house yet."

Savannah grinned from ear to ear. "Well, it's perfect! No, it's beyond perfect. It's amazing, it's stupendous, it's…It's home."

"I can't tell you how happy I am for both of you."

"Well, you gave Leo and me time to look at the house together, and I appreciate that, but now you have got to see this tub." Savannah hooked her arm through Gia's and hauled her toward the hallway, chattering a mile a minute about how amazing the house was.

She wasn't wrong, the master suite was just as perfect as the rest of the house, high vaulted ceiling, a set of French doors set amid a wall of windows overlooking the pool oasis. And the master bath boasted not only a walk-in shower with three shower heads, including a rainfall shower head, but a huge, deep jacuzzi tub you could lose yourself in for hours. In all, the master suite was the perfect retreat, like a tropical getaway within your own home.

Savannah returned to the master bedroom and pushed open the French doors, inviting the coolish breeze inside.

"So, what do you think?"

Gia whirled toward the sound of Mallory's voice from the bedroom doorway.

"Oh, I love it. It's perfect." Savannah flung her arms out to encompass both the room and the yard.

"I'll go ahead and get the paperwork started for you to make an offer," Mallory said.

Gia glanced at Savannah to be sure she was certain. She didn't want Mallory pushing her into something she wasn't ready for. She didn't read any hesitation in Savannah's expression, but still. "You can take some time to talk it over with Leo if you want."

Savannah waved her off. "Nope. We already talked about it. It's perfect. In the neighborhood we wanted to be in, within our price range, and even better, less than a mile away from you, Gia. I could walk over to say hello any time I want."

Gia shivered. Though she often walked around her yard with Thor—and her bear spray close at hand—she hadn't yet worked up the nerve to wander around the neighborhood surrounded by the thick Ocala National Forest.

Savannah's laugher echoed through the cavernous, empty room. "Don't look so stricken, Gia. Not all of us are afraid of every little critter."

Gia didn't argue, simply laughed with her. Savannah grew up in rural Florida, so to her bears, alligators, and giant snakes were the norm. Gia hadn't yet mastered her level of comfort with the Florida wildlife yet, though, in her defense, she was getting better.

"Oh, wait, you know what I didn't realize?" Mallory held up a finger and frowned, then pushed the bedroom door closed gently, with only the softest click. "Unfortunately, there might be one little problem."

Savannah spun toward her. "Problem? What kind of problem?"

"Well…" Mallory shrugged and put on her best pout, her full, recently polished lips accentuating the expression. "It seems your cousin and your fiancé ask an awful lot of questions, ya know? And for some reason they keep coming back to question me."

What was she talking about? As far as Gia knew Mallory had only been questioned the day of Robyn's murder, with a few follow up questions from Hunt earlier this morning. And Gia had seen Hunt grill a suspect before; his questions for Mallory had been tame in comparison.

"I mean, it's not like I haven't already given a complete statement of the events that occurred around Robyn's tragic death," Mallory continued, "and answered everything they've asked, multiple times now."

Gia moved to stand beside Savannah. Whatever game Mallory was playing, she wasn't going to get away with it. "What are you talking about?"

"Well, it makes a girl wonder if she's a suspect, you know?" She lowered her gaze and peered from beneath her thick lashes, a move that might have had more of an effect on an unsuspecting man.

It only served to irritate Gia further.

"And I'm sure it would be a conflict of interest for a suspect in a murder investigation to sell a house to one of the investigating officers." She folded one arm across her body and tapped a dagger sharp French manicured nail against her lips.

Who said anything about her being a suspect? As far as Gia knew, she wasn't suspected of anything, though she did suspect Mallory had lied to Hunt about being late for the tasting. And now here she was trying to manipulate some part of the investigation, though Gia wasn't quite sure just exactly what her goal was.

Mallory's perfectly sculpted brows drew together in a scowl, which Gia suspected she'd spent considerable time practicing in front of a mirror. "It sure would be unfortunate if the sale fell through because of something like that. Don't you think?"

Enough of this nonsense. Gia took a step forward, sucked in a breath, and opened her mouth to let Mallory have it.

Savannah lay a gentle hand against her wrist to stop her, then smiled sweetly at Mallory. "Well, bless your heart, dear."

Uh oh. Whenever Savannah started out with bless your heart in that syrupy tone, nothing good was coming. Oh, well, Mallory had brought it on herself.

Savannah took a step toward Mallory. "You're right, of course."
Wait. What?

Mallory fluttered her lashes. "I'm glad you can see my dilemma. Now, what could we possibly do to resolve it?"

Savannah hefted her oversized bag higher on her shoulder and moved toward the door, continuing as if Mallory hadn't said anything. "And in that case, since you are right and since I definitely want this house, I will contact the listing agent directly and make the offer through him or her. Thank you for your time."

"Wait, what?" Mallory's mouth fell open and her eyes went wide as she stumbled after her.

Gia bit back a grin as Savannah reached for the door knob.

"Wait!" Mallory stepped in front of her and splayed a hand against the door. "You can't do that. I already took the time to show you the house, along with five others I showed your friend this morning."

Actually, it was only four others, but who's counting? Apparently, not Mallory.

"I know, and I appreciate that." With a dismissive nod, Savannah sidestepped Mallory, then once again reached for the door. "Thank you for your time, dear. Much appreciated, but I can take it from here."

Gia bit the inside of her cheek to keep from smiling. Mallory had clearly underestimated Savannah.

"You can't just go somewhere else. That's not legal!" Mallory was on the verge of whining. Clearly, whatever her angle was, she hadn't thought it through before opening her mouth. Rule number one when you want to intimidate someone, know your opponent, which she obviously had not taken into consideration.

Savannah's slight build and innocent, sometimes naïve, disposition often led people to believe she was a pushover. Those people couldn't be more wrong. A lesson Mallory Levine was about to learn the hard way. Under other circumstances, Gia might have felt sorry for the woman. As it was, not so much.

"Of course, I can. I can do business with whomever I choose, and while it might be unethical under other circumstances, it is most definitely not illegal. Especially when the agent in question just tried to blackmail me into something, though I'm not even sure what, to be honest."

Mallory's complexion paled beneath her makeup. "Please, you took what I said wrong. I didn't mean it that way."

"Oh, then what did you mean?" When Savannah tilted her head, her smile was all sugar. "And before you open your mouth and stick your foot back in it, you should know that before I went to work for Gia as a waitress at the café, I was a real estate agent."

"Uh...Oh." Mallory deflated. "Look, I didn't mean anything, I was just saying..."

Savannah propped and hand on her hip. "And for the record, I agreed with you, so what's the problem?"

"You don't understand. I really need this sale, and I don't want to lose it. Please, listen to me."

Savannah pursed her lips and shot Gia a glance.

Gia just shrugged. On the one hand, she really wanted to walk out of there and let someone else sell Savannah the house, and on the other hand, Mallory obviously had something on her mind, and Gia would be lying to herself if she didn't admit to a certain amount of morbid curiosity about what it was.

With a quick glance at her watch, Savannah wrapped her arms around herself, cocked a hip, and tapped her foot. "You have one minute."

"It's not that I have a problem with Captain Quinn or Detective Dumont, it's not even that I mind answering their questions. I certainly want them to find out who killed Robyn. I just want to know I'm off the suspect list, ya know?" Tears once again shimmered just short of falling over her lashes.

"No, not really. Why would you assume you were on the suspect list in the first place?"

"Well, Captain Quinn came back in this morning to ask me questions again, and my experience with the police has been—" She stopped short, a look of horror crossing her face. Clearly she had almost slipped and said more than she'd intended. "Look, I have to get going on this if you want me to put in an offer. While we're here dilly-dallying, someone else could beat you to it."

Savannah bit her lip. "I don't know. I really don't want to run into problems down the line. Like you said, I might be better off with someone else that I know won't have a conflict of interest."

"Please, there won't be any conflict. I shouldn't have said that, and I apologize. I just thought maybe, you know, you could ask those two to look elsewhere for a suspect. Robyn wasn't exactly my friend, but she was once my brother's wife, and I was very close with him, and I did like Robyn, and I most certainly wouldn't have hurt her..." She swallowed hard. "Or worse."

"Who do you think killed her?" Savannah blurted, catching Mallory and Gia both off guard.

"I...I...uh...I have no idea." She whipped the door open. "And like I said, I'd love to hang around and chat, but if you don't want to miss out on this perfect house, I have to get the offer in."

Savannah held up a finger. "All right, fine, but there had better be no problems."

"Oh, there won't be. Thank you." She started through the doorway.

"And Mallory?" Savannah called after her.

She paused. "Yes?"

"Believe me when I tell you..." She smiled and batted her lashes in perfect imitation of Mallory's earlier ploys. "If you pull anything that costs me getting this house, or if you ever try to intimidate me again, I will ruin you."

Mallory swallowed hard and nodded.

Gia watched her walk out, questions swirling around in a chaotic jumble in her mind, questions she'd love to ask at a more opportune moment. Hunt had said Mallory insisted there were real leaves and berries on the cake, though Gia hadn't seen any. She definitely wanted to ask about that. And she really wanted to know what Mallory had stopped just short of revealing about her past experience with the police. But now wasn't the time. This was Savannah's moment. There would be plenty of time to track Mallory down and demand answers later.

Chapter Twelve

Gia snapped her seatbelt closed, looked to be sure no one was coming, and headed out of the development. She thought of stopping home quick to pick up something to wear for the dinner Hunt had unexpectedly asked her out to before they'd parted ways, but she had a nice print skirt and cream-colored blouse at Trevor's that she could wear, so there was no real reason to stop home except that she missed her little house in the forest. At some point over the past year, all the apprehension she'd originally felt about living in such a rural area had faded, leaving her with only the comfort of home and a sense of accomplishment. Her first house. All hers. And she loved every last thing about it. Even the quiet nights, which had been a big enough problem when she first moved in that she'd been forced to sleep with the TV, or her phone before her cable had been installed, tuned to a station that played old movies with lots of screaming, sirens, and explosions to lull her to sleep.

"So," Savannah twisted in the passenger seat to face Gia and slipped on her sunglasses. "What do you think?"

"About?" Gia stopped at a stop sign and hit her turn signal, not that there was anyone around to alert to her intention. She and Savannah were both headed back to the café, so Savannah opted to ride with her and let Hunt and Leo head off to whatever investigating they had to do next.

"Mallory, of course." She slid her glasses down just enough to peer over them and lift a brow. "Don't even tell me you missed her insinuation that this wasn't her first run-in with the police."

Gia laughed. She should have realized Mallory's slip wouldn't have gone unnoticed by Savannah. "No, I didn't miss it, but as much as I wanted to question her on it, you getting the house was more important in that moment."

She clapped her hands together and relaxed back into the soft seat. "It is perfect, isn't it? I just love it so much. Thank you for that, Gia."

"You're very welcome, but don't be too grateful yet. Let's just wait and see if the owners accept your offer."

"Oh, they'll accept. We offered their asking price. I didn't even try to get them to pay any of the closing costs, since I don't want to risk anyone offering higher while we negotiate. So there's no real reason for them to say no."

"I hope you're right." For her own sake as well as Savannah and Leo's. Selfish as it might be, she really wanted Savannah to stay close by. At least then, when Leo worked late, they could hang out together with a bowl of popcorn and some old movies.

"I usually am." She grinned. It was good to see some of Savannah's confidence returning.

"I am curious, though, what made you decide to let Mallory handle the sale?" Gia had fully expected her to walk out and go to someone else.

"She did show us the house, so there's some amount of respect for that, but at the end of the day, even if she ends up getting arrested for Robyn's murder, the sale wouldn't be affected. Someone else in her office would just step in." Savannah dug through her bag, pulled out a pack of gum and offered Gia a piece. Then she unwrapped her own piece and popped it into her mouth before dropping the pack back into her oversized bag, which always seemed to contain anything she needed. "Besides, now we have reason to go back out to her office and grill...uh... I mean, talk to her some more."

Gia couldn't help but laugh. Once again, Savannah's thoughts had run similar to her own. Not that she should be surprised by that. "So what do you think she started to say before she caught herself?"

Savannah pulled out her phone and waited for service. It would be a few miles before she could connect. "That's one of the things I was wondering too. As soon as I can get a wi-fi signal, I'm going to look up her brother, Max, and see what his deal is. Then I'm going to search Mallory's name and see what I can come up with."

"Snoop much?" Gia chided.

"Hey, it's never a bad thing to know who you're doing business with."

"Touché." It was a lesson she'd learned the hard way, so she couldn't argue. "Speaking of, I had an idea for the catering."

"Yeesh, don't remind me." She slouched in the seat. "That's one path I've actively been trying to keep my mind from wandering down."

"Me too, but at this point, we have to consider some other options, so I was thinking of asking Alyssa if she wanted to use the All-Day Breakfast Café kitchen to cook. At least, for the wedding. I was closing anyway, so it won't even interfere with business. The rehearsal dinner is smaller, so I'm sure she can do the cooking for that at Trevor's."

"Seriously? That's a great idea."

"I'll give her a call while you see what you can dig up on the Levines."

"Works for me."

At the first sign of civilization, Gia switched her phone to Bluetooth and dialed Alyssa's number.

A man answered. "Hello, Gia."

"Hey, Carlos, how are you?"

There was a long pause, but Gia couldn't be sure if it was hesitation on Carlos's part or spotty cell phone service. "I'm doing okay, all things considered. How is Savannah holding up?"

Gia glanced at Savannah, who was deeply engrossed in something on her phone. "She's doing well, I think."

"Look, Gia, Alyssa and I totally understand if she wants to cancel the catering contract. Especially considering how up in the air things are with the investigation right now."

"Actually, I'm calling for just the opposite reason. Is Alyssa available?"

"I'm sorry, she's…uh…she can't come to the phone right now."

"Oh, well, that's okay. I was just thinking that, with your business closed down, maybe you could do the cooking for Savannah's wedding at the All-Day Breakfast Café. That way, there would be no question about you being able to get it done."

"Huh…" The hum of the tires against the pavement drowned out any sounds Carlos might have made.

"Carlos?"

"Yeah, uh, sorry. Listen, I'll talk to Alyssa about it, and we'll get back to you. If it's okay, we can stop by the café tomorrow morning and maybe take a look at the kitchen?"

"That sounds great, you can come early, before I open, and I'll give you the tour and you can join us for breakfast if you'd like."

"Sounds good. I'll see you then." He disconnected without saying anything further.

Hmm…weird. He might have been a little more enthusiastic considering he'd have lost the job otherwise. Anyway…

She shoved the thought away for later. It didn't matter right now. She'd talk to Alyssa in the morning and get her opinion, then they could decide whether they needed to change track and come up with a new plan.

Since Savannah was privy to the conversation via Bluetooth, Gia was saved the trouble of having to repeat it. But one thing was nagging at her. Well, more than one thing actually, but one to start. "You know what I'm curious about?"

"What's that?" Savannah answered, frowning at her phone.

"If the cake did have some kind of poison in it, belladonna or something else, how did it get there? Theoretically, Carlos would have been in the kitchen cooking." Gia thought of what it was like on a busy day in the café when Cole was in back cooking. She always loved to visit with customers and pitch in as much as possible in the dining room, even if Willow and Savannah were both there. "Alyssa was most likely bouncing back and forth between the kitchen and the dining room, especially since she was serving, so I guess it's possible neither of them saw anything unusual. Though it seems Alyssa would immediately notice something off about the cake. But Isaac, Jeremy, and Mallory, and Robyn for that matter, were all present in the dining room when the cake was brought in. How could someone have poisoned it right in front of everyone and no one noticed?"

"Hmm…" Savannah tapped a steady rhythm against the dashboard with her nails. She snapped her fingers and spun toward Gia. "Unless the poison was added while the cake was still in the kitchen."

Gia studied her a moment to see if she was kidding, but the expected grin never came. "For that to have happened, either Carlos or Alyssa would have to be the killer, and I just don't see why either of them would kill Robyn."

"Who knows?" She tapped her phone several times, obviously still not getting a clear signal. "What if the rumors are true, and Alyssa and Jeremy do have something going between them. She could have wanted to get rid of the competition."

Gia took her eyes from the road for just an instant to see if Savannah seemed to be kidding. "You can't possibly think that's true and still plan to use Alyssa to cater your wedding."

"Nah, just sayin'. As a motive, it works as well as any."

"I guess, but I just don't see Alyssa killing someone in a jealous fit of rage and then going home to her husband like nothing happened."

"Huh…when you put it like that, probably not." Savannah sat back in the seat and typed something into her search box. "I can't see any reason for Carlos to have killed Robyn."

"No, me neither." If anything, if the rumors turned out to be true, he'd be opening up a position at Jeremy's side, a position his wife just might decide to fill. "And it doesn't make sense for Carlos to have killed her. Unless the poisoned slice wasn't meant for her. Mallory said she gave Robyn her slice; maybe the killer had been targeting Mallory. Or Jeremy, even."

That made more sense to Gia, that Carlos would have wanted to get rid of Jeremy if he was encroaching with Alyssa. And it jibed with what Cole had said about Carlos being jealous and possessive. Still…as a theory, it was weak at best.

"Ugh!" Savannah tossed the phone into her bag.

"No service?"

"No. So annoying." She lowered her face into her hands. "I need this to be over."

"I know." What could she say? Though her heart broke for Savannah having so much stress less than a week before her wedding, especially after Trevor had gone to so much trouble to make sure she could relax, what could she do to help?

"Someone needs to solve this case. And fast."

And there it was. The only thing she could do was try to ask around and at least see if she could clear Alyssa and Carlos, since they were the only two who actually impacted Savannah's wedding. Oh, and Mallory, since her involvement might possibly impact Savannah's hope to buy the house in Rolling Pines. Okay, how hard could it be to clear those three? Even if Mallory's past did turn out to be a little murky, what were the chances she, Alyssa, or Carlos had killed Robyn?

"Anyway, enough talk of murder. Did you book your trip to the Keys yet?"

"Uh." Gia struggled to switch gears from murder to vacation. "No, actually. I was thinking of just telling Hunt about the trip for Christmas, maybe wrapping up a box with some hints inside and letting him help in the planning. Could I borrow some of your brochures?"

"Sure." A slow smile crept across her face, mischief dancing in her eyes. "So, did you figure out what Hunt got you yet?"

"I haven't even thought about it." But now that Savannah had brought it up, especially with that sly smile teasing her, she couldn't help but wonder. "Do you know what he got me?"

"Oh, please, honey, of course I do."

True. Why would she have even questioned that? "Well, are you going to give me a hint or what?"

"Hmm…" She drew her eyebrows together in feigned concentration. "Okay, it's no vacation, but it will certainly allow the two of you to spend more time together."

If she'd said that about Trevor, knowing what she did about Trevor's propensity for dangerous activities, Gia might have gotten a little nervous. But this was Hunt. Mostly they enjoyed quiet walks around her property and cozy dinners, either out or on her couch with Thor, Klondike, and a good movie. "Tickets to something?"

"Tickets." She snapped her fingers. "That's it."

"It is?" She'd have expected to have to work harder for Savannah to dish on Hunt's gift to her.

"Oh, no, not that. Tickets, like parking or traffic tickets. I bet that's what Mallory was talking about."

"Could be, I guess, but what real problem could she have had with the police over traffic tickets?"

"Oh, puh-lease." Savannah stared at her and lifted a brow. "Have you noticed the way she uses her looks to get what she wants?"

"Only when she flirted with Hunt earlier this morning."

"Yeah, well, she doesn't strike me as the type who takes kindly to not getting her way."

"No, I suppose not." And if she tried to get out of a ticket with a cop who wasn't falling for her feminine wiles, it could have left a bad taste in her mouth, though, honestly, Gia expected it to be something more incriminating.

"I'm assuming flirting with either Hunt or Leo, or maybe both, didn't get her anywhere, so she moved on to trying to get me to do her dirty work."

Gia hadn't thought of that, but it did make sense. She couldn't help but wonder what she'd try next.

Chapter Thirteen

Gia hopped out of Hunt's Jeep and smoothed her knee-length print skirt. Maybe she should have gone with something a little shorter, or even with a slit like the one Mallory had been wearing? Nah. That wasn't her style. Besides, the print was all she'd had at Trevor's, and she didn't want to go all the way back home after closing the café.

Hunt closed the passenger door behind her, wrapped an arm around her waist, and kissed her temple. His lips lingered long enough for him to inhale the strawberry scent of her shampoo he loved so much. "Mmm… you look amazing."

"Thank you." Heat flared in her cheeks, and she was glad she'd decided to spend a few extra minutes blowing out her long, usually curly, dark brown hair and adding just enough make-up to enhance her natural look. "So do you."

Hunt wore fitted jeans and a dark green shirt, a color that looked especially good with his dark, shaggy hair just curling over his collar. And what could she say? She was a sucker for a man in work boots. He grinned, and she lost herself in eyes the color of melted chocolate.

"Come on, let's eat, then we'll go back to Trevor's and watch Christmas movies if you want."

"Sounds good. Do you want popcorn?"

"How about s'mores?"

"It's a date." She'd have to remember to save room. Then again, that wouldn't be easy, considering she always left Lakeshore Pier stuffed. She hooked her arm through his, and they started up the pier toward the best seafood place around, one Savannah had introduced her to not long after she'd moved in.

Soft lighting ran along the pier's base on either side of them, spilling into the dark lake and shimmering along its surface. The dark silhouette of the woods surrounding the lake made her feel like a tiny speck amid a giant expanse of forest. The reflections from thousands of tiny, festive lights adorning the front of the building reflected on the lake like a myriad of multi-colored fireflies flitting through the night. The place held a special intimacy when she visited with Hunt.

Since it was late on a Monday evening, they didn't have to wait on the wraparound porch to be seated. Too bad; it was a gorgeous night, soft breeze, no humidity to frizz her hair. "Want to sit on the terrace?"

"I was just thinking the same thing." Hunt approached the hostess and gave his name, then requested a rooftop seat.

The young woman smiled, grabbed two menus, and led them through the dining room and up a flight of stairs to the houseboat turned restaurant's rooftop terrace. She gestured toward a wrought iron table tucked against the railing in the corner. "You got here at the perfect time; the corner table just opened up. Best view in the house."

She wasn't kidding. The view from the corner table overlooking the lake was incredible, and Gia stared, awed by the effect of the decorative lights on the lake, bringing with it the festivity of the season. "What a beautiful night."

"It is." Hunt pulled out Gia's chair, and Gia thanked him and sat.

A breeze whipped off the lake, sending the palm trees swaying and bringing a chill. Gia shivered.

"Are you cold? We could sit inside if you want." Hunt left his menu on the table.

"No, I'm fine, thank you." The cool dry air was a nice change from the heat and humidity of late.

The waitress stopped by to introduce herself, and they ordered drinks and appetizers, the melon balls Savannah had introduced her to on their first visit, and Gia was reminded of their conversation back then. Leo had already asked Savannah to marry him—again—but at that point, she hadn't agreed, though for the first time she hadn't said no either. "Did you know Savannah knew you threated to beat Leo senseless if he didn't propose to her before she moved to New York?"

Hunt laughed out loud, a deep rich sound that drew gazes from the few remaining diners on the rooftop and warmed Gia in a way nothing else could have. He wiped a tear from the corner of his eye. "She never said. I'd have expected a scolding."

"To be honest, I think she appreciated it, but Savannah is too strong willed to be deterred from something that means a lot to her." In an effort to keep Savannah from leaving to pursue her dream of being a dancer, Hunt had tried to make Leo propose, only because everyone knew he wanted to. But Leo hadn't budged. He'd risked Hunt's wrath to give Savannah the opportunity to see what she wanted, and in the end, she'd returned to her home of Boggy Creek and, eventually, to him. "What would you have done if it was you and the woman you loved wanted to leave to pursue her dreams? Would you have been able to stand back and let her go?"

Hunt remained quiet, studying Gia with an intensity that no doubt had her blushing, but she kept her gaze on his, determined not to look away, though the sudden urge to do so surprised her. She had never been shy around Hunt, yet she was suddenly embarrassed that she'd asked such an intimate question.

The waitress arrived and set their drinks in front of them, then took out her order pad, breaking the uncomfortable spell that had been cast between them.

With a wave of nostalgia threatening to overwhelm her, Gia ordered the steak and lobster tails she'd had the first night Savannah had taken her to Lakeshore Pier.

Hunt ordered the same, and when the waitress left, he propped his elbows on the table, folded his hands together, and rested his chin on his hands.

Gia sipped her lemon water, then sat back and waited, giving him the opportunity to return to their conversation or deflect and change the subject.

Finally, Hunt sat back. "No."

Gia lifted a brow, determined to get more of an elaboration now that he'd answered the question. A smile tugged at her. "No, what?"

He leaned forward, capturing her gaze with his and holding it firm. "No, I would not let you go that easily."

A lump clogged her throat, and she swallowed hard.

"If you tried to leave, for any reason, I'd put up a heck of a fight to get you to stay."

Heat flared through her entire body, and suddenly the rooftop seemed too hot. She and Hunt shared a friendly relationship pretty much since they'd first met. They dated casually, spent time together, enjoyed each other's company, even shared deep conversations about important topics. She'd only known him for a bit over a year, but in that time, she'd come to know that he was a good man, a kind man who put others ahead of himself, a man she could trust, did trust. But something had held them back from taking that next step. Gia had blamed it on his job, on her career, on how hard both of them were working to get ahead, but as he stared at her, daring her to open up, to say more, to reveal something of her deepest, truest feelings for him, that something reared its ugly head, and she danced back away from the precipice she could so easily fall over.

She sipped her drink to give herself a moment to bury the more intense feelings, then forced a grin. "Oh, really? And you think you could get me to stay?"

"Never underestimate me, my dear." Triumph danced in his eyes, but he simply smiled and sat back, allowing her the space she needed. As he always had, she suddenly realized. As he had just insisted he wouldn't. He grinned, and the triumph of the moment before turned to mischief. "I know I could get you to stay with me."

Gia laughed, breaking the tension, relieving her of the weight of reality that had just settled on her. She loved Hunt. With all of her heart. And the thought terrified her.

Knowing her as well as he obviously did, and being the kind of man who always put the needs of others ahead of his own, Hunt simply smiled and changed the subject. "So, how's Savannah holding up? I haven't had a chance to talk to her lately."

She shot him a genuine smile of gratitude that he hadn't pushed her. Gia's past with her ex-husband, a man she'd loved with all her heart, a man who'd lied to her, hurt her, humiliated her, and put her life in danger, had left her too broken to ever consider a lasting relationship with another man. Until Hunt. A man she'd initially met because of her ex-husband's untimely death and Gia's discovery of his body in the dumpster behind her café on opening day.

She took a deep breath and switched gears. "She's doing well, I think. Excited about the house and, of course the wedding, but kind of worried about what's going on with Alyssa and Carlos. They're not actually suspects, right?"

Hunt shrugged and sipped his sweet tea. "At this point, everyone's a suspect."

She shared her plan to allow the two the use of the café to cater the wedding. "You think it's safe, right?"

"Do you mean do I think they'll poison the guests?"

"No…" Well, actually, yes, that was exactly what she meant, but the guilt wouldn't allow her to admit it out loud.

Hunt inhaled deeply and leaned back in his chair, running both hands through his hair, leaving him with that slightly disheveled look Gia had come to love.

Whoa! Love? Yes, love. No surprise there, but would her heart allow her to pursue their relationship to another level, or would she run scared?

"I honestly don't know." He folded his arms on the table and leaned forward, lowering his voice despite the lack of diners close to them. "I'd like to be able to discount their involvement completely, but in all fairness, both had access to the cake that was poisoned."

Truthfully, it would have been easiest for one of them to add the poison, considering they'd baked the cake, frosted it, and served it. "But why would either of them want to poison Robyn?"

"We have no motive yet, but it's early."

Unless the rumors running rampant all over town were true. "I'm assuming you've heard the rumors about Alyssa and Jeremy?"

"How could I miss them when Isaac spouts them at every opportunity?" He paused and sat back to allow their waitress to set the melon balls in the center of the table, then thanked her and waited for her to leave before continuing. "Unfortunately, he's not the only one saying it. I've heard them from others as well, but I have no proof yet they're any more than rumors started by Isaac."

"Speaking of Isaac, what ever happened the other day when you and Leo had to rush out?"

Hunt waved it off and speared a melon ball. "We picked him up and brought him home, told him to stay away from Jeremy and Ethan or he'd be arrested."

"Did it work?"

"For the moment, I guess, but who knows for how long. That right there's a powder keg waiting to explode."

She couldn't really blame him if he really believed his mother's killer was roaming free, unpunished, to live his life. "Do you think his claims that Jeremy killed his mother are true?"

Hunt tapped a sugar packet up and down on the table, then turned it over and tapped the other side a few times. "I just don't know. We haven't yet found motive, but he might have had the opportunity to plant the poison."

"Isaac said something about his mother's inheritance from his father, and he made it sound like it was a lot of money. Wouldn't that be reason enough?"

He finally opened the sugar packet and poured it into his tea, then stirred it, clanking the ice against the sides of the glass. "Probably, if Robyn had left everything to Jeremy."

Gia paused, a melon ball halfway to her mouth. "She didn't?"

"Not as far as we know. The only will that's surfaced so far has Isaac as the sole beneficiary."

Gia slouched back in the chair and her breath shot out, the implication in Hunt's words perfectly clear. "Do you think Isaac killed his own mother before they got married so Robyn wouldn't have a chance to change her will?"

Hunt spread his hands wide. "It's a possibility we have to consider."

"Hmm…" One Gia hadn't thought of.

The waitress arrived and set their orders in front of them. "Can I get you anything else?"

"Gia?" Hunt asked.

"No, I'm good, thank you." The aroma of the grilled steak made her mouth water.

"Just give a yell if you do." The waitress nodded and left.

Gia's knife slid through her steak like it was butter, her mind whirling with possibilities. "Do you know anything about Robyn's first husband or his sister getting into any kind of trouble with the law?"

Hunt frowned. "Who, Mallory Levine?"

"Yes."

"Not that I'm aware of, but I haven't thoroughly investigated Max Levine yet, why?"

"She sort of slipped and mentioned her past history with the police after the incident with Savannah."

Hunt lowered his fork onto his plate with a clang. "Incident?"

Uh oh. She hadn't meant to let that slip, figuring Savannah would tell him or Leo if she wanted them to know. One look at Hunt's expression made it clear it was too late to walk back the comment. Oh, well, better they knew what was going on anyway. "Earlier, at the house, Mallory implied there might be a conflict of interest in her selling Savannah the house since she's a suspect in Leo's murder investigation."

Hunt stiffened. "Oh, really?"

"Savannah handled her, and she still wants to buy the house from her, so please don't interfere." The last thing Gia wanted this close to the wedding was a rift between her and Savannah. Still, if Mallory was going to pull something, better to know everyone was prepared for whatever she might come up with.

He rolled his shoulders and picked his fork back up. Some of the tension seeped from him. "Savannah handled her?"

Gia grinned, glad the moment had passed but equally glad Hunt was now aware of the potential problem. "You'd have been proud."

"I usually am." He took a bit of steak and savored it before continuing. "So, what exactly did Mallory say?"

"That's just it, nothing really. Just that her history with the police has been, and then she seemed to catch herself and stopped talking."

"Or she said it intentionally hoping Savannah would pass it on."

Gia hadn't thought of that. Had she fallen right into what Mallory wanted? "Why would she want you and Leo to think she had a history with the police?"

"Who knows? You're assuming it was a negative relationship; maybe the history is a relative in law enforcement or something."

Hmm…what had made her assume she'd been in trouble with the law? Something in the way she phrased it or just Gia's own interpretation? She'd have to remember to ask Savannah's opinion later.

"We've done background checks on everyone and haven't come up with anything yet, but that doesn't mean there's nothing there, just that we might have to look deeper."

"I got the impression Mallory was lying about being late to the tasting." Since she was pretty sure she couldn't have arrived when she said she did without Gia seeing her. "Why would she do that if she wasn't guilty?"

Hunt shrugged and swallowed a bit of lobster. "Could be anything. If she has some past criminal history and doesn't want to be involved, which kind of jibes with the stunt she tried to pull with Savannah, saying she wasn't there might get everyone to back off and leave her alone. Or she could be afraid being there early would have given her opportunity to poison the slice of cake Robyn ate and wants to remove herself from the suspect list from the get-go. She may also be harboring some amount of guilt if she thinks it was the cake she gave Robyn that killed her."

"It was only the one slice that was poisoned?" Gia dipped a piece of lobster in melted butter and took a bite. The flavor burst on her tongue and she barely refrained from moaning.

"As far as we can tell. No one else got sick, and the remaining cake was tested and none but the remnants on either Robyn's or Mallory's plate had any traces of poison."

"So it could have been Mallory's cake that was poisoned and not Robyn's?" That was a twist they had to consider.

"It's possible, since no one seemed to be a hundred percent sure which dish belonged to whom. Robyn ate both slices and pushed both plates aside, and neither of their fingerprints were found on the dishes. Only Robyn's fingerprints were found on both forks."

"Were anyone's fingerprints found on the dishes?"

"Only Carlos and Alyssa's."

Gia choked on her sip of water. "Seriously?"

"Don't get too worried about that. If Carlos plated the slices and Alyssa served them, which coincides with their statements, then that's within the realm of possibility." He wiped his mouth and sat back.

She tried to remember if she'd touched her plate so far during dinner. Not that she could recall. The waitress had placed it in front of her, but sometimes you turned your plate or pulled it closer or set it aside when you're finished, as Hunt had just done. No matter how hard she concentrated, she couldn't recall if she touched her plate. If she wound up poisoned by something in her dinner, would her fingerprints show up? Then again, what if the poison was meant for Hunt? They'd ordered the same thing, who's to say the plates didn't get mixed up? Which once again went back to could Mallory have been the target? "Does it seem weird to you neither woman's prints were on the plates?"

Hunt called the waitress over and ordered coffee for him and herbal tea for Gia before he answered. "I don't know, and there are no surveillance cameras inside the dining room, so we may never have a complete picture of what went on inside. But we have people collecting footage from any other surveillance cameras along the street, and we put word out asking for anyone who might have been taking pictures in the area that morning to come forward. At least then we might be able to figure out exactly who came and went and when."

Gia nodded, but she was only half paying attention to what he was saying, because her mind had already begun to wander down another path, one it couldn't seem to deviate from.

"So, if it was Mallory's cake that was poisoned, it's possible she was the target all along and Robyn was only..."

"Collateral damage?" He nodded. "It's possible."

"And now Mallory could still be a target."

"Yes."

"And Savannah will have to continue to meet with her if the sellers accept her offer on the house."

"Yeah."

Suddenly Gia didn't feel quite as good about finding Savannah the perfect house.

"I can see the wheels turning, Gia." He stared at her a moment. "Gia..."

"What?" At least he hadn't told her not to get involved, which he knew full well she would since the whole situation was affecting Savannah.

"Don't worry, I know the drill; stay out of trouble, keep Savannah out of trouble, and blah, blah, blah…"

Hunt laughed. "Actually, I was just going to say be careful."

She narrowed her eyes, searching his expression for the slightest hint if he was just teasing her.

As usual, his poker face gave away nothing.

"Look, we both know you're going to ask questions. You can't help being nosy."

"Hey." She pouted. "I prefer to think of it as inquisitive."

"Okay," he relented. "Inquisitive, another one of the things I love about you."

Now he was pushing it.

"And I know you can't help it if people come into the café and gossip and you overhear things." He cleared his throat, and she almost laughed out loud. He knew her too well. "But, please, be careful. We don't know what we're dealing with right now, and there's no way to tell what is going to happen next, but I feel like we're missing something, and I have a hunch this whole thing isn't over."

Chapter Fourteen

The next morning, Gia flipped on all of the coffee pots behind the counter at the All-Day Breakfast Café, then turned to head to the kitchen and almost tripped over Savannah, who was bent over stuffing her oversized gold bag on a shelf beneath the counter. "Oh, sorry."

"It's okay." Savannah stood and offered a sort-of half smile, then lay a hand on the counter and took a deep, shaky breath. She looked pale.

"Are you okay?" Gia rested a hand on her arm. "You feel cold."

Savannah let out a sound somewhere between a laugh and a cry, and tears pooled in her eyes. She shook her head and looked down.

"Hey?" Gia leaned over to look up at her. "What's wrong? Do you feel all right?"

"No, I mean yes, I mean…"

"Come on." With a firm grip on her arm, Gia led her around the far end of the counter and guided her onto the first stool they came to. Thankfully, they hadn't opened yet, so there were no customers to deal with. Earl hadn't even arrived yet. "Sit for a few minutes. Do you want something to drink? Water? A diet soda?"

Savannah waved a hand, then patted the stool next to her. "I'm good, just sit with me a minute."

"Okay." Keeping a close watch on Savannah, Gia slid onto the stool beside her. "Are you sure you're all right?"

"I am." She wiped tears that had spilled over and rolled down her cheeks, then laughed. At least some of her color had begun to return. She started to say something then paused and laughed again.

"Want to let me in on what's so funny?" Because Gia had no clue. And considering they were usually so in tune with one another, that bothered her.

"I bent over to put my bag on the shelf, and I remembered I'm going to have to change the name on my driver's license, and this… like a tidal wave of realization came over me." She looked Gia straight in the eye, all of her fear and joy on full display. "In three days, I'm going to be Mrs. Leo Dumont."

Gia wasn't sure what to say. She'd just been thinking about their conversation last year at Lakeshore Pier when she'd sat on the rooftop with Hunt last night. She recalled Savannah's fear of losing herself too much in a man, as her father had once done for her mother. Then, when her mother was killed, her pa retreated, unable to come to terms with losing the love of his life, and became a shell of his former self. Savannah hadn't been sure she could marry a man who had chosen such a dangerous career, even if it was in the small, usually safe town of Boggy Creek, no matter how much she loved him. "Did you ever speak to Leo about your feelings about him being with the police department?"

"No. I never did." She heaved in a deep, shaky breath. "It's who he is, Gia, how could I ask him to change that?"

Oh, boy. It was definitely a little late for this conversation. "Savannah, if you're uncomfortable with that, or if you're unsure about what you're doing, you need to talk to Leo."

"I know. It's just…" She glanced at the clock.

"Hey." Gia gripped her chin and pulled her gaze back to her. "Don't worry about what time it is."

"But Alyssa and Carlos—"

"Can wait outside until we're done."

Savannah threw her arms around Gia's neck. "You're the best."

Gia set her back. "Then talk to me. Tell me what's wrong?"

"Nothing, actually." She laughed. "I think I just had a moment, ya know. That instant where you suddenly realize something you've been looking forward to, planning, thinking about on some level for most of your life is about to happen."

"And it terrifies you." Gia knew the feeling all too well. Hadn't it happened on a lesser level just last night when Hunt had once again tried to talk about his growing feelings for her, a conversation she steered away from every time he broached the subject?

"Exactly."

"Look, Savannah, whatever decision you make, you know I'll support you. You are my sister, and I will stand by your side no matter what, and I would never try to sway your decisions. That said, as your sister, I will give my opinion."

Savannah rolled her eyes.

Gia punched her arm. "Hey, I'm trying to be supportive here."

This time when Savannah smiled it held all the warmth Gia was used to. She reached out and gripped Gia's hand. "Yes, you are, and I appreciate it more than you know."

Gia knew. It was the same way she'd always appreciated Savannah's caring advice, even when she chose not to listen and even when some of the sentiments weren't easy to hear. "Well, as far as I'm concerned, you have found the perfect man. He's kind, loving, patient, and that's just in general. He also loves you with every last ounce of his being, and I know you feel the same about him."

"I do."

"Savannah, loving someone with everything in you is not a bad thing. It's a beautiful thing that not everyone is fortunate enough to ever find."

"And if something happens..." She sobbed softly and finished on a whisper, "and I lose him?"

"Aww, honey." Gia stood and gathered Savannah into her arms. "We will pray every day that doesn't happen, but that's something that's just not up to us. It's out of our control, and you can't spend your life afraid to love anyone because you might lose them. And if it ever does happen, then we deal with it. Together. Like we've done since the day we met. We'd have no choice, but you would be surrounded by love, between your family and me. And don't forget, in three days you will be Mrs. Leo Dumont, but you will also still be Savannah Mills."

She sniffed and nodded against Gia. "You're right."

"Of course, I am." Gia laughed and bit back her own tears and threw back the words Savannah often said to her. "I wouldn't have said it if I wasn't."

Savannah laughed out loud and shook her head. "What am I going to do with you?"

Gia shrugged. "For starters, you could try taking my advice."

"Well, since you're right and it's such good advice, I'm going to share it right back with you. I would never interfere in your relationship with Hunt, and you know I'll support you no matter what, even if Hunt is my favorite cousin—and if you tell him that I swear I'll deny it—and even if you do break his heart, but I've always kind of regretted not trying harder to talk you out of marrying Bradley."

"It is what it is, Savannah. If we're being completely honest, you did tell me exactly what he was, and you tried to talk me out of it. I was the one who didn't listen." This was one walk down memory lane she didn't want to share right now. Nor did she want to discuss where her and Hunt were headed. It was so much easier to just keep deluding herself into believing their relationship wasn't progressing because they were both so busy with work.

She looked around the dining room to see what still needed to be done before they opened. She'd come in early to finish up just in case Alyssa and Carlos stopped by, though she had her doubts Carlos would even pass on her message.

"Well, that being the case…" Savannah continued undeterred. "Though I would never say I told you so, I will say you should listen a little more closely to my advice this time. Hunt loves you, Gia, with all his heart. He understands what you've been through, and he's been so patient, and he will continue to be, I'm sure, but it hurts my heart to see the two of you dance around any kind of intimacy or commitment. If I didn't think you loved him back just as fiercely, I wouldn't say anything, and I'm not telling you what to do, but if you want my advice, you should stop holding him at arm's length. Isn't that basically what you just told me? You can't hold love at bay just for fear of being hurt."

Gia nodded. She was right, of course, but it didn't make it any easier to face the demons of the past and let them go for good.

A knock at the door brought a rush of relief.

Gia turned and saw Alyssa waving from the walkway.

"You do always find a way out of this conversation, don't you." Savannah grinned and hopped from her stool.

"Maybe because it wasn't meant to be had."

She caught Gia's gaze and shrugged, mischief alight in the deep blue of her eyes. "I guess we'll see, won't we?"

Choosing to ignore the comment, Gia hurried to open the door. She could only deal with one crisis at a time, and since Savannah was getting married in three days, with or without a caterer, Savannah's dilemma had to come first. She unlocked the door to let Alyssa and Carlos in, then locked it behind them and left the closed sign in place. "Good morning."

Alyssa hugged Gia then stepped back and rubbed her hands up and down her arms. "It's chilly out there—"

Gia's phone had read fifty-nine degrees that morning, headed up to seventy. Hardly chilly by her standards.

Alyssa shrugged out of her peacoat. "—I think we're having winter."

If this was winter, Gia would take it.

Carlos nodded in greeting, took Alyssa's coat, and hung it over a chair back.

"Carlos told me about your idea, and it's amazing. That's so kind of you, Gia."

"Of course, I'd love to help. Hopefully, I have everything you need to make it work."

She rubbed her hands together for warmth. "Oh, I'm quite sure we can make it work. Plus, Trevor offered to let us use his amazing kitchen too."

Trevor's kitchen, with its stainless-steel commercial grade stove, two ovens, and dishwasher left Gia with a serious case of kitchen envy.

"So between the two, I'm sure we can do everything we need."

Savannah offered coffee or something to eat, but Alyssa and Carlos both declined, saying they had things to do, though Gia couldn't imagine what with their business closed down.

"Um…" Savannah twisted her fingers together in a nervous gesture Gia wasn't used to, though she'd become accustomed to the rhythmic nail tapping that often accompanied a bout of anxiety. "Please don't take this wrong, but… uh… would it be okay if we went back to my original cake choice?"

Gia held her breath, hoping the two wouldn't be insulted but totally understanding Savannah's reluctance to serve her guests the same cake that had just killed a woman.

Alyssa gripped Savannah's clasped hands in one of hers. "It's no problem, Savannah, I actually already made a note to ask you about that. I don't plan to offer that cake any more. It would seem…I don't know, disrespectful somehow."

Gia breathed a sigh of relief. "Please, come sit for a minute or two. I have coffee already made, and I just took out a fresh batch of muffins."

The two looked at each other for a moment, then nodded and followed Gia to the counter. They each sat, leaving one stool free between them.

Savannah sat on Alyssa's far side, and Gia rounded the counter. She poured coffee, then offered a selection of muffins from the trays she'd brought out earlier to cool so she could restock the glass-covered cake dishes on the counter.

Carlos took a banana chocolate chip muffin.

"Mmm…that smells delicious." Alyssa chose a cranberry, one of Gia's new recipes for the holidays. "But this will have to do since I'm allergic to chocolate."

"How about I'll let you know when I make a batch without the chocolate chips?" Gia offered, happy she'd decided against the cranberry, white chocolate ones she'd originally planned on. She left nuts out of the banana muffins, since a lot of people were allergic, but she hadn't thought about those people with chocolate allergies.

"That sounds perfect, thank you."

"Sure thing." Gia plated two more cranberry muffins and slid one in front of Savannah. The most obvious place left for Gia to sit was on the empty stool between Alyssa and Carlos, but that seemed weird, so she kept her plate in front of her and opted to stand facing them across the counter.

Silence screamed through the café as the four nibbled on muffins and sipped coffee, and Gia was hard pressed to find a topic that didn't include murder. "You guys know Trevor pretty well, right?"

"Sure." Carlos answered, narrowing his eyes. "Well enough, I guess. Why?"

Alyssa remained quiet.

Gia hesitated, but then figured what the heck? Someone had to say something to cut the tension Carlos and Alyssa had ushered in with them.

"I was thinking of getting him a GoPro for Christmas—you know, the one with the strap you can wear on your head to capture things like bungie jumping and sky diving from a first-person perspective—but I realized I don't know if he has one. Do you happen to know?" She sure hoped he didn't since the gift was already wrapped and under the tree in hers and Savannah's suite at Trevor's mansion. She'd originally thought it would be great for filming when he went kayaking, and had even thought of getting one for herself since she enjoyed the scenery so much whenever he took her, and then the salesman had told her all the other great uses he might get out of it. It had seemed perfect. Too perfect, considering he could have gotten one for himself if he'd wanted one.

Carlos was already nodding.

Gia's heart sank.

He swallowed his bite of muffin then took a sip of coffee. "He'd like that a lot. He's talked about getting one before, and maybe even starting one of those vlog things everyone's doin' nowadays, but he never did get around to it, far as I know."

"Oh, thank you. I'm so glad to know he'll like it. He's not easy to buy for."

"No, I'd imagine not."

And with that the silence returned, like a vacuum threatening to suck them all into a void of awkwardness.

Thankfully, Alyssa returned to the business at hand, and Gia took a big bite of muffin. "So, Savannah, do you want to go back to your original cake, or would you like me to stop by with pictures for you to look at for something different?"

"No, thank you, but I think the original one is good. It wasn't that I didn't love that one, just that the cascade of mistletoe and berries pouring down the other one was so beautiful."

"You know, I could do the same thing with different flowers, maybe poinsettias or holly?"

"Oh, yeah?" Savannah tapped a nail against her coffee cup. "Hmm... maybe, but aren't poinsettias poisonous as well."

"Oh, I don't use real flowers. Only fondant and icing, sometimes candy if needed."

"So how do you think the nightshade got onto the cake without you guys noticing?" Though she tried to clamp her teeth together and stop the flow of words before they erupted, Gia failed miserably.

Carlos ground his teeth together, his jaw clenched.

Alyssa just shook her head. "You know, I've asked myself that same thing about a million times. We made the whole cake, though a smaller version than we'd have made for the wedding, and left it on the counter just inside the kitchen door."

Gia kept her mouth shut, since she had no idea if Hunt had shared his suspicions that only the one slice, or maybe two, had been poisoned.

"It sat there through the group tasting all of the other foods, so I suppose someone could have added the real leaves and berries." She frowned. "Though I don't see how I wouldn't have noticed that."

Carlos chimed in. "There was such a nice breeze that day that I opened the back door from the kitchen because it got hot back there with all the ovens and stove burners going, so I suppose someone could have come in—"

Maybe the elusive Ethan, who might or might not have been hanging around earlier than he'd admitted to, depending on who you asked.

"Plus, the door between the kitchen and the rest of the shop was open so Alyssa could run back and forth, and the restrooms, lounge, and a table with a phone are all right there outside the door."

Since Gia hadn't gone into the back of the shop, she had no idea of the layout past the dining room and lobby. "What is the lounge for?"

When Carlos didn't answer, Alyssa took over. "Mostly because we had extra space, but it also gives customers some privacy if they want to talk about what they want, or a place to take younger children to entertain them if they act up, or make a phone call to a relative who couldn't attend the tasting. Pretty much an all-purpose room for the convenience of our guests. And since the restrooms are on the far side of the lounge, you have to pass through it to get to them."

Carlos once again took over. "I suppose it wouldn't have been too difficult to poke your head in on the way by and add a handful of berries or leaves. The counter with the cake would have been out of sight from most of the kitchen, and I had a lot to do that day, what with them wanting a million different choices…"

"None of which they could agree on," Alyssa added.

Since they both seemed willing enough to talk about it, and no matter what might be going on between them in private, they seemed to have each other's backs and be presenting a united front on this matter, Gia pressed. "What about after the cake was cut?"

"After Alyssa put the whole cake on a tray and rolled it out for them to see, she returned it to the kitchen where I cut generous slices for each of them."

"What about mine and Savannah's slices?"

Carlos just looked at her.

"I cut those myself," Alyssa said. "After I served the others, I came back and cut a couple of small ones for you two and set them aside until you came in."

So, theoretically, anyone, including a random stranger who walked in the back door, somehow snuck past Carlos who was cooking in the kitchen, poisoned the cake, then slid unnoticed out either the front or back door, could have done it. The thought of it all started to give Gia a headache, and she suddenly found a new appreciation for the work Hunt and Leo did every day. "When you served the cake to Robyn's party, was everyone there?"

Alyssa chewed on her bottom lip, her gaze searching out Carlos's.

He nodded. "It's not anything the police haven't asked, Alyssa. And I doubt Gia or Savannah plan on gossiping about whatever you tell them."

"Oh, no, of course not," Gia quickly reassured them. "Whatever you tell me is between us."

"Well, when I brought the cake in, the room was empty. I don't know where everyone was." She blushed and lowered her gaze. "To be honest, I didn't really care. Their constant non-stop bickering had already given me a headache, so I just set the slices out in front of each place setting, including the one guest who hadn't shown up yet, and went back to the kitchen. The next I heard from any of them was when you came in and all the screaming started."

"You didn't see Isaac and Robyn come back in?"

"Nope. I served the cake and went back to my office to take a couple of ibuprofen for my headache."

Savannah finished off her muffin and brushed the crumbs from her fingers onto her plate. "So that means at some point after you set the cake slices out, someone could have added the poison to Robyn's?"

"I suppose," Alyssa admitted.

"We saw Robyn and Isaac out front, then they went inside and Isaac came back out again alone to make a phone call. Did you see him come back in?" Gia asked Alyssa.

"No. I must have been in my office or the kitchen during that time."

"What about Jeremy? Do you know where he was?"

Her gaze shot to Carlos, then skipped back to Gia.

Gia realized her mistake a moment too late. If Alyssa had any idea where Jeremy was when Robyn was poisoned, she had no intention of mentioning it in front of her husband. But Gia couldn't help but remember the span of time when she and Savannah had entered Rinaldi's and Alyssa had been nowhere to be found. Had she been somewhere with Jeremy? If so, she might be his only alibi. And he hers.

Chapter Fifteen

Gia wiped down the butcher block counter-top on the island in the center of the café's kitchen. She'd just finished dicing potatoes for home fries and still had to cut up the peppers and onions. She set the giant stainless-steel bowl of potatoes on the counter beside the sink and got to work chopping vegetables. If she did not only enough for the home fries, but for omelets the next morning too, she'd save herself prep time later.

Savannah stuck her head through the doorway and held up a credit card. "Hey, Gia, got a sec?"

"Sure." She tossed the rag into the hamper. "What's up?"

"Jeremy Nolan is out front. He just finished dinner with a friend"—her disapproving lifted brow told Gia it was a female friend—"and tried to pay with this." The credit card she handed Gia had Robyn Hackman's name on the front.

When she turned it over, Robyn's signature was on the back. "Hmm."

"What do you want me to do?" Savannah worried her bottom lip.

A quick glance at the grill told her Cole had everything under control. "Don't worry about it. I've got it."

Savannah nodded and left.

Gia followed her out and approached the register where Jeremy waited alone. "I'm sorry, sir, but there seems to be a mistake?"

"What do you mean?" He frowned and glanced at Savannah, who was refilling cake dishes with muffins and discreetly eavesdropping.

He didn't seem to recognize her, so Gia didn't say anything about recognizing him from the tasting. Better to see what he was trying to do first. She held up the card. If he tried to say he was Robyn Hackman, she'd call Hunt and let him deal with it. "This credit card. It's in the name Robyn Hackman."

"Oh...I...uh..." He studied her for a moment, his mouth and eyes wide in a horrified expression that seemed a bit too practiced. She could almost imagine him in front of the mirror perfecting it. Then he went for a sheepish smile. "I am so sorry. It's my fiance's card. I must have given you the wrong one by mistake."

"No problem. Mistakes happen." Though she had a feeling he knew exactly what he was doing.

He pulled his wallet out of his pocket and handed her a card with his name on the front.

"Thank you." She rang the purchase with no problem, but now what to do? Should she return Robyn's card to him or keep it and give it to Hunt? She really didn't have the right to confiscate it, and it could well have been a mistake. She handed both cards back to him, had him sign, and wished him a good day. She'd just tell Hunt about the incident and let him decide what, if anything, to do about it.

"Well?" Savannah appeared at her side the instant the door fell shut behind Jeremy. "What do you think?"

"Honestly?" She watched him climb into a car out front, with a woman waiting for him in the passenger seat. "I think he tried to get away with using his fiance's card, and when he couldn't, he acted repentant, apologized for the mistake, and paid with his own card."

Gia checked the side of the register, where the pin pad sat in plain view. "Why didn't he use the pin pad?"

Savannah shrugged. "No idea, maybe he didn't see it. He just handed me the card, and when I looked at it, Robyn's name was on it."

"Weird." Since there was nothing more she could do about it, she took a moment to shoot Hunt a quick text letting him know what happened, then returned to the kitchen. "All right, I'm back. Thanks, Cole."

Cole set two plates on the dining room cut-out for Savannah to serve, then turned to Gia. "Need me to do anything else?"

She glanced at the clock over the cut-out to the dining room. Almost four o'clock. The lunch rush had ended two hours ago, and Cole had been handling grill while Gia did prep work. While she couldn't close for the week, she was trying to get out as early as possible so she and Savannah could do wedding and Christmas stuff. "Nah, I think I'm good, thank you."

"You bet. I don't mind staying if you and Savannah want to head out early?"

As much as the thought appealed, she'd been absent from the café a bit too much lately, and she realized she missed it. "I'll be okay, thank you, though. And I appreciate you coming in to open all week. At least, I'll get to sleep in a little. Maybe. I hope."

Cole laughed then peered through the cut-out and crooked his finger at someone in the dining room. "I diced the ham already, so you don't have to do that. And there are steaks marinating in both refrigerators for steak and eggs, since that seems to be your biggest selling dinner item."

"Thanks, Cole. You're the best."

"Any time, dear." He pulled his apron off over his head, wadded it into a ball and made a two-point shot into the hamper.

"Knock, knock." Cybil Devane, a woman who had become a good friend to Gia since the first time she'd found her wandering in the middle of the forest, poked her head in and grinned. "Everyone decent?"

"Woman, I haven't been decent in sev-uh-in a long time." The corners of Cole's eyes crinkled as he laughed.

"Come on in, Cybil. Sit. It's so good to see you." Gia hadn't seen Cybil in a few weeks, and she always enjoyed her company. "Do you want something to eat or drink?"

"No, I'm good, thank you." Cybil pulled a stool from the counter and sat.

The first time Gia had met Cybil, the older woman had been wandering through the woods, a long, flowing hooded cloak concealing most of her body, giving the appearance of a frail stooped woman. She'd come to know Cybil was anything but. While she was petite, and very thin, she had the same kind of spunk as Savannah, and Gia adored her.

Cybil patted her flat belly. "Cole and I are going to walk, and I don't want to do that on a full belly."

Gia couldn't blame her. To Gia going for a walk meant strolling along Main Street to the park, maybe doing some window shopping along the way, or taking Thor to walk one of the numerous walking trails dotting the area. Cybil gave whole new meaning to the phrase, often hiking miles and miles through the woods with her newest addition, a beagle mix she'd adopted from the same shelter Gia had gotten Thor from. She thought nothing of making that trek, even after dark, which it would be soon. Gia worried about her wandering the deepest parts of the forest alone, but she always insisted she'd been ambling through those woods since she was a kid and wasn't about to stop now. Unfortunately, the loss of her husband had left her walking alone. Until now, apparently. Gia didn't push the subject; she was just glad Cybil had found someone to walk with.

"So, what's new and exciting?" Cybil's deep blue eyes sparkled. Her jeans, sweatshirt and hiking boots didn't quite suit her the way the long, dark cloak did, with her long, thick, salt and pepper hair hanging down the front of her body from beneath the hood. The first few times she came upon her, Gia had been eerily certain she held some kind of psychic powers.

Gia continued to chop vegetables while she chatted. "You mean other than the murder at the caterer like a week before Savannah's wedding?"

Cybil tilted her head and studied Gia. "I suppose that is enough. How's Savannah taking it?"

"Better than I would be, for sure." Gia sighed. After the intense scrutiny, she'd been hoping for some words of wisdom.

Cybil only grinned and twisted back and forth on the stool, sending her long hair swinging back and forth. She wasn't much for staying still. Again, like Savannah. "I'm sure everything will work out just fine."

Gia longed for a return to the time when she'd have assumed that was a premonition, but she'd pegged Cybil way wrong. "Me too. It's just frustrating when Savannah's caterer is on the suspect list, and the woman's place of business is closed down while rumors of her infidelity with the deceased's fiancé abound."

Gia hadn't meant to blurt all that, but Cybil exuded that special kind of warmth that just invited you to open up. With a quick glance over her shoulder into the dining room to be sure no one could overhear their conversation, Gia continued. "That's all anyone's been able to talk about all day."

"Well, you know how it is once rumors get started."

Gia did, all too well. She knew exactly what it was like to be on the suspect list in a murder investigation. She knew the way strangers and acquaintances watched from the corners of their eyes when you walked into a room, how even friends glared with suspicion when they thought you weren't looking. She'd have to reach out to Alyssa when her husband wasn't around—whenever that might be—to see how she was really holding up.

"And don't forget…" Cybil reached across the counter and patted Gia's arm, then sat back. "Just because you can sympathize with someone's circumstances, doesn't mean that person is not guilty."

Gia's gaze shot up, and she nicked her finger with the knife. "Ouch."

"Oh, dear, are you alright?"

She hurried to the sink, dropped the knife inside, ripped off her gloves, and washed her hands, lathering good despite the sting of the soap in the wound. The juice from the onion she'd been cutting stung a whole lot worse.

Cole stood over her shoulder, staring down at her finger, Band-Aid held at the ready.

"It's okay." Thankfully. She had to be more careful.

Cole wrapped the Band-Aid around her finger tight enough to cut off the trickle of blood. "You two sit and chat while I finish cutting the vegetables, since Gia's multitasking skills leave a lot to be desired."

"I'm sorry, dear, I didn't mean to catch you off guard like that." Cybil chewed on a thumbnail, clearly distressed.

"No." Gia waved her off. "It was totally my fault. I won't lie and say I've never wondered if Alyssa could have had anything to do with Robyn's murder, but I've kind of been going on the theory that just because someone's spreading rumors doesn't mean she's guilty."

"Of course, that's true," Cybil agreed. "But it doesn't mean she's innocent either. Only the courts can decide that, which they will once Hunt and Leo finish their investigation."

"Yes, I'm sure." Gia frowned. Cybil was a tell it like it is kind of person. In fact, her first statement to Gia had been that she was following the wrong path. Boy, had she been right. Hmm…maybe there was some solidity to her statement. A fact Gia really didn't want to consider. "Do you know Alyssa?"

She shrugged one very slim shoulder. "We've met."

Gia waited, but she didn't elaborate. "I take it you're not a fan?"

"I don't know her well enough to offer an opinion one way or the other, but I did attend an event she catered, and that husband of hers followed her everywhere. Every time she turned around, she practically ran into him." She nodded knowingly. "That can get old real quick."

"I would imagine." Gia's thoughts turned to Hunt, who seemed to be willing to give her as much space as she needed. He never gave her a hard time if she wanted to hang out with friends, simply met up with her a different time. Even when one of her best friends was Trevor, a young, handsome in an endearing sort of way, perfectly eligible bachelor.

What would it be like to have someone on you constantly, everywhere you went, not in a loving, caring, enjoying time together kind of way, but in an I-don't-trust-you, stalkery kind of way? Suffocating. Could that have pushed Alyssa into an affair? Come to think of it, why was Carlos so possessive? Was it a fault in him, a lack of the ability to trust? Gia could certainly understand that. Or was it because Alyssa had given him reason not to trust her?

Cybil grinned. "Don't think so hard, dear. You're going to hurt yourself. The only thing I know about Alyssa that matters right now, is that the food at the event she catered was amazing."

Gia's mouth watered at the thought of all the food they'd tasted, and she realized she hadn't eaten anything but one cranberry muffin all day. Maybe she could talk Savannah into stopping by Xavier's to pick up dinner on the way home. With any luck, Hunt, Leo, and Trevor would be able to join them. Though Trevor usually kept the shop open late, he'd been closing earlier this week in order to tend to any last-minute preparations. Besides, by the time they went all the way out to Xavier's and back to Trevor's, it would be late, so he might be home anyway.

"If you're good, then, Cybil and I are going to take off." Cole scraped the last of the peppers off the knife into the full stainless-steel bin, set the bin aside for Gia to cover, and dropped the knife into the sink. Then he kissed her cheek. "Behave, and stay out of trouble."

Gia grinned. "Now you sound like Hunt."

"And that's a bad thing?" He winked. "Listen, I already made Harley's dinner. It's in the fridge, so you can just heat it up and leave it out back before you go."

Harley was a homeless man who hung around the neighborhood. Because he couldn't bring himself to go inside buildings, he most often roamed around the park. He'd become a good friend to Gia and Savannah, and Gia always left dinner on a table beside the back door for him. "Thanks, Cole, you're the best."

Cybil hugged her and said goodbye.

Once they were gone, Gia peeked into the dining room to be sure there were no orders coming in. Acid burned in her stomach. If it was going to be at least ten before they got to eat dinner, she was going to need something to hold her over. Again, she peered through the cutout at the empty dining room.

Savannah strode through the room setting everything back in place. She changed placemats, replaced dirty cushion covers on the seats, and restocked condiments.

"Hey, Savannah?" Gia called through the cutout.

She hefted a bus pan onto her lip and looked up. "What's up?"

"Have you eaten anything today?"

"Not since this morning. Why? You hungry?"

"I was thinking barbeque for dinner later," Gia said.

She considered for a moment. "Yeah, that works."

Gia's stomach growled. "But do you want to split an omelet now to hold us over?"

"Sounds good." She returned to working even faster.

Gia tossed some of the peppers and onions Cole had finished cutting onto the grill along with a handful of diced ham from the fridge. While it heated, she put together the home fries and scooped out two small helpings. She scrambled a couple of eggs and added them to the mixture on the grill. As much as she'd love to add cheese and bacon, she refrained, since this wasn't actually dinner. She definitely didn't want to be too stuffed to eat barbeque.

When the omelet was done, she split it onto two plates and added them and the home fries to a tray, then carried it out into the dining room.

Since no customers had come in, Savannah had already set a table for them and poured drinks. "I hope lemon water was okay? I didn't figure you'd want coffee or soda now."

"No, lemon water is perfect, thank you." Gia set the food out, and they both sat.

"I hadn't even realized how hungry I was." Savannah opened her napkin and spread it on her lap, then dug in.

"I didn't either, until Cybil said something about attending an event Alyssa and Carlos catered. I'm pretty sure it was the memory of the bruschetta chicken that drove me over the edge."

Savannah laughed. "I guess that was a good choice then."

"Indeed." Since a customer could walk in any minute, Gia didn't linger over her food, just started to eat.

"Oh," Savannah pointed at Gia with her fork. "Mallory called."

"Is everything okay?" If that woman gave Savannah any more trouble—

"Fine. I have to stop by tomorrow morning to sign the papers and drop off the deposit so she can make the offer. Leo is meeting me out there; do you want to come?"

"Sure, I'd love to." It might give her another opportunity to question Mallory. Who knew? Maybe she'd slip up about her past again.

"Thanks." Savannah took another bite, chewed, and swallowed. "Leo called too."

"He have anything to say?"

Since her mouth was full, she just rolled her eyes, then swallowed. "They had to pick Isaac up again."

"Seriously? What for?" Wow, did that guy ever learn his lesson?

"Apparently, he was stalking Jeremy and Ethan, sitting outside Jeremy's house until all hours of the night. Jeremy called nine-one-one and insisted Isaac tried to break into the house," Savannah said.

That seemed kind of extreme, even if Isaac did think Jeremy killed Robyn. "Did he actually try to break in?"

She shrugged and sipped her water. "Leo wasn't sure. There were pry marks on the back door, and they did find Isaac sitting out front, but he swears he never left the car, and he offered to let them search the car, which they did, and there were no tools, not even the stuff you'd need to change a flat tire."

"Even I have that much in my car."

Savannah held up a finger. "Exactly."

"Huh…so what did they do? Arrest him?"

"Nah, just another warning, since they didn't find any evidence that he tried to break in. Not even any fingerprints on the door, though he could have worn gloves."

"And ditched them with whatever tools he used. Are they searching the bushes and stuff by any nearby houses?" Gia asked.

Savannah stared at her, lifted a brow, then grinned.

"Oh, all right." So she sometimes forgot she wasn't the detective. Of course, Hunt and Leo would have known to search the area.

"I think you missed your calling. You should have been a detective."

"Ha ha." But maybe she wasn't completely off base. Gia did love solving puzzles. "You know. I was thinking."

Savannah's fork stopped partway to her mouth.

"Don't be a smart aleck."

"Did I say anything?" She lowered the fork to the plate.

"You didn't have to, and you know it." Gia smirked at her. "Just for that, I might not share what I was thinking now."

"Okay." Savannah shrugged and went back to eating.

Hmm…Gia hadn't expected that. Savannah was usually pretty gung-ho to go along with whatever Gia had in mind. "Okay, fine, you twisted my arm. I'll tell you."

Savannah sat back to listen. "Is this plan of yours, whatever it is you were thinking about, going to get me into trouble with Hunt?"

Gia paused. "Does it matter?"

"Not really," she shrugged, "just curious."

"Well, I don't think it will anyway. I was just thinking it would be nice to bring a basket, maybe some bagels and muffins and stuff, to Isaac and

Jeremy." After all, she hadn't offered either of them her condolences. And if one or the other let something slip while she was there, then so be it.

"And you think the two of them are going to share breakfast together without one or the other of them winding up in jail?" Savannah's eyes went wide in mock terror.

"Ha ha. No, I was thinking of bringing each of them their own basket."

"Why?" She sipped her water.

"Because it would be a nice thing to do." Mostly.

"And?"

Gia feigned innocence. "And what?"

"Gia, I have been friends with you for a long time, and you are a kind woman. A good woman. When tornadoes hit Boggy Creek last year, after you first moved here, and you didn't even know anyone and were still thinking about moving back to New York, you opened the café to help, donated whatever you could, and tried to help anyone in need. So don't take it wrong when I say, that story ain't no relation to the truth." Savannah picked up her fork and went back to eating.

"Oh, okay, fine. I just wanted to poke around a little. That slip of Mallory's at the house yesterday has me wondering what her past relationship with the police has been, and no one I've talked to seems to know much about her. I figure either Isaac or Jeremy should, and maybe they'll let it slip. I'm sorry, but I don't love the idea of you doing business with someone I don't know anything about, especially when said someone was present during a murder and tried to blackmail you once already. Plus, I want to offer my condolences."

"Okay."

Gia opened her mouth to further her argument, then paused. "Wait. Okay? That's it?"

"Yup. I'll go with you." She waggled her eyebrows up and down. "But you already knew that before you asked. You had me at, I was thinking."

Chapter Sixteen

Gia set two baskets on the back seat of Savannah's blue mustang convertible. They'd already dropped Thor at daycare and stopped into the café to make up the baskets, filling them with bagels, muffins, and an assortment of teas and coffees. "You think that makes a nice gift for a condolence call, don't you?"

"Sure thing. Especially if by condolence you mean snooping." Savannah slid her sunglasses on and hopped into the driver's seat.

Gia scowled at her, then climbed into the passenger side. "You make it sound like I have no compassion."

With a quick glance over her shoulder down Main Street in the early morning, pre-traffic hour, Savannah pulled away from the curb. "I'm only teasing you, Gia. It's a nice gift and a nice thought, both of which come from a good heart. The snooping is just a bonus."

Well, when she put it like that, it was an assessment Gia could live with. "Do you have the check for the deposit?"

"Leo's bringing it."

"I don't understand why you're putting a down payment when the seller hasn't even accepted your offer yet?" It seemed foolish to Gia to put down money on something you didn't know you'd get. What if the seller said no?

"It's not the down payment, just a good faith deposit to show we're serious about buying and not wasting everyone's time."

That made sense, she supposed. Gia put on her own sunglasses as they headed toward Mallory's office. Hopefully, Mallory would be on time. They still had to visit Isaac and Jeremy, and Gia hoped to make it back in time for the lunch crowd. "Why didn't I have to do that when I bought the house?"

"Uh…" Savannah winced. "We…ell…"

"You paid the deposit." It wasn't a question. She didn't need to ask, since she could already tell she had. Gia had been adamant she'd wanted to pay everything when she bought her house, even though she hadn't been able to get down to Florida to see it at the time and Savannah had handled the entire purchase. "I thought I—"

"Enough. I know what you said, and on the morning I found the house you were in court. After court, you called crying about having to listen to testimony from Bradley's mistresses." She reached out and squeezed Gia's hand. "What was I supposed to say, oh, hold that thought I need a thousand dollars?"

Gia squirmed. She remembered that day, and it had been a particularly stressful one. Having to listen to other women describe their relationships with Bradley as they tried desperately to provide false alibis had been sheer torture. "I don't know what to say, Savannah, thank you. And I'll pay you back every dime."

"You will do no such thing." She patted Gia's hand once more and returned her hand to the wheel. "That was a gift, Gia. Think of it as a housewarming gift."

Savannah's upbeat phone call a few days later to tell Gia about the house she'd found, along with the tons of pictures she'd texted and emailed, had pulled Gia through the worst of the trial, and then Gia had fled to her new home and never looked back.

Well, that wasn't exactly true. She'd spent the first year or so creating mental pro and con lists about living in Florida or New York. But somewhere along the line, Boggy Creek and its inhabitants had just become home, and she'd stopped looking back. Now, she simply enjoyed the present and looked forward to the future. A future that might be about to change drastically as her best friend in life got married and started a family. She pulled off her glasses and looked at Savannah. "Have I told you how much I love you?"

Savannah's lips quivered as she smiled. "As much as I love you. And you have shown it in so many ways you don't have to tell me."

Gia let her head fall back against the seat.

Seeming to sense her need for a quiet moment, Savannah switched on the radio to a soft rock station and cracked open the window. And in that one instant, Gia knew her life couldn't get any more perfect. Unless maybe she allowed her full feelings for Hunt to emerge, allowed him into the part of her heart she'd kept closed off since Bradley's betrayal.

She jerked upright.

Savannah laughed. "I figured that was coming."

Gia shot her a dirty look. "What are you talking about?"

"It's those quiet moments, when everything in life seems about as perfect as it can get, when the thought of maybe getting married and starting a family sneaks on up and blindsides you."

"Whoa, don't get ahead of yourself now." Family? Who said anything about family? She was barely willing to admit to thoughts about a committed relationship with Hunt.

"Uh huh." She nodded knowingly, flipped on her turn signal, and pulled into the real estate parking lot. "Come on. Don't want to keep your true love waiting."

"I'm choosing to ignore you." Gia climbed out of the car.

Hunt and Leo hadn't arrived yet, so she and Savannah headed inside.

Mallory sat at her desk, her hair piled in a complicated braid of some sort, her V-neck almost low enough to show her belly button.

"Guess she figures Leo and Hunt are coming," Savannah muttered.

Gia figured the same.

When Mallory saw them, she stood and smoothed a skirt so short you could see almost—in Savannah's words—clear to the top of the Christmas tree. "I thought Leo was coming with you?"

Savannah smiled her sweetest smile, the one she reserved for those rare occasions when she either didn't like or didn't trust someone. In this case, it might be both. "He'll be along."

"Great. Do you want a cup of coffee or something while we're waiting?" She gestured toward a coffee station at the far end of the waiting room. As if Savannah wasn't capable of looking over the papers without Leo present.

Savannah cut her off before Gia could accept the offer. "Nah, we're okay, thanks."

Mallory shrugged and turned away. "Suit yourselves."

Gia started to say something, but Savannah pinched her arm discreetly and nodded toward the parking lot.

Isaac stood beside Mallory's car, his gaze darting back and forth between Savannah's convertible and the real estate office.

Savannah leaned toward Gia and whispered, "That guy's as nervous as a long-tailed cat in a roomful of rocking chairs."

"No lie." Gia watched him look around, then bend over on the far side of the car. "What do you think he's doing over there?"

"I don't know." Savannah glanced at Mallory, who had returned to her desk and buried her nose in whatever papers she was shuffling, and lowered her voice even further. "But I don't like it. I can't help remembering the slice of cake that poisoned Robyn could well have been Mallory's."

"And it could have been her someone was trying to kill, not Robyn." Hmm… What to do… Even though Gia didn't much care for Mallory, especially after she gave Savannah such a hard time, not to mention flirting with Hunt. At the same time, she didn't want to see the woman wind up dead. Gia took a step away from Savannah and held her gaze, then spoke loud enough to get Mallory's attention and raise the alarm that Isaac was messing around by her car. "Is that Isaac?"

As usual, Savannah caught right on. "You mean the guy by the black car in the parking lot?"

Mallory's chair shot back and hit the wall as she surged to her feet. "My car?"

Gia tried to look surprised that Mallory had overheard, but it didn't matter. Mallory was staring intently out the window as she hurried across the office. "Where?"

Gia pointed out the window. "I thought it was him standing beside your car, but then he bent over, and I haven't seen him stand up again."

Mallory barreled through the door and started across the lot.

Savannah stared after her in wonder, then let out a low whistle. "Boy, she can really move on those spiked heels, huh?"

"No kidding. I'm not gonna lie, that's pretty impressive." Gia pushed through the door after her, just as Hunt pulled into the parking lot.

"What do you think your doing?" Mallory stood at the far side of her car, fists planted on her hips.

Isaac jerked upright and whirled toward her. "Mallory. Uh…I…uh…"

Hunt kept an eye on the two of them as he slammed his door shut behind him and approached Gia and Savannah.

Leo watched Mallory and Isaac as he stopped and kissed Savannah hello.

Hunt kissed Gia's temple in a gesture of affection she'd come to enjoy, then he frowned. "Something going on?"

"No idea. We were inside waiting on you two, and I noticed Isaac bent over beside Mallory's car. When I mentioned it, she went rushing out there to confront him." Gia tried her best to relay the information quickly enough that she didn't miss whatever went on between the two. She needn't have rushed, since the two of them just stood staring at one another, Mallory like a lion on the hunt, Isaac jittery as the prey she'd cornered.

"Wait here," Hunt said.

As if she'd do anything else.

Hunt strode toward the confrontation, his professional smile firmly in place. When he reached the pair, who were still glaring at each other, he stopped. "Everything okay over here?"

"Um…yeah." Apparently bolstered by Hunt's presence, Isaac puffed up his chest. "Why wouldn't it be?"

He pointed a finger back and forth between the two. "Just curious why the two of you are glaring daggers at each other out here on this beautiful morning."

Isaac took a couple of steps, then staggered and caught himself against the car.

Mallory sneered and shook her head. "I asked you what you're doing out here bent over next to my car?"

"Nothing. Besides, it's not your car. It's mine."

"What!" Mallory's eyes went wide. "What are you talking about?"

Isaac slapped the trunk of the car. "This here was my daddy's car, and it should have been left to me."

Her lips twisted into a half-smile, half-grimace. "Except your daddy knew you were a no-good drunk who'd probably wind up wrapping it around a tree, so he left it to me instead."

"What else did he leave to you, huh, Auntie?" Isaac lurched toward her.

She danced back out of the way, graceful as a ballerina on those blasted shoes that made her legs seem like they went on forever before disappearing into that little scrap of fabric that passed for a skirt. "I don't know what you're talking about."

Gia couldn't deny a burning case of shoe envy, though they wouldn't do her a bit of good, since she'd probably just fall off the darn things.

Leo chuckled. "Looks like Isaac might be taking another ride with us."

Savannah elbowed him in the side. "Five bucks says Hunt loses his cool in less than a minute."

"You're on." Leo's grin widened. "It's going to take him at least two minutes."

Savannah looked at her watch.

"You know exactly what I'm talking about," Isaac whined. "And it's not like I was going to drive the car, I was just looking to lay down in the back seat for a few minutes and collect myself."

Mallory huffed and turned to Hunt, completely dismissing Isaac. "Remove him, please."

Isaac took one step forward and cocked his fist.

"Hey," Leo called and started forward.

Isaac swung.

Mallory must have caught the movement from the corner of her eye, and the woman who had been as adept as a stilt walker only moments before staggered and fell against Hunt's chest.

Isaac's swing missed Mallory's head by less than an inch. Instead, his fist plowed into Hunt's jaw.

Hunt's eyes went wide.

Savannah looked at her wrist and grinned. "Eighteen point oh five seconds."

Hunt struggled to right Mallory—who seemed fully intent on playing the damsel in distress and clinging to him for all she was worth, and fend off Isaac—who seemed to have completely lost his mind and was still trying to get ahold of Mallory, though his reflexes didn't seem coordinated enough to allow it.

Gia couldn't help rooting for him a little bit, not that she'd ever condone him hitting his aunt, but he could at least get ahold of the woman and pull her off Hunt.

"That's it." Hunt shoved Isaac back against Leo, who grabbed hold of him. He then straightened Mallory, stepped back, and pointed at Isaac. "You are under arrest this time. I've tried to be patient with you, tried to respect the fact that you just lost your mother, but taking a swing at a woman just pushed my patience past their limit."

"Yes," Savannah whispered and pumped her fist. "And the winner is...*moi.*"

Hunt grabbed hold of Isaac's shirt front and yanked him from Leo's grasp, then whirled him to face a towering oak tree. "Keep your hands where I can see them."

Leo glanced back at Savannah.

She held up her hand, wiggling all five fingers.

He swiped a hand over his mouth to cover his grin.

"But you don't understand." Isaac tried to turn toward Hunt, but Hunt kept firm pressure against his shoulder, holding him in place.

"Hands on the tree," Hunt demanded.

"But—"

"But nothing. You have the right to remain silent, I suggest you use it."

Isaac deflated, his shoulders slumping as Hunt cuffed him, led him to his Jeep, and stuffed him inside.

Leo stood by the side of the car while Hunt approached Mallory and took out his notebook. After a few quiet questions Gia couldn't hear, he flipped the notebook closed and turned his back on her. With a quick glance over his shoulder to be sure Leo had Isaac under control, Hunt strode toward Gia and Savannah. He used the back of his hand to swipe a trickle of blood from the side of his mouth.

A smile played at the corners of Savannah's mouth. "Getting slow in your old age, huh?"

"Ha ha." Hunt grinned. "Not so fast, cous, it wasn't Isaac's punch that caused the bleeding, that barely landed."

"Uh huh," Savannah teased. "A likely story."

"Don't you be spreading no rumors now." He pointed a finger at her. "I had just opened my mouth to tell Isaac to back off when Mallory's head hit my jaw, and I bit my tongue."

Savannah laughed out loud.

"Yeah, funny for you, maybe, but I hate that crunching sound when you bite your tongue." He shivered.

Gia dug through her bag for a wet wipe and handed it to him. She'd have tried to clean his face off herself, but she doubted he'd appreciate the gesture in front of his attacker.

"Thanks." He took the wipe from her and opened it, then cleaned off his chin. "Did I get it all?"

"Yeah, your good."

"Good. Wouldn't want to give Isaac the satisfaction of thinking he bested me." He crumpled the wiped and stuffed it back into the wrapper, then pocketed it. "Looks like I'll have to catch up with you guys later."

Savannah's smile fell, and her good-natured teasing slipped away. She lowered her gaze. "Looks like I'll have to wait to put in my offer now."

"Don't be silly." Hunt propped a finger beneath her chin and lifted it until she made eye contact. "I can handle Isaac by myself, and Mallory seems no worse for wear."

Probably because she'd gotten the opportunity to cozy up close to Hunt. Gia dismissed the less than charitable thought, along with the small pang of jealousy it brought, an emotion she was not only surprised by but had no clue what to do with.

"If you guys can drop Leo off at the station when you're done, I don't see any reason you can't take care of business here." He slid a strand of Savannah's hair behind her ear and smiled at her, so softly it sent a wave of love crashing through Gia. Despite the fact that Savannah had five brothers, she and Hunt had grown closer than any of them growing up. "You know I'd do anything for you, cous."

She nodded and gave him a quick hug. "I do know, Hunt, thank you."

He kissed the top of her head and stepped back. "Any time, kiddo."

"Hey." Her playful grin returned. "Maybe later I'll buy you a cup of coffee."

"You've got to be kidding me." He propped his hands on his hips. "How long?"

"Just over eighteen seconds before I knew you were going to blow, another ten for you to untangle yourself and yell."

He seemed to consider that for a moment, pursed his lips, then nodded. "What did Leo say?"

"Two minutes."

"Hah. He deserved to lose if he doesn't know me better than that by now." Hunt turned and jogged back to the car.

And Gia once again lost her opportunity to talk to Mallory. She had a list of questions fully prepared this time for after the signing, figuring she could stall for a few minutes once Hunt and Leo took off. Now that Leo would be present until they left, she might never get to ask her about the real leaves and berries on the cake, or her past involvement with the police.

Chapter Seventeen

Savannah bounced in the driver's seat as she pulled out of the police station parking lot after dropping Leo off. "And now we wait."

"You think they'll accept, right?"

"I do." She nodded and stopped at the only traffic light around for miles. She held up a hand, her fingers crossed. "Mallory already spoke to the listing agent to let him know we were planning to offer their asking price, and she said they're anxious to sell. We shouldn't have any trouble getting the mortgage, so I don't see a problem."

"When should you hear?"

The light turned green, and she looked both ways before starting through the intersection. "It shouldn't take too long, especially since the listing agent already got in touch with them to let them know an offer's coming."

"That's good, at least." Waiting wasn't easy for Gia, and she suddenly realized how much Savannah had done for her when she'd been buying her own house and the café.

"Hey, look at that?" Savannah pointed toward the side of the road and slowed down.

"Look at what?" Gia didn't see anything but an old thrift shop on the side of the road.

Savannah pulled onto the grass bordering the road and hit her turn signal, then looked over her shoulder and swung a U-turn.

"Where are you going?" Gia scanned the road but didn't see anything but woods.

With a small squeal, Savannah pulled into the gravel driveway and parked beside a weathered wooden sign laying against a stack of tires, whose white lettering, that read *Antiques*, had long ago faded almost completely. "It's perfect."

"What's perfect?" A beat up, rusted pick up truck that might once upon a time have been green, unless the remaining flakes were some kind of mold or moss, sat lopsided on three tires beside the sign. She couldn't possibly mean that.

"Look, on the front porch." Savannah pointed toward a collection of what to Gia's untrained eye appeared to be junk that had been piled high enough to spill over the railing and onto the patch of weeds that passed for a front lawn. A string of old-fashioned Christmas lights, with half of the old fashioned, giant, multicolored bulbs burnt out, sagged from the ceiling above the whole mess.

"Sorry, Savannah, this is one time we are just not on the same page." Because Gia could not find a single thing amid the clutter that would have piqued Savannah's interest.

"Come on." She shifted into park, turned off the car, leaving her keys dangling from the ignition, and hopped out.

Gia followed. "Where are we going?"

"Don't you see it? Look." She pointed toward the far corner of the porch.

Two rocking chairs made from logs, their finish long ago stripped away by the elements, were stacked atop one another against the railing at the front corner of the porch.

"How did you even see those from the road?"

"They're perfect, aren't they?" Savannah clasped her hands together and hurried up the rotting porch steps, which creaked beneath her slight build.

Gia chose her footing more carefully, afraid the decaying wood would give way any second and send her crashing through into whatever den of critters might be living underneath. When she could have sworn she heard a low hiss, she threw caution to the wind and ran up the remaining step.

Savannah waded through the mess, shifting aside an old electric heater, a rusted bicycle with only one wheel, and two wooden barrels.

Hmm…they would look great with checkerboard tops sitting out in front of the café, maybe with a couple of wrought iron chairs for each. She could imagine Earl and Cole out there lounging over a game while people stopped to gossip over the latest news in the Boggy Creek rumor mill. Okay, she had to have those barrels.

When she reached the rocking chairs, Savannah tilted her head to get a better look. "They seem to be in good shape. Here, help me."

Gia wedged herself between an old refrigerator and what looked like it might be a car radiator, though she couldn't be certain. "What do you want me to do?"

"Help me lift it over the rail. We'll put it over onto the grass."

One chair had been stacked atop another upside down, and two of the arms had gotten tangled together. Gia worked to shift them apart while Savannah lifted. Together, they managed to get one of the chairs over the railing without damaging it any further than it already was and with no injuries other than a large splinter in Gia's thumb. She plucked it out while Savannah bent to pull an old tricycle out from where it lay on its side, one wheel caught up in the chair's legs.

"Howdy, there, ladies." An older man in faded jeans and a flannel shirt, a piece of what looked like straw clenched between his teeth, stood on the porch just behind them scratching his head. "Can I help you with somethin'?"

Savannah stood and rubbed her hands together to get rid of some of the grime, then held one out to the newcomer. "Hi, I'm Savannah Mills, it's nice to meet you."

The stranger took her hand, seemingly oblivious to the dirt still covering her palm. "Cooter Grimes. Please to meet you, ma'am."

Savannah returned her attention to the second chair. Now that it seemed to be free of any encumbrance, she shifted it toward the railing.

Cooter winced and shifted from one foot to the other. "I certainly don't mean to be rude or nothin' to a couple of such lovely ladies, but would you mind if I ask what're y'all doin'?"

Savannah paused and straightened. "We're trying to get this chair over the railing."

He frowned. "Where y'all going with Aunt Birdie's chairs?"

Uh oh. Something about Cooter's behavior seemed off, not that of a man eager to make a sale. Gia looked over at Savannah.

"Once I sand them down and refinish them, they'll be just perfect for the front porch of my new house. I can just imagine rocking beside my new husband, watching the sun set over the forest," she rambled, seemingly oblivious to Cooter's odd behavior.

"Uh...well..." He glanced at Gia as if for confirmation, or support, or something, and she imagined her chances of getting those cool barrels rapidly dwindling away. "See, the thing is, those ain't actually for sale."

Savannah stopped short, the second chair halfway over the railing. "Excuse me?"

Gia stepped in. "I'm sorry, we saw the Antiques sign out front and thought you were open for business."

"Oh, my." Cooter started to laugh, a long deep belly laugh that made you want to laugh right along with him. "Well, I can't say it's the first time this has happened."

"You mean, you're not an antique dealer?" Savannah's cheeks blushed a deep red that crept all the way up to her hairline.

"No, ma'am." He sighed and gestured toward the dilapidated wood-plank ranch behind him. "This here's my home, been livin' here nigh on fifty years, born right there in that back bedroom and I ain't never left since."

Gia would have pegged him for at least a decade older than fifty.

"Oh, my gosh, I am so sorry." Savannah started to wrestle the chair back onto the porch.

Gia grabbed the back and helped her pull. "Please, forgive us. We didn't mean any offense. Savannah simply saw the chairs as we were passing by and fell in love. We thought the sign was a sign for a business. We'll put everything back just the way it was."

They got the chair onto the porch, and Gia started toward the stairs to boost the second chair up to Savannah.

"Ah, well, hold on now." Cooter wiped his face with a red bandana, then stuffed it back into his pocket. "You say you're getting married, are ya?"

"I am, yes." Savannah nodded. "In three days, actually. My friend, Trevor, is having my wedding at his house, and Alyssa and Carlos Rinaldi are catering it…"

Cooter's friendly blue eyes went icy, and he pulled the straw from his mouth and spat over the rail.

"And my fiancé is a detective with the Boggy Creek Police Department, so I most definitely didn't mean to steal anything."

Gia lay a hand on her arm to stop her from rambling.

Cooter tilted his head and studied her. "You talkin' about Trevor from Storm Scoopers?"

Savannah heaved in a deep breath.

"You know Trevor?" Good thing. At least, he'd vouch for them if Cooter decided to press charges.

"Sure, I know Trevor. Nice guy. And he makes a mean banana split." Cooter patted his considerable belly.

"He sure does." As Gia knew firsthand, since it was one of her weaknesses.

"Ahh…" Cooter scratched his head, pulling a few strands of long gray hair free of the pony tail hanging down his back. "I'll tell ya what, ma'am;

since you're a friend of Trevor's and all, and you seem to be so smitten with them, you can have ole Aunt Birdie's chairs."

"Are you serious?" Her mouth fell open.

"Not like she's usin' 'em now, anyway." He guffawed and slapped his leg. "I'd help you get them into the car, but I had back surgery a few years ago and cain't lift the way I used to."

"Oh, no, don't worry about it at all." Savannah waved both hands. "Gia and I can get them, no problem. How much would you like for them?"

At this point, Gia figured Savannah would pay just about any price Cooter wanted.

"You just fix 'em up nice and enjoy 'em. My grandpappy made those chairs for my grandmammy for their wedding. A long line of Grimes babies got rocked in those chairs, and since I'm the end of the line, maybe it's time to pass 'em on to someone who will appreciate the beauty of grandpappy's craftsmanship."

"Oh, I assure you, I most definitely appreciate them. They don't make stuff like this anymore." Savannah rubbed a hand lovingly along the back of the chair at her side.

From what Gia could see, she was telling the truth. Even after who knew how many years out on the porch, in all kinds of weather, and though the finish had long ago begun to weather, the chairs themselves were still solid. The spindles all firmly attached and in place. The arms and legs and rockers didn't give an inch when they'd been prying them apart.

She glanced at the barrels again, wondering if she should push her luck and offer a fair price for them, then thought better of it. But first chance she got, she was heading out to rummage sales, thrift stores, and antique shops in search of something similar. And if she didn't find it, maybe she'd even stop back. Not like they were going anywhere.

"Are you sure I can't offer you at least a little something for our intrusion on your time?" Savannah asked.

"Are you kidding me? Talking to two beautiful ladies ain't never an intrusion, ma'am. You take those chairs and enjoy them, and when you are one day rocking your babies on your front porch, you think of an old man who spent his life taking care of his family. A good man, who don't deserve to be forgotten once I'm gone."

"Thank you so much, Cooter!" Tears shimmered in Savannah's eyes. "I promise you I will always think of your family. And you, for being so kind."

Cooter's face turned purple. "Well, thank you kindly; that's much appreciated. Now, I'll let ya'll get to takin' your chairs home, while I get back to work."

Gia wondered briefly what kind of work he'd been doing. If his grandpappy had passed down his knowledge of furniture making, Cooter stood to make a fortune. "Thank you so much, Cooter. That is very kind of you."

"Sure thing." He nodded.

"If you get a chance, be sure to stop by the All-Day Breakfast Café in town and say hello. I'd be happy to treat you to a nice meal on the house."

"Could you make it steak and scrambled eggs with home fries?" His eyes fluttered closed, and he sighed.

Gia smiled. He'd obviously eaten dinner there before, since that item was off her dinner menu, and enjoyed it. "Absolutely."

"Well then, you got yerself a deal, pretty lady."

After Cooter went back inside, Gia ran down the porch steps so Savannah could hand the chair over the railing to her. "What a nice guy."

Once Gia had the chair set on the ground, Savannah met her on what passed for the front lawn. "He sure is."

"And a good thing he knew Trevor."

"No kidding." Or the entire ordeal might have gone differently, and Savannah could well be explaining to her fiancé why she'd been caught red handed robbing the man of his chairs.

"Then again, Cooter's been here his whole life; I bet he knows pretty much everyone in town." Savannah stood admiring her chairs, or maybe considering how to get them to the car. Grandpappy had made those chairs out of some heavy logs.

"How is it you don't know him?" It seemed to Gia Savannah knew almost everyone in Boggy Creek.

Savannah swiped her hair out of her face with the back of her wrist. "He probably never needed a real estate agent."

Hmm… She looked back at the house where Cooter had been born and raised. True enough.

"But I'd bet my pa and some of my brothers know him." She tilted one of the chairs back and started to drag it down the lawn.

Probably. Savannah's extended family was huge, and most all of them were born and raised and went on to raise their own families in Boggy Creek. Gia grabbed the other chair and started to haul it toward the car. "Speaking of knowing everyone, did you happen to catch his reaction when you mentioned Alyssa and Carlos?"

"No, I didn't notice. Why?" Savannah huffed.

"Oh, no reason. It just seemed like maybe he didn't like them." Gia looked back at the house, then at the rocking chairs and Savannah's mustang sitting in the driveway. Now they were going to have to fit the chairs into the car somehow. Along with the baskets Gia had packed for Isaac—who was most likely sleeping off a bad night at the Boggy Creek Police Department—and Jeremy. Oh, well. They could always head out to visit Isaac tomorrow, provided Hunt released him.

Thunder rumbled overhead, way too close. A burst of wind sent a pile of dead leaves skittering from where they'd gathered against an old picket fence that had seen better days but still stood strong and proud. Perhaps one of Grandpappy Grimes's creations.

Savannah stopped when she reached the car, and Gia set her chair upright next to Savannah's. They were going to have to drop them off somewhere, either Gia's or Savannah's pa's house before going back to the shop. "Where do you want to store them for now?"

"I don't know." She stared at the car, then up at the darkening sky, and chewed on her lower lip. "First, we need to get them into the car somehow."

"Wait here." Gia reached in and grabbed one of the baskets off the back seat. She hurried back up the porch to Cooter's front door and knocked.

The door swung open immediately, as if he'd been standing right next to it, and Cooter looked up at the dark sky. "You ladies need a hand after all?"

"No, we've got it, thank you, but I wanted to give you this." Gia held out the basket of bagels and muffins. "And to thank you again for being so kind to Savannah."

"Aw, you didn't have to do this." He peeked through the cellophane to see what was inside. "But I sure do appreciate it, ma'am. Those muffins smell delicious. Please, tell me there's a banana chocolate chip in there."

Gia grinned. "There's two."

"Oh, my mouth's a waterin' already. You done made my night."

"Thank you. I always love to hear that someone enjoys my cooking."

"Well, I most certainly do. I didn't realize you owned the café, but I've been going in there since you first opened and the Bailey sisters started raving about your cooking. Those two ain't easy to please, for sure."

Gia couldn't agree more, but she kept her mouth shut. Wouldn't want anyone to get the impression she was bad-mouthing anyone, especially someone who obviously recommended her café. "Do you mind if I ask you something, Cooter?"

"Not at all. What's up?"

Savannah shielded her eyes and looked up at the sky.

She was going to have to hurry. "Feel free to tell me it's none of my business, but when Savannah mentioned Alyssa and Carlos Rinaldi earlier,

I couldn't help but notice your reaction. Is there some problem with the two of them?"

"The two of them, no. I got no quarrel with Alyssa; she seems like a nice enough woman, though I don't know her well. Carlos on the other hand, well I don't mind sayin' exactly how I feel about him. And when your business with him is done, you might want to steer clear."

"Why?" She didn't want to push it, and in about two minutes, Savannah was going to be standing out in the pouring rain, but she couldn't help her inquisitive nature.

"Going back, I don't know, about twenty years now, I guess, when my younger brother was still with us, bless his soul, Carlos Rinaldi beat him to within an inch of his life."

Gia gasped before she could catch herself. "Oh, no. That's awful. Why would he do that?"

"They were at a bar, closed down now, but a good place to grab a beer after work at one time." Cooter shrugged and set his basket inside the door, then leaned against the doorjamb as if he had all day to chat. "Monty didn't do nothin' but ask Carlos's girlfriend at the time, Becky Seaverson if memory serves, for her opinion on the music the band was playin'. Sure, he might have had a little too much moonshine, and he was a little sloppy with it at the time, but he didn't disrespect no woman. Not even drunk."

"Were you there when it happened?"

"Nah, I heard about it after the fact, wanted to go after Carlos and give 'im a talkin' too, but Monty wouldn't hear nothin' about it. Said it was his own fault for bein' too friendly with Becky. Everyone knew better, and he didn't want to cause no trouble for her. That's the kind of guy he was, ya know, more worried about what Carlos might do to her than what he'd done to him."

When Cooter stopped talking, Gia left him be, hoping he'd reveal more without her having to prod.

"Anyway, that was a long time ago, and Becky, she smartened up and dumped him, then married an insurance salesman and had herself a pack of kids. And Monty, well, he stayed away from Carlos after that, married 'imself a good woman, then both of 'em died in a car crash a few years later."

"I'm so sorry for your loss."

"Thank you, ma'am. Been a long time now, but I still think about Monty every day, and rememberin' how he suffered that beatin' makes me want to thrash Carlos all over again." He stood and shook off the dour mood, then smiled. "Anyway, thanks for the basket and the trip down memory lane."

"You're very welcome. And thank you for making Savannah so happy. Be sure to let the waitress know you're there next time you come into the café, so I can come out and say hello."

"I'll be sure to do that, ma'am. Thanks again."

She left him to whatever work he needed to get back to and reached the car as the first fat raindrops splattered against the roof.

Savannah had the driver's door open and the seat pushed forward, and she was trying to wrestle one of the chairs into the back seat. She'd already moved Jeremy's basket to the front. "Dag nab it!"

"What happened?"

"I broke a nail." She held up her right hand, the pointer finger nail broken all the way down to her fingertip. "I can't get married like this."

"All right. Just relax, Trevor set up an appointment with Tina for Friday morning, remember? She's coming to the house."

"Still." She studied her finger, which looked about an inch shorter than the rest. "I can't walk around like this until Friday."

"Then I'm sure Tina can fit you in." The rain started to fall harder.

"Four days before Christmas?"

"She always fits you in, Savannah."

"Right. Okay, that's true. I'll give her a call and see if she can just fix this one nail for me. It shouldn't take long."

"See, everything's fine. Now..." Gia gestured toward the chairs, one of which was hanging out of the car. "You do realize these are not going to fit, right?"

"They'll fit." She shook her hand and stood back, leaving the chair's back wedged between the seat and the doorjamb, the bottom half still outside the car. "We just have to be smart about it. It's like a puzzle, you know?"

"If you say so." She just hoped Savannah could solve it quickly, because in about two minutes they were going to be soaked.

"I do." She pulled the chair back out, climbed into the car, and turned it on, then took the convertible top down. Raindrops bounced off the seat. "Okay, grab one end."

Together, she and Gia lifted the chair and lay it on it's back across the back seat. Then they grabbed the other chair, turned it the opposite way, and lay it on top of the firsts one. Though they were still precariously balanced, and one over ambitious pump of the gas would surely send the top one flying off onto the road behind them, at least they were in. But now what to do with the basket?

The sky chose that moment to open up, unleashing a torrential downpour that would probably fill the small car in a matter of minutes.

"Just get in." Savannah hopped into the driver's side and couldn't close the door.

"Here." Gia lifted the chairs so Savannah could get the door to close. Once the door was closed, she ran around to the passenger side. Not wanting to open the door and have the same problem, she lifted the basket off the seat and set it on the rocking chairs. "Roll down the window."

"I can't; it's raining," Savannah said, her expression serious.

"Savannah, I'm getting soaked."

Savannah laughed and rolled down the window for Gia to climb in. "I got news for you, honey, you ain't gonna be any less soaked once you get in the car."

Very true. Gia settled into the wet passenger seat, grabbed the basket from the back, and settled it onto her lap.

"I figure we have to go back to the café anyway, so maybe we could just put the chairs in the upstairs apartment for now."

"That's a great idea. I hadn't thought of that."

"Do you still want to try to go see Jeremy?" She gestured to the rain-soaked basket. "After we go back to the café to fix that mess up, anyway."

"We'll see. First, let's see if Isaac was released. I'd like to see him first."

"Good idea, since that one seems to be quite willing to run his mouth."

If they were going to get any helpful information, it would most likely come from him.

"True, and hopefully, he'll be happy to talk about whatever is going on between him and Mallory, especially after the incident this morning." With a plan in place, Gia settled in for the long, soggy ride back to the café.

Chapter Eighteen

Gia held her soaking wet shirt away from her skin and aimed the blow dryer at the worst of the wet spots. She needed to do her hair too, but her wet clothes had her freezing. Being cold hadn't been a problem since moving to Florida, but it did make it feel a little more like the Christmas season. With holiday music playing softly from the speakers and the café decorated for Christmas, the warm weather had seemed out of place. Still, it was better than being cold, which she now realized.

A knock at the door interrupted her.

"Come in," she yelled without turning off the dryer.

The door eased open and Hunt poked his head inside her office. "Hey, got a minute."

"Sure." Reluctantly, she turned off the dryer. "Come on in."

He pointed at her clothes. "I saw Savannah on my way in. She said she was going up to the apartment to get dry clothes, and she'd grab some for you too."

"Oh, great." Thankfully, she'd left leggings and T-shirts upstairs in case she ever decided to stay over. Even though Savannah was smaller than her, she should be able to find something that would work for her. Gia unplugged the hair dryer, wrapped the cord, and stuffed it back into her bottom desk drawer. The desk Savannah had put in the café until Gia could afford something better, the desk Savannah's pa had made her, that she'd taken to New York with her, and that Gia had stubbed her toes on more times than she could count. "I'm going to have to buy a desk."

Hunt frowned. "Okay, I'll bite. Why?"

"Oh, sorry. Just thinking out loud." Gia grabbed the sweater off the back of her chair and put it on. It would do until Savannah got back. She grabbed a brush from her top drawer and started tugging it through the tangled mess of wet curls. "The desk is Savannah's. Her pa made it, and she loaned it to me. Now that she's getting her own house, she should have it back."

"Come here." Hunt pushed the office door shut, then took the brush from her hand and set it on top of the file cabinet. He wrapped his arms around Gia from behind and rested his chin on her shoulder.

She leaned back against him, grateful for the warmth of his embrace. "You're going to get soaked."

"Don't worry about it." He nuzzled her neck, sending a different kind of chill rushing through her. "I won't melt."

Gia wrapped her arms around herself, gripping Hunt's arms. "What brings you by, other than warming up your girlfriend who had to ride all the way home with the top down in the pouring rain thanks to your crazy cousin."

"Hey," he laughed. "She's your friend. At least I can say she was born into the family; you actually chose to befriend her."

She couldn't argue with that logic, so she changed the subject. "You're done early. I figured you'd be at the station most of the day."

He leaned against the desk, taking her with him. "Nah, I just read Isaac the riot act, gave him a severe warning about going near Mallory again, and dropped him off home before heading back to the station."

Gia turned to face him and kissed his lip where it had started to bruise. "You let him go? Just like that? Even after he hit you?"

Hunt shrugged it off and slid onto the desk. "You were there. It wasn't like he hit me on purpose. If Mallory hadn't moved, he'd have hit her, instead."

"Yeah, well…" The thought did appeal. Shocked at the thought, Gia mentally reprimanded herself. "I think maybe you're turning into a big softie in your old age."

"It's not his fault dear old Aunt Mallory has a way of provoking him."

"Seems everyone does, if you ask me."

"Could be. He does have a bit of a temper, but he's mostly harmless."

"So, you don't think he killed his mother?" Gia grabbed the brush from the cabinet, plopped onto the chair in front of her desk, and went back to work on her hair.

Hunt folded his arms across his chest. "I mean, I wouldn't go that far, especially since he's the sole beneficiary as far as we can tell now, but time will tell."

"Ow." She tugged through a particularly tough knot. "I suppose it will. What about Jeremy? Is he a suspect?"

"Right now, everyone's a suspect, but I don't have any evidence that leads me to believe Jeremy had anything to do with Robyn's death." He frowned. "At the moment, we can't even be completely sure she was the intended target."

"So, you think it was Mallory the killer was after?"

"Could be. Seems the most likely since she's the one who gave her slice of cake to Robyn."

"But why would someone want to kill Mallory?" Unless it was the girlfriend of some guy she hit on.

"Isn't that the million-dollar question? And once we can answer it, we'll probably know who killed her."

Gia had come to love discussing Hunt's cases with him. While he often stopped by the café, hung out for a while if he had time, had something to eat, she couldn't be a part of his world in that way. Not that she couldn't stop by the station and say hello, but she didn't often. Chatting about his cases allowed her to share in his day. Plus, she enjoyed the fact that he trusted her enough to confide in her and often considered her opinions. "Have you found any proof that Mallory was at the caterer earlier than she admitted to?"

"No." He boosted himself onto the desk to sit, then clasped his hands between his knees, settling in for a chat. "But we did find a surveillance camera a block over that shows a man walking away from Rinaldi's and rounding a corner. The quality of the footage is awful, and the man is only seen from the back, but the build and hair color is in line with it having been Ethan Carter."

"Jeremy's best man? You think he was there and left before he showed up after Robyn was killed?" She set the brush aside and sat on the chair across from him, slipping her shoes off and tucking her cold feet beneath her.

"We think it's possible. Now that we know what direction the man was headed, we're trying to find footage he shows up on again, or a video that shows a car leaving the area he was last seen in. Anything that might point us in the right direction. At least then we might luck out and get a tag to run."

"And if it's his?"

He shrugged. "It shows he was in the area and lied, so we can pick him up as a person of interest and bring him in for questioning. Rattle the cage a bit and see what happens."

"Why didn't you bring Isaac in for questioning?" It didn't seem like Hunt to keep picking someone up and releasing him.

"We did. A few times now. But we didn't get anywhere. As much as he's all bluster while he's accusing Jeremy of murder in public, once we get him alone in an interrogation room all he does is whine for a lawyer. Isaac wants to talk, but he most definitely does not want to answer questions."

"Hmm…" Maybe she'd have more luck getting him to open up than the police had, since he might not perceive her as a threat. Plus, he'd seen her with Hunt a couple of times now, so he might think she'd be able to sway him. Little did he know Hunt if that was the case, but it could work to her advantage.

"Gia." Hunt's tone changed, his voice deepening in warning.

"Yup?" She realized she'd zoned out for a second and winced.

"That 'hmm…' sounded like you're up to something."

"Not at all, just thinking I should try to get something done soon." True enough.

"Uh huh." He eyeballed her from the corner of his eye. "Just make sure you leave the investigating to us."

"Of course." Certainly, a condolence call wouldn't be considered investigating. But just in case, it probably wouldn't hurt to wait until afterward to mention it.

He hopped off the desk and held a hand out to her. "Anyway, I've got to get going. We just stopped by because Leo had to drop something off to Savannah, and I wanted to stop in and say a quick hello."

Disappointment surged. With the chill of her wet clothes still embracing her, she'd love nothing more than to cuddle up with Hunt and forget all about murder, even for a little while. "Are you going to be staying at Trevor's tonight?"

"Yeah, as long as nothing breaks on the case. Leo and I are planning to stay out there until after the wedding."

"I still can't believe they're getting married in three days." No matter how long they'd been planning it, the date seemed to be flying up on her faster than she could comprehend.

"No, me neither." Hunt studied Gia, his expression soft, as if she'd caught him in an unguarded moment. He seemed like he was about to say something, then shook his head as if he'd changed his mind. "Anyway, I'd better get going. And, Gia…"

"Yeah."

"Next time it rains, put the top up." He winked and walked out.

Her gaze lingered on the doorway he'd just walked through. Could she really have a future with Hunt? Could she envision herself sharing the rest of her life with him, starting a family, growing old together? She wasn't sure. But the one thing she was absolutely certain of was, if she was going to share her life with anyone, it would be Hunt.

Savannah shoved the door open and tossed a bag onto Gia's desk. "There you go. Dry clothes."

Not a minute too soon. She'd just started shivering again. "Thanks, Savannah, you're a lifesaver."

"It's the least I could do considering I'm the one who got you soaked in the first place." She hopped up onto the desk next to the bag and let her legs swing. "Thanks for that, by the way."

"No problem." She grinned. "Shivering put me in the holiday spirit."

Savannah laughed. "I do have to admit, that was the only time of year I enjoyed the cold weather when I lived in New York. There was something so magical about walking down thirty-fourth street, all bundled up in that big thick coat, gloves, hat, scarf pulled over my nose and mouth so my lungs wouldn't freeze when I breathed, especially when it snowed. I loved the big fat flakes that clung to my eyelashes when I was trying to take in the Christmas decorations in the Macy's window. Throw in one of those amazing big pretzels from the corner stands, and it was just about perfect."

Abandoning the thought of changing into dry clothes, Gia dropped onto the chair in front of the desk. "When we lived together in New York, in the beginning, at least, did you think you would stay?"

Savannah tilted her head and stared off into space for a couple of minutes. "I don't think so. I think on some level I always knew Boggy Creek was my home and always would be, but I just couldn't bring myself to settle down into that life until I at least tried to pursue my dreams."

"Do you ever regret the years you lost there? Years you could have been here with Leo, starting your life together?"

"No," she answered without a moment's hesitation. "If I hadn't gone, I'd always have wondered what it would have been like, if I could have made it on Broadway, ya know? Now, I always have the knowledge that I tried, that I got to take dance classes with real Broadway stars, that I had the courage to follow my dreams, and that I met you. That's one thing I wouldn't change for the world."

"Even though you ended up hating living in New York?"

"Are you kidding me? I appreciate everything I have here so much more than I ever could have if I hadn't experienced something else, all the things I used to take for granted when I was young." She leaned forward, propped her elbows on her knees, and clasped her hands together, her expression turning serious. "Sometimes, it's the difficult times in our lives that make us be able to appreciate the joy in a way we couldn't have if life had been easy. All we can do is learn from our mistakes, take those lessons with us, and move on to something better."

Gia had no doubt the conversation had just changed track from a fun reminiscence to something deeper. She also had no doubt it had something to do with Hunt. "And what happens if we repeat the same mistakes? It's not like we have control over what other people do."

"No, we don't. So we have to learn to make better choices in the people we surround ourselves with. And if we get hurt, then we get hurt. The joy of loving someone so completely is worth the risk."

Gia lowered her gaze to her hands in her lap. Why couldn't she just let go and love as freely as Savannah seemed to do so easily?

"Anyway." Savannah jumped off the desk and patted Gia's shoulder. "That's enough words of wisdom for today. Ponder that while you change into dry clothes and I go get this nail fixed. Tina squeezed me in, but if I don't hurry I'm going to miss the appointment. See you in a bit."

Gia said good-bye, then quickly changed into dry clothes. Instead of blow drying her hair, she simply pulled it up so the wet strands wouldn't hang down the back of her dry shirt. She'd have to wear it up in a little while anyway when she took over the grill from Cole. But for now, if she hurried, she could put together a new basket and go have a chat with Isaac before Savannah returned. At least then, if he freaked out or turned out to be a killer, she wouldn't be putting Savannah at risk.

Chapter Nineteen

Gia shifted the basket she'd brought for Isaac to free up a hand so she could ring the doorbell. While she waited to see if he'd open the door, she looked up and down the quiet street. Though she'd expected to have trouble entering the gated community without a code or an invitation, the arm had lifted as soon as she'd pulled up to the gate, and she'd driven right in.

The house Isaac had shared with his father before his death last year, and his mother before her recent demise, sat at the end of a dead-end street. The white house with black shutters and a black shingle roof was the largest on the block, and boasted a variety of nooks and crannies all highlighted by reverse gables. A thick row of overgrown azaleas blocked any view of the street and driveway, giving a sense of privacy, and making Gia a little nervous. Not that it would matter anyway—probably—if Isaac decided to kill her inside the house, chances were none of the neighbors would hear her scream, with or without the thick foliage to serve as a barrier.

The red front door opened with a squeak, and she spun toward it.

Isaac stared at her, confusion furrowing his brow, anger clenching his fist around a half empty beer bottle. "What do you want?"

Okay. She thought about turning tail and running, but it was probably too late for that. Besides, her curiosity wouldn't allow it. "Hi, Isaac. I'm Gia Morelli. I was at Rinaldi's when your mother took ill."

He narrowed his eyes and studied her. "You tried to save her."

"I did, yes. With my friend, Savannah, and I'm very sorry we weren't able to." A fact that would be sure to haunt her forever. Was there anything more she could have done? If she'd gone to the dining room when Robyn had first screamed, would the outcome have been different? Hunt had said there was an antidote; would that minute or two have given the doctors time to administer a lifesaving dose?

She swallowed the lump threatening to choke her.

"Come on in." Isaac stepped back and held the door open.

"Thank you." She held the basket out to him as she stepped into the marble tiled foyer. "I just wanted to stop by and drop this off for you and offer my condolences on your mother's death."

"Thanks." He took the basket without looking at it and headed toward the back of the house.

Gia followed, taking her time as she crossed the living room, past a fireplace, the mantle decorated with a Christmas village and covered in faux snow. Though no Christmas tree held a position of prominence in the large picture window, a small one graced the far corner of the room with nothing but a few strands of lights, many of the bulbs burnt out, and a silver star on top.

Isaac dropped the basket onto the kitchen table, then set his bottle unopened on the counter beside the sink. "You want something? A drink?"

"No, I'm fine, thank you." And now that she was standing there in his kitchen, she was at a total loss as to what to say to him.

He yanked a chair out, the legs scraping loudly against the terra cotta tile, and flopped onto it. "You can sit down if you want."

"Thank you." Gia took a seat across the table from him. At least it was some protection if he came at her. "How are you doing?"

He slid down in the seat, his legs splayed in front of him beneath the table, and Gia wondered how much alcohol he'd consumed that day. "Been better."

"I'm sorry to hear that. You and your mother must have been very close."

He frowned. "What makes you say that?"

She had no clue. "Uh…I don't know. I guess because you were at her tasting."

He made a rude noise somewhere between a snort and a grunt. "Yeah. That."

She'd made a mistake coming here. She started to stand.

"Hey, sorry, I didn't mean nothing." He sat up straighter. "You don't have to go."

She lowered herself hesitantly back onto the chair.

He crinkled the cellophane wrapping the basket, seemingly more for something to do than any interest about what was inside. "You were there this morning. At the real estate office, right?"

She hesitated, unsure if she should answer him, then finally decided it didn't matter. He had to have seen her there. "Yes, I was."

He sniffed and shook his head. "Good ole Aunt Mallory. Gotta love her, right?"

"I...um...sure...I guess."

He stared at her a moment. "Did you come for anything else besides to drop off this basket and to apologize for letting my mother die?"

Gia cringed. "No, I'm sorry to have bothered you. I'll be going now."

"Nah, you ain't gotta leave. Not like I have anyone else to talk to now." His gaze raked up and down, making her squirm. "You date that cop, right?"

"Um, yes, I do." A fact he'd do well to remember if he decided to do away with her or anything.

He sat up straighter and propped his forearms on the table. "Well, maybe you can give him a message for me."

Gia braced herself for whatever message he might have for Hunt.

"Tell him I said thanks."

Surprised, Gia perked up. Maybe this wouldn't be a wasted trip after all. "For what?"

"You know, for not arresting me and all after I hit him. You can tell him I'm sorry too. I didn't mean to hit him, but Mallory gets me so mad sometimes I can't control myself."

"I'm sure he realized it was just an honest mistake." Though Hunt did not take kindly to a man taking a swing at a woman under any circumstances. It was part of his charm.

"I think he said he did, but I was a little too messed up to remember for sure."

"And now?" she asked.

Isaac seemed depressed, and maybe lonely, but he didn't seem drunk. His words were clear, not slurred. He'd walked in a perfectly straight line from the foyer to the kitchen, no staggering or stumbling.

"Now, I'm sober as could be." He flung a hand out toward the beer bottle. "You caught me just as I was about to get started."

"Oh, well, I'm glad then." Even though she had no clue what to say to him, she didn't want to leave him alone, concerned he might need help. "Is there anything I can do to help? Do you want to talk?"

"Talk about what? The fact that my mother cheated on my father and now they're both dead?"

"Cheated with Jeremy?" Normally, she'd never have asked such a thing, but since Isaac seemed to want to toss around accusations, as he had every other time she'd seen him, who was she to ignore him?

Isaac slouched in the chair once again and sulked. "He was Mallory's boyfriend first, you know?"

"Who, Jeremy?" Well, that was new. She hadn't heard that anywhere, and you'd think it would be news, especially considering Robyn had possibly been killed by Mallory's slice of cake.

"Yup." He took a napkin from the holder on the table and mopped his brow. "She brought him home, hanging all over him like they was something special. Then they started hanging around, the two of them and that other jerk, Ethan. And before you know it, Jeremy, Ethan, and my dad were best buds, doing everything together. Good ole Auntie Mallory, who hadn't come around the house in years, all the sudden showed up with those two in tow and wrecked everything."

"How did Jeremy go from dating Mallory to marrying your mom?" With Mallory as her maid of honor. Gia's head swirled.

"I don't think they were dating at all. I think Mallory showed up with that creep, and he set his sights on my mom from day one. I think the two of them schemed to kill my father and my mother and take the inheritance."

"I don't understand. If both of your parents were gone, wouldn't you have inherited everything?" She didn't dare repeat what Hunt had told her about him being the sole beneficiary, though she found it hard to believe he didn't know.

"Mallory convinced my father I was too irresponsible to handle it and should have a babysitter to make sure I didn't squander it all."

So where was that will?

"It wouldn't be the first time that witch tried to con my old man out of money, and he always fell for it." He slammed the side of his fist against the table, and Gia jumped. "He just couldn't accept what she was. And when the other two showed up, he took them at face value too, just accepting everything they said as if it were gospel truth. Even when I told him I caught my mother and Jeremy together in the garage, locked in an embrace that was far from innocent."

Seemed Jeremy got around, first Mallory, then Robyn, then Alyssa, if gossip were to be believed.

Isaac lurched to his feet and began to pace, back and forth across the small kitchen, arms flailing wildly. His voice grew louder as he continued to rant. "But he believed them instead of me, said I was mistaken, or drunk, or lying, but let me assure you, that time I was stone cold sober. And now he's gone. And so's my mom. And for what?"

He dropped back into the chair, folded his arms on the table, and lowered his head onto them.

Gia wasn't sure what to do. The desire to get up and go to him, maybe lay a hand on his shoulder or try to offer comfort nudged her forward. The fact that Hunt had told a much different version of who stood to gain from his parents' demise held her rooted in place. No, the best thing she could do for him was to keep him talking, maybe figure out who was to blame for all of this and hold them accountable. "What happened after your father passed away?"

Isaac jerked upright. "You mean after he was murdered?"

"If that's what happened."

"It is. I'm sure of it, though the police haven't found any evidence." His eyes went wide, eager. "Do you think you could get your boyfriend to open his case again? Maybe investigate what happened?"

Oh, boy. Hunt would not be amused if she asked him to do that. "Maybe, if you think you can show some kind of just cause."

"My father was taken to the emergency room, but they couldn't save him. The doctor there said it was possible his heart had given out before the accident. When I insisted to that stupid cop that he took his medication regularly and couldn't have had a heart attack, the guy said I couldn't know that for sure. All he offered was a snide, placating smile when he told me people skipped or forgot to take their medication all the time."

Something wasn't adding up. There seemed to be too much confusion around Max's death. Was it possible it was related to Robyn's in some way? "What did the autopsy show?"

"There was no autopsy." He squeezed his temples between his hands. "My mother refused to have one, after counsel from Mallory. Then, a few months later, Jeremy paid a condolence call, and the rest, as they say, is history."

"If there was suspicion his death wasn't an accident, there would have been an autopsy regardless, I'm sure." Actually, she wasn't at all sure, but it seemed reasonable to assume that his wife, who'd have been the most likely suspect, wouldn't have gotten to make that choice.

He snapped his fingers and pointed at her.

Something about the move seemed off, fake, contrived.

"Here. Wait here." More animated than she'd seen him, he jumped out of the chair and ran down the hallway, then pounded up the stairs.

While she waited for him to return, she stood and stretched her back, then wandered around the kitchen. A pile of dirty dishes filled the sink and spilled over onto the counter and all the way to the stove, garbage was piled high in the pail, knocking the top askew, a stack of mail sat unopened on a small desk tucked into the corner of the kitchen.

Gia approached the desk. With a quick glance over her shoulder, she paused to listen. The sounds of someone rummaging around upstairs trickled down the hallway.

Gia sifted through the mail, mostly bills, a lot of bills, in both Robyn and Jeremy's names. Very little of the mail was addressed to Isaac, and what was seemed to be mostly Christmas cards. Did the man child have no responsibility? No job? No bills?

Nothing seemed suspicious, though she didn't know exactly what she was looking for. A copy of the will naming Isaac, or someone else, as the beneficiary might be helpful. A picture of Robyn standing in a pumpkin patch, Jeremy standing beside her lifting an ear of sweet corn in toast, both of them grinning widely, sat in a frame on a shelf that ran across the top of the desk.

Gia picked up a Christmas card out of the pile, one of the beachy ones with a light strewn palm trees and Merry Christmas written in the sand. Personally, she preferred the wintry scenes for her cards. She opened the card and read the generic *Wishing you a very Merry Christmas* written in italics in the center. Below that, scrawled in sloppy cursive were the words, *Here's to a job well done! See you on the beach in Waikiki soon, bro.* It was signed *Ethan.*

She flipped it over, but it wasn't addressed to anyone. She looked over her shoulder, then frantically searched through the pile for an envelope. Nothing that matched the size and shape of the card.

The phone rang, shattering the silence, and Gia's heart shot to her throat. What if Isaac came downstairs to answer it? She hurriedly tried to make sure everything was in order and bolted across the room, as Isaac's footsteps pounded back down the stairs.

By the time he reached her, she was still out of breath, but at least she'd managed to swallow her heart back down into her chest, where it thumped wildly against her ribs.

He didn't seem to notice as he shoved a bottle of pills at her, nor did he pay any mind to the ringing phone. "See. Look. You can count them."

She looked at the bottle. "Count what?"

"Dad's heart medicine." He ripped the bottle back out of her hand and pointed to the label. "See, the date's on there, when he picked up the prescription, and the exact number of pills he should have taken is what's missing from the bottle."

"Okay, so that means he probably did take his meds, but it doesn't prove he didn't have a heart attack." Plus, he could still have had pills left from his previous prescription before he started this one, or Isaac could have dumped a few down the toilet, so the number of pills missing from the bottle didn't really prove anything. But Isaac's frantic plea might.

"Just show them to Captain Quinn, okay? Promise?" Beads of sweat trickled down the sides of his face.

"Yes, I'll show him." Gia agreed, just grateful he hadn't realized she was snooping. She dropped the bottle into her bag just as the answering machine picked up the call and told the caller to leave a message.

"Isaac, look, it's Jeremy." He blew out a loud mechanical sounding breath on the machine. "I need to talk to you. I have something to give you. I'll be home any time after ten tonight. I'll be waiting for you to stop by."

Well, that let out stopping by Jeremy's tonight, if he was going to be out until late.

"That'll be the day, you con artist." Isaac's face turned purple as he grabbed the closest thing he could reach, a salt grinder from the table, and threw it full force at the machine. It hit and knocked the machine and phone to the floor with a crack.

Gia jumped, startled by the sudden move.

Isaac let out a scream, ran across the room, and kicked the machine, which bounced off the glass sliding door that opened to a small herb garden on the back deck.

Gia backed toward the door, careful to give him a wide berth. "I'm sorry, but I have to get going now. I've already been gone from the café too long."

Isaac just nodded and waved at her, then yelled after her down the hallway. "Don't forget to give my dad's medicine to Captain Quinn."

Another loud crash preceded a string of curses that followed her out the door.

Chapter Twenty

With the stop by the station to drop off Max's heart medication to Hunt, who simply took her involvement with a sigh and a shake of his head, Gia had been gone from the café longer than expected. She parked out in front, still her preferred parking spot, though at least now she could take the garbage out back to the dumpster without having an anxiety attack, and hurried up the front walk, enjoying the quick moment of warmth at the coziness of her very own place, especially decorated for Christmas.

The holiday cheer continued as she opened the front door and sent a cluster of bells jingling. Someone, probably Savannah, had thought to play *It's a Wonderful Life* on the TV hanging behind the counter, the volume loud enough to hear but not loud enough to be intrusive. A number of customers sat at the counter enjoying the movie while they ate.

Willow waved. She seemed to have things under control, and Savannah sat at a corner table with a man who looked vaguely familiar, though Gia couldn't quite place him. Too bad, she'd been hoping to discuss her conversation with Isaac and get Savannah's take on it, but several customers sat perusing menus, so they were about to begin the dinner rush. It would have to wait until later. Oh, well. Nothing that wouldn't keep.

"Gia, hey." Savannah waved her over.

As she weaved between the tables to the far side of the café, shaking off the disappointment that Savannah was busy, Gia paused to say hello to a number of customers she was beginning to recognize since they came in so often. It sent a burst of pride rushing through her.

Savannah started talking before Gia made it all the way to the table. "Hey, Gia, you remember my friend, Tom, don't you?"

Uh oh. That meant she should know him, but she just couldn't place the face or the name. She settled for a smile and nodded toward Tom.

Seemingly sensing her dilemma, Savannah rushed on. "Tom Prichard, the reporter?"

"Oh, right, Tom." She held out a hand. "Sorry, it took a minute, but I do remember you. It's nice to see you again."

Tom stood and shook her hand, then pulled out the seat between him and Savannah, who sat across the table from him, and gestured for Gia to sit.

"Thank you." She sat and pulled herself in closer to the table. "I only have a minute, but how have you been, Tom?"

"I'm doing well, thank you." He returned to his seat. "How are you?"

"Good, just trying to balance getting ready for the wedding with holiday preparations and work. You know how it is."

"Oh, believe me, I do. This is going to be my little girl's first Christmas, and my wife is going all out." He beamed with pride, and Gia had a feeling she wasn't the only one going all out.

She'd met Tom's wife, Cindy, once or twice when they'd come in for breakfast, and the woman was completely devoted to their little one. "How is the baby? Chloe, right?"

"Yes." His smile held such love, she was thrilled she'd been able to pull up the curly haired baby's name. "She's perfect, thank you."

"Tom has a new podcast," Savannah interjected, seemingly over the small talk.

"Fairly new," he added with an adorable smile. "It's been around for a while; it's just not real popular yet."

"It will be, though, I bet." Savannah scooted closer and lowered her voice. "He does true crime segments and cold cases and the like. Mostly local stories."

"Oh, wow, that sounds interesting." Gia would have to check it out. She'd begun to develop an interest in the history of Boggy Creek. Maybe because the town was so small, and she was beginning to know so many of its residents, she loved hearing all about local lore. "You'll have to give me the information so I can listen while I'm cooking."

"Sure thing." He grinned that aww...shucks grin again. "Thanks."

Savannah tapped her nails against the table top. "Listen, Gia. Tom was just telling me about an old story I think you'll find real interesting."

"Oh, yeah?" She turned her attention to Tom.

With a quick glance around to be sure he wouldn't be overheard, he shifted forward and lowered his voice, his expression turning more somber. "So, Chloe hasn't been sleeping much of late, teething according to my wife, and Cindy's been exhausted, so I stopped in to pick up take-out for dinner."

Gia's gaze shot to Savannah.

Savannah rolled her eyes. "Which I've already ordered and gave him a cup of coffee to keep him awake while he waits."

Tom lifted the cup in acknowledgement and took a sip. "So, Savannah and I got to talking about the Hackman case, and Mallory Levine in particular. I was just telling her about the history between her and her brother, Max. A real love-hate relationship those two had."

Now he'd caught Gia's interest. "You knew them?"

"Nah, not really, just from around, but I make it my business to know the history of all of Boggy Creek's residents." His mouth fell open in an O almost as wide as his eyes. A crimson blush rushed across his cheeks. "I...uh..."

"It's fine, Tom, no problem." Though Gia didn't love the idea of everyone in Boggy Creek knowing her business, especially the ugly truth of her past with Bradley, she couldn't stop the rumors or the speculation. Those who'd become important to her didn't judge.

"Anyway," Tom continued, probably happy just to move past the awkward moment. "Mallory's been in trouble with the law before."

Now that piqued Gia's curiosity, though she couldn't claim it surprised her. But why wouldn't Hunt know that already? "What for?"

Tom's leg bounced up and down. The man definitely needed sleep more than caffeine. "Forgery. Apparently, she rented a house years ago and furnished it by running up a bunch of credit cards that didn't belong to her."

Hmm...Gia didn't know what she'd expected, but somehow it wasn't forgery. Maybe growing poisonous substances, but not credit card fraud. "Was she convicted?"

"Nope. They were her brother's and Robyn's cards, and Max refused to press charges. She was never actually even arrested."

"Oh?" No wonder Hunt hadn't mentioned it.

"Nope. Max intervened, paid everything, and it all got swept under the rug."

"How do you know all this if she wasn't arrested for the crime?"

He lifted a brow and smiled. "People talk to me."

She could see why. He had that boy-next-door quality that invited trust. Besides, in her experience with Boggy Creek, people loved to talk. There wasn't much you couldn't find out if you were willing to listen.

He spread his hands wide. "So, there you have it."

"What about Robyn?" And how had she and Mallory moved past it to become close enough that Robyn asked Mallory to be her maid of honor?

"I couldn't find much, but supposedly, even though she wasn't happy, she let it go. But she was pretty furious that Max made good on the money to the credit card companies without Mallory having to pay it back." He paused then snapped his fingers. "Oh, and I did hear a rumor recently that Mallory was trying to lay claim to Isaac's inheritance."

"Wait? Isaac's?" Just like Hunt had said.

"Uh huh."

"But Isaac's been swearing up and down Jeremy killed his mother for the inheritance." And he'd said Mallory was left in control of the money.

He sipped his coffee, and Gia resisted the urge to reach out and stop his leg from bouncing. "Yeah, except Jeremy didn't inherit a thing. Unless there's another document, the will on record indicates everything was left to Isaac. And it was a substantial sum."

That was nothing she didn't already know from Hunt, but something wasn't adding up regarding the will. So far, it seemed that something was that Isaac was lying, but why? And how could he think he'd get away with it? "Is that the only time Mallory was ever in trouble?"

He shrugged and took another mouthful of black coffee. "As far as I could find. Unlike the rest of the players in the case."

"Oh yeah?"

"I've been following the case closely, researching all the players, because I'm thinking of featuring it on my podcast this weekend. I think doing a current crime, something that's hot right now, might bring more listeners."

"That's probably true. Especially if it might involve a local scandal."

"Exactly." He slid to perch on the edge of his seat, warming up to a subject he clearly had a lot of interest in. "So, I did preliminary research on all of the people who were at Rinaldi's the day it happened. Not you and Savannah—I'm pretty sure you guys were just in the wrong place at the wrong time."

Good to know.

"But the others all have histories of one sort or another. Take Isaac; he's been arrested numerous times, for everything from drunk and disorderly to driving while intoxicated, to assault in the cases of many a bar room brawl, though he only has a handful of convictions that never even netted him any jail time."

Not surprising, considering the temper tantrum he threw earlier. But she'd wait until she and Savannah were alone before delving into that.

"Then there's good old Jeremy, the grieving fiancé. Thing is, Robyn's not the first significant other he's lost. The man's already gone through three wives, all of whom were widowed within the year before he married them." He lifted a brow. "And all of whom had been left a substantial inheritance."

How could Hunt not know about that? If Tom had found the information, surely Hunt would have been able to. She shook her head and laughed at herself. Of course, Hunt would know that. He'd just chosen not to share the information with Gia. It wasn't like she was his partner or anything.

"And all of whom died soon after the wedding," Tom continued, clearly fascinated by the subject. "And each time, even though his marriages all took place in different states, Ethan was there with him. Sometimes real friendly, other times not showing up on any radar, simply lurking in the background."

Gia pondered that and thought there had to be some proof his marriages had been legitimate and just coincidentally ended in tragedy. Otherwise, Hunt would probably have been able to work with the other jurisdictions to make an arrest. Of course, that would probably take time.

"And let's see." Tom ticked off one finger at a time. "That's Mallory, Jeremy and Ethan, Isaac, and…who else? Oh, right, the Rinaldis."

Savannah sat up straighter. "What about them?"

"Well, I couldn't find anything on Alyssa, other than the rumors she was involved with Jeremy, but Carlos is another story altogether."

Gia's stomach sank.

"His temper has landed him in lock up more than once. Way more than once. Getting into fights with men he thinks are eyeballing his wife seems to be a hobby. Some beating recipients press charges, others admit they may have acted inappropriately and let the matter drop without bringing criminal charges, though a few have pursued civil cases. Which is why he and Alyssa are so far in debt. Between the cases he's lost and the lawyers he's paid to defend him, they owe out quite a substantial amount of money."

"Even so, I don't see how he or Alyssa would benefit financially from Robyn's death."

"Me neither." He drained the last drops of coffee from his cup.

"Can I get you another?" Savannah asked.

"No, thank you. If Chloe decides to sleep at all tonight, I don't want to be too hyped up on caffeine to conk out."

It might be too late for that.

He pressed a button on his phone, then slid his chair back. "And I do have to get going. Thank you for a lovely chat, ladies, and I really hope you'll both tune into my podcast and subscribe; it's called Boggy Creek Under the Magnifying Glass. Catchy, huh?"

"It certainly is, and I can't wait to listen." Gia shook his extended hand. "It was good to see you again, Tom. Say hi to Cindy for me, and be sure to give Chloe a kiss."

"You got it, Gia. Thanks."

She left Savannah to ring him up and see him out, hoping to catch Cole before they got any busier. She found him standing in front of the grill, using a spatula as a pointer as he counted off what he needed to fill the remaining orders.

"Hey, Cole." She went straight to the sink to wash her hands and get gloves so she could help.

"Hey, there. How's it going?" He grabbed a carton of eggs and started cracking them into a large stainless-steel bowl.

"Everything's good."

"You ready for the wedding?"

Actually, the wedding wasn't nearly as prominent in her mind as it should be. "As ready as I'll ever be, I guess."

He glanced up to study her for a moment, then returned to whisking eggs. "It's not like she's moving away or anything."

Gia shrugged. "I know, and she's waiting to hear if the offer she made on the house by me is accepted. Everyone thinks it will be, and then she'd be close by, but it's just not the same as living with me, you know?"

He nodded. "I do."

"Anyway…" She waved a hand to dismiss the subject she didn't really want to think about any longer. "I wanted to talk to you quick, before we get too busy."

"Are you expecting a big dinner rush?"

"It's already getting crowded out there."

"Huh, I figured with nothing new happening on the case, at least as far as I know, things would settle down a bit."

"You'd think." Unless people were congregating in anticipation of news. With a killer on the loose, that wouldn't be surprising. "Maybe it's just because everyone's busy shopping and getting ready for the holidays. No one's got time to cook."

He considered. "That could be true."

Gia scanned the row of tickets and started doling out bowls of home fries, grits, and gravy, then filled all of the toasters with bread or bagels.

"So, what did you want to talk to me about?" Cole poured the egg mixture over several piles of meat and vegetables already sizzling on the grill.

"First off, I want to tell you how much I appreciate all the extra hours you've taken on lately, and assure you I will be picking up the slack again as soon as the wedding is over." And she couldn't wait. Not that she didn't love having the time with Savannah, but it was time for her to get back to working her café the way she loved.

"You know it's not a problem. I love being here." He continued to scan orders and cook as he spoke.

"Yeah, well, I don't ever want you to feel like I'm taking advantage of your kindness."

He paused and caught her gaze, apparently sensing the seriousness in her tone. "I've never felt that way, Gia. You know how much I enjoy working here. I hated retirement. I was bored out of my mind, and I couldn't find anything that made me feel happy. Then I met you, and all that changed."

Joy filled her heart, and a huge smile forced its way past any apprehension she'd had that he might be unhappy working so much. "Thank you for that, Cole, and thank you for everything you've done for me. I couldn't have done all of this without you."

"Sure, you could have." He winked. "It would just have been a bit more challenging."

She laughed. At least he didn't underestimate his worth. "You're right, it definitely would have, and in the beginning, when you first agreed to work for me, I was just starting out, and I couldn't afford to pay you much, but now, things have gotten better. Business has really picked up since then, and a good part of that is thanks to you, not only because you're an amazing cook, but also because you've come up with some wonderful recipes and ideas. You're always looking for new ways to increase sales, and I can't tell you how much I appreciate that, and I'd like to give you a raise."

His eyebrows shot up. "You know you don't have to do that."

"I do, and thank you for that, but I want to. And I can afford to now." She kissed his cheek.

"Well, thank you very much, then. What an awesome Christmas gift."

"Sure thing." They continued to work in tandem with each other, neither of them getting in the other's way, like a well-choreographed dance routine. "But it's not your Christmas gift. That you'll get at midnight on Christmas Eve with everyone else."

"At midnight?" He handed her a plate with an omelet on it.

She added a toasted, buttered bagel and placed it in the cutout. "Yup. That's what Trevor said. Exactly midnight, we open Christmas gifts."

Cole laughed and shook his head. "That boy really is taking this whole organization thing to a new level."

"Tell me about it."

"Hey, Gia." Savannah's knock against the doorjamb interrupted. "You got a minute?"

"Yeah, is something wrong?" She stripped off her gloves and dropped them in the garbage pail.

"No, but Jeremy is out front, and he asked if he could talk to you for a minute—and by asked I mean insisted—said he has to tell you something."

Hmm... What in the world could he want with her? "Did he give you any clue why?"

"Nope, sorry." She waggled her eyebrows up and down. "And believe me, I asked."

"All right." She started toward the door. "I'll be right back, Cole."

He waved the spatula, distracted, already moving on to the next ticket in line. "No problem."

Gia scanned the dining room on her way through to the counter where Jeremy paced a trench in the floor, only pausing occasionally to glance out the front window. Everything seemed to be in order, customers chatted amiably—many with shopping bags boasting logos from a number of stores along Main Street piled beside them—while they waited to have their orders taken or be served. The half-full umbrella stand dripped water onto the floor, and for just a flicker of an instant, she wished it was snow being tracked in instead of rain water. She'd have to grab a mop after this and take care of the puddle.

The scent of gingerbread hovered in the air from a tray of freshly baked cookies they'd just sorted into the cake dishes on the counter. Holiday joy embraced the cozy space and filled Gia near to bursting. She smiled as she approached Jeremy.

"Ms. Morelli." He nodded toward her but didn't extend a hand, so Gia kept hers at her sides and waited to see what he wanted.

"Hello, Mr. Nolan." Rather than telling him to call her Gia, she kept it professional, figuring she'd let him set the tone for their conversation. She strode to keep her expression neutral, not to let the curiosity consuming her to show on her face. "What can I do for you?"

He stopped in front of the register, maybe a foot away from her, invading her personal space but not quite confrontational, and propped his hands on his hips. "I know you talked to Isaac."

Her eyes widening probably gave away her surprise but, otherwise, she remained silent, shooting for indifferent. So what if he knew? Then again, how did he know? Isaac, maybe?

He pointed a finger at her. "I went by the house and saw your car there, watched you come out."

The hairs on the back of her neck prickled. Hunt would read her the riot act for sure if he knew she'd been oblivious to his surveillance. Annoyance prodded her temper, but she squashed it. At least he'd kept his voice low. The last thing she needed in the middle of a nice holiday crowd was a scene.

Savannah continued to serve meals to a nearby table, her attention fully focused on what she was doing, no outward sign she was eavesdropping, which Gia knew full well she was. If Savannah hadn't reacted, it was likely no one realized what was going on.

"I'm sorry, Mr. Nolan, but I don't see how my paying a condolence call to the son of a woman I tried to save concerns you."

He pounded a fist against the counter.

Conversation around her drifted off, as more and more customers became aware of an issue at the front of the café.

"Everything about that evil, lecherous liar concerns me." His voice rose, took on a more desperate note.

The front door opened inward, giving Gia an excuse to take a few steps back and distance herself from what was fast becoming a confrontation.

Savannah caught Gia's eye and drew her brows together.

Gia gave her a quick, hopefully imperceptible, shake of the head. No, she did not need Savannah to run interference, but she appreciated the gesture.

Carlos Rinaldi, his hands full of bags, held the door open with his back for his wife to precede him.

Alyssa hurried through balancing a stack of trays and grinned at Gia. "Sorry to interrupt, but is it okay if we put some of this stuff away in the back so we'll have it ready to go on Friday."

Gia summoned a smile. "Of course. Come on in."

"Thanks." Alyssa shifted the trays to clear the door, sending a number of shopping bags hung over her wrist swinging.

"Here, let me get that for you, hon." Jeremy, a completely different man from the one who'd stood in Gia's face only moments ago trying to intimidate her, reached for the trays, brushing his hand along Alyssa's arm in the process.

"That's it." With no warning, Carlos dropped all of his packages on the floor. The sound of several things breaking shattered the sudden silence. He cocked his fist back and swung for all he was worth, nailing Jeremy's jaw full force.

"Hey," Gia reached for Carlos's arm.

Jeremy staggered back, stunned, his hand against his face, and caught himself against the counter beside the register.

Carlos shook Gia off and pounced on him before he could recover.

Customers scrambled to get out of the way.

Gia tried to step between them, to at least keep Carlos from killing the other man, and earned herself an elbow to the ribs from one of them. She doubled over, more stunned than hurt.

Cole grabbed her shoulders and moved her aside. He stepped in front of Carlos and held up his hands. "That's enough, man."

Carlos tried to surge past him.

Savannah reached Jeremy, grabbed his arm and tugged, trying to remove him from the situation. If they could get him out of the way, they might have some hope of calming Carlos.

Jeremy shoved her and sent her sprawling on the floor.

Rage ripped through Gia. How dare he? She grabbed the nearest umbrella from the stand, a big black one with a pointed metal top. She poked it into Jeremy's throat, hard enough to get his attention, not hard enough to do any permanent damage. She hoped.

He jerked upright, tearing his attention from Carlos and turning on Gia.

She pulled the umbrella back a bit and poked him again. "That is enough."

"Hey." He glared at her, keeping Carlos in sight from the corner of his eye. He flung a hand toward him. "What are you poking me for? He's the one who started it."

"Yeah, but he's not the one who knocked down my friend." A quick glance around showed Willow helping Savannah to her feet and Cole with a choke hold on Carlos. "Now shut up, stand there, and be happy this umbrella only found its way to your throat, because I assure you, it could have been worse."

His mouth opened and closed a few times before he finally settled on glaring silently.

"Good choice." Gia lowered the umbrella but kept a close watch on him. "Savannah, are you all right?"

"I'm fine. I'd have knocked him on his keester myself if you hadn't gone all Samurai with the umbrella."

Gia laughed, along with a few nervous customers who kept a wary eye on the two fighters.

"I'm outta here." Jeremy started for the door.

Cole relinquished his hold on Carlos to Alyssa and went after him.

Gia held out a hand to stop him. "Don't worry about it, Cole. Better to let him go and diffuse the situation. Hunt can track him down later. Thank you, though."

On his way past her, Jeremy kept a watchful eye on Cole and leaned close to Gia. "I came in here to give you a warning, but now you can just fend for yourself."

Gia watched after him as he strode through the doorway, leaving her with a giant mess to clean up and a million questions pinging rapid-fire through her head.

Chapter Twenty-One

Gia chastised herself, not for the first time, but she ignored her own warnings as she hurried up the walkway to Jeremy's front door.

"You're sure about this, right?" Savannah kept pace at her side, half jogging to keep up with Gia's longer stride. "Even after he came into the shop yesterday and acted like a horse's backside?"

"He said he came in to warn me about something but that now I could fend for myself." He'd also never gone to the police to file an assault report against Carlos, and since Gia hadn't pressed charges against either man, there wasn't anything Hunt or Leo could do, especially considering Jeremy had fled the cafe before Hunt and Leo had shown up. But she didn't have much of a choice. Being that Carlos had thrown the first punch, he'd have been arrested, and that would have messed up Savannah's wedding. Though Hunt understood her reluctance, he hadn't completely agreed with her. He'd wanted to at least have a talk with the other man, but she'd convinced him to let it drop. "I didn't press charges, but I do want to know what he was talking about when he said he'd come to give me a warning."

Savannah nodded and looked around the run-down neighborhood. "And what if he won't tell you?"

"Then I'll go back to work." She reached the front stoop and only hesitated for a moment before ringing the bell. His small ranch sat on a postage stamp size property between two others that looked just like it. Paint and pieces of stucco had peeled and cracked in numerous places, and rust stains ran down the wall beneath one window.

Savannah cupped her hands around her eyes and tried to peer through the grime on the window without actually coming in contact with it. "Now what?"

What could they do? It wasn't like she could track him down if he wasn't home. She had no clue where else to look. She shrugged and started back down the walkway toward the car, then paused and detoured to the driveway. "Here, let me boost you up so you can peek in the garage windows and see if there's a car in there."

Savannah looked around. "Seriously? Are you trying to get me arrested on the day before my wedding?"

"Oh, please, like Leo's really going to arrest you." Probably.

She cocked a brow. "It's not Leo I'm worried about."

Oh, right. So Hunt could be a problem, but even he wouldn't arrest her on the day before her wedding. Most likely.

Gia looked up and down the street and scanned the neighboring houses. When she didn't see anyone, she knelt on one knee and cupped her hands together.

Savannah shook her head but propped a hand on Gia's shoulder and one on the garage door, then placed her foot in Gia's cradled hands and boosted herself up to see into the row of windows along the top of the garage door.

"Well?"

She dropped down and brushed her hands off. "Yup, there's a car in there."

"Okay, so now what?"

Savannah went back to the front door and rang the bell, then knocked a couple of times. Still nothing.

A cracked concrete walkway led around the side of the garage. Gia peered around the side. A chain link gate hung from rusted hinges, propped open with a crumbling cinder block. She returned to the front stoop, where Savannah stood with her hands on her hips staring at the door as if willing it to open.

Gia tried the knob. It turned easily. She looked at Savannah for her opinion.

She simply shrugged and blew her hair off her forehead.

With a deep breath and warning bells clanging in her head, Gia eased the door open and poked her head inside. "Hello? Jeremy?"

Dust motes drifted lazily in those shafts of morning sunlight that were strong enough to penetrate the build up of grunge on the curtainless front window. A couch that sagged in the middle sat facing a brick fireplace covered in black soot. A big screen TV took up the space above the fireplace from the mantle almost to the ceiling.

"Is anyone home?" Savannah waited with her lower lip caught between her teeth.

"I don't think so, but the door's open, so we could just take a quick peek and see if he's here."

"We could, except that's considered breaking and entering."

"Technically, it's just entering if the door's open."

"Ya think?"

She shrugged. She actually had no idea, but it sounded good, and she really wanted a quick peek at the pile of paperwork sitting on a milk carton in the far corner of the room. "Probably."

"Sounds good." Savannah shoved the door open and walked in. "Hey? Anyone home?"

Silence screamed back at her.

Gia made a beeline for the paperwork. If she was only going to have a few minutes, that was one thing she was determined to look at. She shuffled through a stack of bills—mostly a month or two behind, a smattering of Christmas cards—mostly from women, and a couple of receipts—one with a note jotted on the back that read tomorrow am. The receipt was dated the week before but she had no way of knowing if he'd written the note then or more recently. Either way, it was something he was supposed to do within the past week. She picked up a piece of printer paper and turned it over. The page was covered with Robyn's first and last name—written over and over again in cursive. She had no idea what to make of that.

Disappointed, Gia moved onto the kitchen.

Savannah's footsteps moved down the hallway toward the bedrooms.

Several manilla envelopes stood in a napkin holder in the center of the table. Gia lifted one up and turned it over in her hands. Not sealed. She slitted the top open enough to see inside. Last Will and Testament stared back at her. Okay, there's no way she should look at that. She should absolutely put it back just as she'd found it and move on. Or even better, get out of there.

"Do you notice something, Gia?" Savannah stood in the doorway, her tour of the house apparently complete.

Gia gripped the envelope tighter. "What do you mean?"

"Look around." She gestured all around her.

Gia did as she instructed, figuring Savannah wanted her to notice something on her own, probably to see if she'd come to the same conclusion Savannah had about something. The white sink held no dirty dishes, but rust stains marred the surface beneath the faucet and around the drain. The counters were bare but for a coffee pot and a toaster. The faux terra cotta linoleum floor was peeling up in the corner beside a sliding door that led to a weed choked yard.

"It's not upkept very well, dusty but not particularly dirty. More aged."

Savannah shook her head. "I know I'm a woman, so it's probably different, but just think about all of the wedding preparation stuff that's spread all over Trevor's mansion right now."

Savannah wasn't kidding, you couldn't even move around without tripping over something wedding related, from Savannah's gown hanging in a spare room to keep it safe from Klondike and Pepper, to lists of last minute things to do, travel brochures for their honeymoon, and a make-up case Gia had to move every time she went to sit at the table.

"Now look around here, even in the bedrooms, there's nothing. No mention or sign or anything that someone was supposed to be getting married any time soon."

"Hmm…that is weird." Even Hunt and Leo's suite at Trevor's had signs of the impending nuptials. She'd had to duck both tuxes on her way in to say goodnight just the other day.

"What's that?" Savannah gestured at the envelope still clutched in Gia's hand.

"Something I should put back where I found it and get out of here."

Savannah took it from her. "In other words, something you really want a peek at."

"Exactly, but let me do it." She took the envelope back. "If either of us gets in trouble for this, better it's me."

Savannah shrugged but let Gia keep the envelope. With a quick prayer they wouldn't get caught, she slid the will out and skimmed over the pages. "Uh oh."

"What?" Savannah looked over Gia's shoulder.

"This looks like Robyn's will. It's dated a couple of weeks ago. Hunt said Robyn left everything to Isaac, but according to this, she left everything to Jeremy." Gia pointed to the only line that mattered.

"Do you think it'll stand up in court?" Savannah asked.

"I don't know. I'm not sure what's required." She flipped to the back page. Robyn's signature was scrawled along a line at the bottom of the page, a signature that looked almost exactly like the one she'd found written over and over again on the printer paper on Jeremy's desk. Had he been practicing forging it? She ran and grabbed the paper, then compared the two. "Look at this. Do you think Jeremy forged the signature?"

Savannah lifted her hands to the side then let them drop. "I have no idea, but I don't see any other signatures on the document, witnesses or anything, nor is it notarized, so I don't know if it's legal."

"I'd think if it was, he'd have come forward with it by now."

"Question is, did he make it up after Robyn was killed and backdate it, or did he write it up a couple of weeks ago in anticipation of her demise?"

Though it was also possible Robyn had done it herself before her death, it didn't seem likely. Gia stuffed the pages back into the envelope. "Let's get out of here."

"How are we going to tell Hunt and Leo about this?"

"Are you crazy? We can't tell them."

"We have to, Gia. We have no choice."

Ugh…why did she have to be right? She stuck the envelope back with the others, exactly as she'd found it. Her hand hovered above the napkin holder for another moment before she snatched another envelope and riffled through the contents. "This just gets stranger and stranger?"

"What's that?" Savannah stared out the back window, sulking.

"Another will, this time Jeremy's."

That caught her interest, and she started to turn toward Gia, then stopped when something outside caught her attention.

"What?" Gia shoved the will back into the envelope without checking the signatures, though she did skim enough to know he'd left everything to Ethan, and dropped it into the napkin holder. "Is someone out there?"

Savannah unlocked the sliding door and pushed it open, cringing when it screeched in protest. She stepped outside.

Gia followed.

Weeds covered most of the yard, but Savannah's attention was on a potted plant in the corner of the weathered deck. "Do you know what I think that is?"

"What?" It looked like it could be a holiday plant of some sort, green leaves, red berries. The only thing out of place about it was that it was the only thing in the yard that appeared to be cared for. The dark soil in the pot looked freshly turned, as if it had just recently been planted. Gia reached toward it.

"No, don't." Savannah slapped her hand away. "I'm no expert, but that looks an awful lot like the pictures of belladonna I saw in the article I read to you."

Gia jerked back, as far from the plant as she could get, and leaned against the deck railing. She glanced down into the knee-high weeds and caught sight of something nestled among them. She looked closer. Jeremy Nolan lay amid the weeds, his eyes open and staring straight up. He didn't blink. "Uh, Savannah?"

"Yeah?" she answered, distracted by the pictures of plants she was scrolling through on her phone. "Put that away and call Hunt. Now."

"What?" She whirled toward Gia.

Gia started down the two steps from the deck to the yard. Though she was pretty sure, she had to make sure he had no pulse and there was no way to save him. "Get out of here, now, and call Hunt."

She started to bend over Jeremy.

A figure darted from the side of the deck and barreled into her, knocking her to the ground.

Shock held her immobile. Fear of whatever critters might be stalking her amid the high grass propelled her into motion. She scrambled to her feet and went after the fleeing figure. "You may as well stop running, Ethan. I already saw you."

All right, that was stupid. The man had just bowled her over fleeing the scene of a murder. And yet…something about his expression seemed off. Instead of the guilt Gia would expect to see, stark terror was etched into his features.

He stopped and held up his hands. "Please, it's not what you think. I didn't mean to knock you over; I just wanted to get out of here before you saw me."

Savannah was already on the phone, presumably with the police, standing right next to the sliding door where she could flee at a moment's notice.

"What are you doing here?" Gia demanded, as if she had every right to be there.

His hands shook wildly, and sweat soaked his light blue t-shirt. His gaze darted around the yard like a cornered animal.

Speaking of animals…Gia scanned the ground as she hopped up onto the bottom step. Facing a potential killer was one thing, venomous snakes something else entirely.

"I just stopped by to talk to Jeremy. I heard about the ruckus in your shop, and I wanted to see if he was all right."

"Just being a good friend?"

"Yeah, like that, exactly." He nodded frantically, like a bobble head. "So, you understand?"

"I understand I found you standing over your so-called friend's body."

He squeezed his eyes closed tight. "I didn't kill him. Or anyone."

Though she couldn't explain why, maybe it was just seeing how terrified he was, she believed him. She had a feeling he was just checking in on his friend, as he'd said, and happened across his body. Of course, it could be he was terrified of going to prison. "If that's the case, why run? Why not call the police and report the crime?"

"I would have, but then I heard you and your friend out front yelling for him, and I got scared. I didn't want to get caught here and have the police think it was me who killed him."

For the first time, what he was saying didn't ring true. He might or might not have killed Jeremy, but he'd had no intention of calling the police.

Sirens wailed in the distance.

"Well, they're on their way now, so you'll get your chance to tell your side of the story. Besides, the police will be able to determine the time of death, so they'll know if he died recently or hours ago or last night."

Ethan grabbed a rusted shovel from where it was propped against the deck railing—whether it was put there recently or had been rusting there for decades, Gia couldn't tell. He flung the shovel at her.

She ducked aside and covered her head, as it hit the stair railing and bounced off.

Ethan turned and fled.

Chapter Twenty-Two

Somehow, after explaining how they came to be at Jeremy's house and stumbled across his body and had a run in with Ethan, to Hunt and Leo, who were not amused to say the least, Gia and Savannah made it back to Trevor's mansion just in time to start the wedding rehearsal and dinner.

Though Gia didn't expect them to make it, Hunt and Leo ran in only a few minutes late, and all seemed to be forgiven. Unfortunately, Ethan had been long gone, and they hadn't been able to track him down.

They ran smoothly through the wedding, in an empty space Trevor had set aside for the purpose since he refused to allow anyone to see where the actual wedding would take place until the day of.

Alyssa placed a tray on a stand beside the long table where the entire wedding party sat. She started clearing empty plates that once contained the best chicken cordon bleu Gia had ever eaten.

"Everything was amazing, Alyssa, thank you." Gia stood to help clear the dishes.

Alyssa took two plates from her hands and set them on the tray. "Oh, no. This is your night off. You sit and enjoy Savannah's last night as a single woman. I've got this."

"Thank you, Alyssa, for everything." Gia returned to her seat between Hunt and Savannah.

She grinned and cleared a small stack of plates. "Let's see if you're still as grateful after dessert."

"Dessert?" If Gia tried to stuff in another bite, she was going to have to open the top button on her jeans. She most definitely should have gone for something with an elastic waistband.

Alyssa hefted the tray of dishes and hurried to the kitchen, only to return a moment later with a cart filled with a smorgasbord of desserts. There were several kinds of tarts, pastries, smores, and crème brulee, just to start. "If I keep eating, I'm not going fit into my dress tomorrow."

Alyssa laughed. "Sorry, but I'll take that as a compliment."

"As you should." As tempted as Gia was to indulge, she resisted.

Until Savannah popped half an éclair onto Gia's plate. "Eat up, sister. If I'm eating, you're eating."

Well, when she put it like that. Gia cut a small piece and tested it. "Oh, no. I'm going to have to finish my half."

"Hurry up about it, because there's a napoleon with our name on it next." Savannah pointed to a delicious looking cake with her fork.

"Oh, fine. You only get married once, but Monday I'm starting a strict diet."

Savannah laughed. "Good luck with that."

Hunt's cell phone rang, and he checked the caller ID, then excused himself to answer. Throughout dinner, talk had stayed focused on the wedding and the upcoming holiday, but with dinner and most of dessert finished, while they lingered over coffee and awaited Hunt's return with what could only be bad news for him to have interrupted Savannah's rehearsal dinner to take a call, the subject inevitably returned to murder.

"So," Trevor asked. "Did you guys find Ethan?"

Gia and Savannah had filled him in on the details of their day while they'd been getting ready for the rehearsal.

Leo wiped his mouth and sat back, then pushed his plate away. "Nah, not yet. We have an APB out on him, though. He'll turn up sooner or later."

"Are you done, Gia?" Alyssa asked.

"Yes." She tossed her napkin onto the plate. "And everything was amazing, thank you."

"Of course. I'm happy you enjoyed it." She picked up Gia's dessert plate and set it on a large, full tray she held against her hip, then hefted the tray and started toward the kitchen.

Gia finally gave in and discreetly undid her top button. "Do you think it was Ethan that killed Jeremy?"

The tray Alyssa was carrying crashed to the floor.

Gia jumped up, but Trevor and Cole were closer and beat her to helping clean up. Gia took Alyssa's arm and led her away from the broken glass. "Are you okay, Alyssa?"

"Oh, my, I'm so sorry."

Savannah came up on her other side. "Don't worry about it. You didn't get hurt, did you?"

"No, no, I'm fine, I..." She sucked in a shaky breath that ended on a half sob. "Are you talking about Jeremy Nolan? He's..."

"Oh, Alyssa." Gia took her ice-cold hand in hers. "I'm sorry."

She hadn't even thought about how Alyssa might react to news of Jeremy's death, or the fact that she might not have heard. Surely, the rumor mill was already up and churning.

"No, no. It's... I just hadn't heard, and it took me off guard, ya know?" She shook her head, lowering her gaze to the mess on the floor everyone was working together to clean up. Her hands shook as she smoothed her ponytail.

Carlos rushed into the room from the kitchen. "What happened? I heard a crash."

Alyssa straightened and avoided making eye contact with anyone. "It...it was me, I'm sorry. I dropped the tray of dishes. I don't know what happened; it just slipped out of my hands."

"No big deal." Savannah shot him a big smile. "It happens to me all the time."

He nodded to Savannah, studied his wife for a moment, then turned and left without even asking if she was okay.

"I'm sorry, Alyssa, I didn't realize you hadn't heard."

She nodded and sniffed, then took the tray with everything on it from Trevor and bolted for the kitchen.

Savannah watched her go. "Hmm. A bit of a strong reaction, don't you think?"

"I don't know. It could really just have caught her off guard like she said. First Robyn, then Jeremy. Even if nothing was going on between them, it could be kind of shocking, especially since she was working with them to cater their upcoming wedding."

"True." Savannah still stared at the kitchen door, frowning. "I guess."

Hunt poked his head in the door and spoke quietly. "Leo, I've gotta go. They just picked up Ethan, and they're on their way to the station. And it turns out Jeremy also died of belladonna poisoning. They found traces in an empty tea cup and a canister of loose-leaf tea on the counter."

Leo looked back and forth between Savannah and Hunt, clearly torn between wanting to stay with her and needing to go with Hunt.

"Go, silly." Savannah kissed him hard. "I'm going to spend my last night as a single woman with Gia."

"Are you sure?" he asked.

"Positive. Go. And keep Hunt out of trouble."

"Same goes." He gave a sidelong glance toward Gia and winked.

"Ha ha." Gia poked him in the side, then kissed Hunt goodbye and turned to Savannah. "So, are you?"

"Am I what?"

"Going to keep me out of trouble."

She lifted a brow and a slow grin spread across her face. "I don't know. What did you have in mind?"

"Well, it is the night before your wedding, so I will totally understand if you just want to hang out here and chill, maybe make popcorn with chocolate chips and watch a Christmas movie." Truth be told, that was probably a better option than what Gia had in mind.

"And what's behind door number two?"

"Well." Gia pitched her voice low enough not to be heard by the others still mingling in the room. "I've been thinking about the plant we found at Jeremy's, the one you thought might be belladonna."

Savannah nodded. "Leo confirmed it was when I spoke to him earlier."

"Don't you find it a little odd he'd have left it right there on his deck after killing his fiancé? Besides, that plant looked newly planted, as if—"

"As if someone had taken part of a larger plant and transplanted it."

"Exactly." That, combined with the wills and the page of signatures they'd found added up to one very sloppy killer. Or, someone was trying to set him up. And somehow, that one made more sense. "It's perfect really, too perfect. Robyn dies of belladonna poisoning, and a belladonna plant miraculously shows up in Jeremy's yard. In addition to that, a will naming Jeremy as the beneficiary happens to be sitting on the table beside a page of Robyn's signature forged over and over again, all conveniently found in a dead man's home pointing to him as the killer."

"So, what, are the police supposed to now believe he had a sudden attack of guilt and poisoned himself?"

Gia shook her head. Who knew what the killer expected?

"So, what do you want to do?" Savannah asked.

"Oh, I don't know. I was thinking of taking a late-night stroll to work off some of the fabulous food Alyssa served tonight. Like, you know, maybe past a few people of interest's houses, maybe just to take a quick peek in their yards, see if they have any plants back there that they shouldn't." What could that hurt? It's not like anyone should be up and about at that time of night.

"Sure, why not?" Savannah shrugged. "At least, it'll keep me from fretting about tomorrow. Where do we start?"

Probably not the way most brides worked through pre-wedding jitters, but hey, whatever worked.

They spent a few minutes chatting with the few remaining members of the wedding party, then begged off and said goodbye, assuring everyone they'd see them tomorrow evening at the wedding. After walking Thor and settling him in their suite, Gia and Savannah headed to her car. They'd debated taking him with them, but in the end decided not to. Gia didn't want to leave him alone in the car if they decided to get out and walk, but she couldn't really take him on the off chance he spotted a squirrel or some other nocturnal creature and decided to bark and draw attention to them. Attention was the last thing they needed.

Savannah accelerated down the dark, mostly deserted road. "Where do you want to start?"

Gia didn't dare say Carlos and Alyssa's house, though now would be the perfect time, since they were still at Trevor's and probably would be for a while cleaning up.

Savannah glanced over at her before turning her attention back to the road. "Go ahead, you can say it. Alyssa did act overly upset when she heard about Jeremy's death. And both she and Carlos did have the opportunity to poison the cake."

"Alyssa says she was in the back room, taking a much needed break from the bickering right before Robyn collapsed." But since everyone seemed to have been conveniently elsewhere in the few moments before Robyn's death, it didn't really matter what she claimed. Someone was lying. They had to be, because she didn't poison herself. "But, I can't figure out a reason for her to have wanted to kill Robyn, regardless of whether or not she and Jeremy were having an affair."

"No, me neither, and that's not just because I don't want my caterer arrested on the eve of my wedding. I really don't see why she'd have killed her. Even if her and Jeremy were together, Alyssa's still married."

"True, unless maybe Carlos is next on the list." But it didn't feel right, and if that was the case, why then turn around and kill Jeremy? "There's always a chance she had a motive no one has uncovered yet."

"I guess, but it's not really jibing for me." Savannah shrugged. "Now, Carlos, on the other hand, is a beast. He went after Jeremy in the café the other day for no real reason."

Gia cringed, knowing she and Savannah were going to disagree on this. "Jeremy did rub his hand against Alyssa's, and at the tasting when we were trying to revive Robyn, he had his hand a little too comfortably on her back. Don't get me wrong, I'm not condoning what Carlos did, but Jeremy was acting a bit suggestively, almost daring Carlos to strike out."

"So you're saying he got what he deserved?"

"No, not at all. I'm just saying maybe he provoked him on purpose for some reason, or maybe he was just being disrespectful and causing trouble. Either way…"

"Either way, Jeremy pushed Carlos's buttons before he got hit," Savannah finished.

"Yeah." So, Carlos might be on the suspect list for Jeremy's murder, but Gia just couldn't come up with any reason he'd have killed Robyn. "I guess maybe Alyssa could have killed Robyn to get her out of the way, then Carlos could have found out and killed Jeremy to keep Alyssa from running off with him."

"Hmm? I don't know." Savannah shook her head. "That seems pretty far-fetched."

Gia had to agree. "Besides, poison doesn't seem like the weapon of choice for someone as prone to violence as Carlos is. It seems he'd be more likely to do something more impulsive, like blow up and kill someone in a fit of rage."

"True." It didn't take long to eliminate the presence of belladonna at Carlos and Alyssa's. Though their landscaping was beautiful, in an out west desert kind of way, with lots of rocks and boulders and cacti, there were no lush plants and definitely nothing that looked like the pictures of belladonna Savannah had pulled up on her phone. They hurried back to the car before anyone could spot them and demand they explain their presence.

Gia shut the door quietly. "Now what?"

"What about dear old Mallory?"

"What reason would Mallory have had to kill Robyn?" If what Tom had told them was true, Mallory owed Robyn a debt. Even if it had been Max's idea to pay off the credit cards she'd basically stolen and not hold her responsible, Robyn still had to have agreed since some of the cards were in her name.

"Jealousy, maybe? Because Robyn got her brother's inheritance. While Mallory might have been left in charge of Isaac's money, which hasn't been proven by any other way but his say so, she didn't seem to have any of her own. Plus, there's still the question of her involvement with Jeremy on some other level, since they were supposedly dating before he and Robyn got together and before Max died. Maybe the two of them were in cahoots, working together to get rid of Max and Robyn and get everything?"

"Could be, I suppose. Where was she supposedly when the murder happened?" Gia tried to remember where each suspect claimed to have been in the moments when the poison had most likely been planted. "The bathroom, I think, right?"

Savannah looked up Mallory's address. She set her phone back in the cup holder without bothering to punch the address into the GPS and pulled out. "The bathroom, which was right past where Carlos and Alyssa supposedly left the cake sitting."

"So she could have had opportunity."

"Could have." Savannah nodded. "And motive, but did she have the means?"

"That's what we're about to find out. Maybe." They rode in silence, each lost in their own thoughts, out past Gia's development. Despite talk of murder, and their current mission, Gia enjoyed the peace of their surroundings. The thick forest could make you imagine you were the only beings around for miles and miles.

When Savannah turned, Gia double checked the address. "She lives on the corner a little ways up. At least that should make it easier to see into the yard."

"Let's just hope this time we find something." Savannah parked got out of the car, but she didn't lock it. No sense making a sound that would draw attention, and they weren't going far. Besides, the neighborhood appeared to be deserted. And unlike the Rinaldi's development, the houses here were set on anywhere between one and five acres of property, with no street lights, so their presence should go unnoticed.

Gia strolled beside Savannah, two friends out enjoying a late night walk if anyone happened to look out their windows. Though it didn't seem likely, since the few houses they could see already had their curtains and blinds closed. Light spilled out from a few upstairs windows, and flickering lights announced several occupants were watching TV.

Mallory's cottage stood on a corner, a split rail fence surrounding the back yard. Easy enough to climb over. "Why don't you wait here and make sure no one comes, while I go check the back yard?"

Savannah rolled her eyes. "Like that won't look suspicious. Do you need help over the fence?"

"Ha ha. I think I can handle this one." She swung herself up and over, then brushed her hands off and looked around. A porch light had been turned on, but from what Gia could make out of the interior, it seemed pitch black. The driveway was empty. "Do you think she's out?"

"I don't know, but let's take a quick peek in the yard and get out of here before we get caught. I don't want to spend my last night as a free woman in a cage."

Gia laughed out loud, then slapped a hand over her mouth.

Savannah nudged her with an elbow to her still sore rib. "I'm glad you think it's funny."

"Oh, stop. You're not going to jail."

"You don't think?"

Gia paused and studied Savannah in the moonlight. "Look at it this way, we're actually doing Hunt and Leo a favor."

Savannah's eyebrows shot up, and she stopped short to stare at Gia. "Okay, I give up. How in the world do you figure that?"

"Well, they wouldn't be able to search these yards without a search warrant, and we can."

It was Savannah's turn to laugh, though she didn't have to cover her mouth since she had the sense to do so quietly. She resumed her trek into the yard. As they passed a low row of azaleas, Savannah grabbed Gia's arm and yanked her down.

Gia dropped instantly, crouching next to the nearest bush, hoping it would provide cover from whatever Savannah had seen.

Savannah put a finger to her lips, then pointed toward the garden at the back of the house.

A figure clad all in black, including a hooded sweatshirt, the hood pulled low over his eyes, stood in the small puddle of light given off by Mallory's back spotlight. His hand rested on the handle of a shovel partly dug into the ground, his head tilted as if listening for something. He must have heard them coming.

Gia froze, barely breathing, despite her lungs begging for air.

After a moment, the figure wiped his forehead with his sleeve and resumed digging.

Savannah put her lips right against Gia's ear and whispered, "Can you tell who it is?"

Gia tried to keep her voice barely a whisper as she struggled for breath. "No, can you?"

"Uh uh. What do you want to do?" Savannah looked back the way they'd come.

"Can you get any deeper into the bushes without making any noise?" Because they either needed to hide or run, and if they ran, she'd never know what the figure in black was up to. She only hoped she wasn't gong to stumble across another body when he left.

Chapter Twenty-Three

Gia followed Savannah farther into the bushes, wedging herself between the fence and an azalea. At least, with the open split rail design at their back, they could make a quick escape if need be. Thankfully, Mallory had recently laid mulch beneath the bushes, and it didn't crunch beneath their feet. A carpet of dead leaves would have given them away for sure.

Gia slid her phone from her back pocket. She couldn't snap a picture, afraid the flash would go off, but maybe she could video whoever it was. Keeping the camera cupped in her hands, she hit the camera icon and checked to be sure there was no blinking light to alert the intruder to their presence. Satisfied she wouldn't blow their cover, she held up the phone and tried to film the stranger through the bushes.

Savannah shifted a branch aside to give her an unobstructed view.

The figure was careful to stay out of the small circle of light cast by the spotlight beside the rear sliding door.

Gia filmed him digging. At least, she was pretty sure it was a man.

Guilt niggled at her. What if someone was injured or could be saved while she and Savannah crouched in the bushes watching their assailant? Maybe they should just call Hunt and Leo and keep an eye on the house from the car. She couldn't do that. With the low fence, the stranger could escape from any side and they'd lose him. Since she couldn't positively ID him, she had to wait until she could at least get a glimpse of his face on camera.

Besides, what if he was just innocently gardening. At this time of night. In the shadows. Dressed like a cat burglar.

Okay, probably not.

The man stopped digging and jammed the shovel into the ground to the side of the hole.

Gia let out the breath she'd been holding as quietly as possible, relief flooding through her. If he was done digging, the hole wasn't big enough to conceal a body. But what on earth was he doing then?

After a quick look around, the man disappeared into the shadows between the bushes on the far side of the yard.

Gia started to stand, to try to see where he was going, but Savannah grabbed her arm.

A second later, he emerged from the bushes dragging something with him.

"What the…" Savannah let out on the softest breath. "Is that what I think it is?"

Gia tried to zoom in, get a good video of whatever he was pulling that Savannah seemed to recognize and still trying for a shot of his face under the hood.

He pulled a bush until its roots dropped into the hole, then hurriedly shoveled dirt back in around it. The crunch of the shovel hitting the dirt and the intruder's harsh breathing filled the night. Could it be Ethan? Had he killed Jeremy and planned to frame Mallory for his murder? For Robyn's murder?

The man patted down the dirt, then gathered handfuls of dead leaves from beneath a large oak at the back of the yard and scattered them underneath, apparently trying to make it appear as if the plant had been there all along. He propped his hands on his hips and looked around, then grabbed the shovel. Apparently satisfied his midnight gardening had gone unnoticed, he shoved his hood off and hefted the shovel over his shoulder.

Isaac.

Gia jerked back and stepped on a branch. It cracked beneath her weight, the sound like a shotgun blast in the silence.

Isaac stopped and stood perfectly still. He scowled toward the row of bushes, bending to look underneath. "Who's there?"

She stopped the camera and felt behind her for the fence. They had to get out of there. If they crawled underneath, they could bolt for the car. Isaac would still have to go through the bush and over the fence. They might be able to make it, especially Savannah, who was much faster than Gia.

Something moved against her hand.

Gia squealed and shot to her feet, desperate to get away from whatever it was.

Isaac shifted the shovel to a two-handed grip. "Who's there? I won't ask again."

Savannah started to stand, but Gia put a firm hand on her head and kept her in place. There was no reason both of them needed to get caught.

Gia inched sideways toward a gap where she could wiggle through, desperately trying not to think about whatever critter had brushed against her hand still scurrying around her feet somewhere. She held her hands up where Isaac could see them. Could she run? If he chased her, Savannah could get away and call for help. But if he hit her with that shovel, she might not get back up. "Isaac? Is that you?"

"How do you know my name?" He strode toward her, his head on a swivel as he tried to look everywhere at once, the shovel now raised over his shoulder like a batter warming up for a swing. "Who are you? And what are you doing there in the bushes?"

She tried for a smile then gave up. He probably couldn't see it, anyway, since she was standing in shadows. "Isaac, it's me. Gia Morelli."

"Gia Mor...why were you following me?"

For the first time, a trickle of fear seeped in. It was late at night, in a dark secluded yard, and she was either standing face to face with a killer or with someone who had a lot of explaining to do. The fact that Savannah was still hidden was the only thing that helped her maintain any kind of composure. "I wasn't following you, I..."

"Then what are you doing here?" he hissed between clenched teeth.

Think, think, think. Even with Savannah working with Mallory to buy a house, it didn't give her reason to skulk around the woman's house in the middle of the night.

"Answer me!"

"Friends of mine are buying a house, and Mallory is the real estate agent handling the sale, and she called today to say that their offer was accepted." True enough, at least that part. Savannah had been beyond thrilled, as had Gia since they would now be neighbors. If, of course, Gia lived through the night. She didn't dare give Isaac enough information to figure out who Savannah was. Thankfully, she hadn't been with Gia when she'd gone to visit him. Hopefully, he'd had too much to drink before their run-in at the real estate office to remember her. "Unfortunately, they were leaving to go out of town for the holidays, and I have a wedding to attend tomorrow, so I said I'd drop off the paperwork Mallory needed tonight so she could get started. I'm supposed to put it in her mailbox. It's kind of a rush sale. So, no one wanted to wait until they got back. Cause they'll be gone for a while."

Okay, Gia, shut up now. She bit down on her tongue, hard, to stop the flow of words.

"So what were you doing hiding in the bushes?"

"I saw someone creeping around back here and got scared, and I wanted to make sure no one was robbing Mallory's house." Okay, at least that sounded legitimate, unlike the rest of the nonsense she'd spewed so far.

He swiped a hand over his mouth and lowered the shovel. "All right, listen. I don't want to have to hurt you."

"That's really good, because I don't want that either. So we are definitely on the same page there."

Bouncing the shovel up and down in the dirt, he looked around. "Did you give your boyfriend my father's medicine like I asked you to?"

"I did, as soon as I left your house I stopped by the station and dropped it off."

"Did he tell you what they found?" Isaac couldn't stand still, bouncing from one foot to the other, fidgeting with anything he could get his hands on; his sweatshirt string, the shovel handle, his hood.

"No, but he probably wouldn't. He's not in the habit of discussing his cases with me." Okay, that one was a big fat whopper. Hopefully, she wouldn't die before she could ask forgiveness.

He shook a finger and started to pace back and forth in the narrow space between the side of the house and the bushes, the shovel swinging from his hand. "Okay, all right, I think maybe we can make this work."

"Pardon?" She held her breath as he strode toward the bushes, praying fervently he wouldn't see Savannah crouched there.

He turned, and she let out a sigh of relief.

He pointed a finger back and forth between the two of them. "You and me, we can make a deal."

"We can?"

"Sure. Everyone has a price, right?"

She hesitated.

He took a step toward her, his grip on the shovel tightening.

"Sure, uh, yeah, I'm sure everyone wants something." Like right now, she wanted to live through this encounter.

"That's good. Right. What is it you want?"

"Pardon?"

"I need to make sure no one knows I was here, and you must need something. As soon as I get my inheritance, I can pay you whatever you want to keep your mouth shut. Anything. Just name your price."

Could this kid possibly be this stupid? She was dating Boggy Creek's chief of police, for crying out loud. "You know what? I'm sure we can work something out. After all, you're related to Mallory. It's not like you were doing anything wrong."

"Right." His head bobbed frantically up and down. "Yeah, I was just doing some work around the house for my dear Aunt Mallory, to make up for the scene I caused at the real estate office. It's a surprise, you know."

"That's very nice of you." His excuse actually sounded more plausible than hers. Gia took a step backward. When he didn't protest, she took another. "I'm sure she'll appreciate it."

"Oh, I won't tell her it was me." His eyes widened, and he grinned eagerly. "That's why I want you to keep it a secret. Like a Secret Santa thing, like that, only instead of a gift, I did some yardwork for her."

"That sounds like a great idea." She took two more steps back, and the fence pressed into her back. Huh, that wasn't a lie. If he were telling the truth at all, that would be a really nice thing to do for someone. "I may do that next year for a few of my friends."

He stopped nodding and stood perfectly still.

She inched sideways down the fence toward the front of the house. No way was she turning her back on him to go over the fence and run, at least not until she'd put some distance between them.

"You're not buying it, are you?"

"Wha—"

"You don't believe me!" he screamed.

"Then why don't you tell me what actually happened?" What difference did it make at that point? He clearly didn't trust her, and probably planned on killing her before he left, so why not try to find out what was going on. Especially when it would also serve to buy her time to escape. "Why did you kill your mother?"

He gaped at her, mouth hanging open.

She held her breath waiting to see if he'd answer or just kill her and be done with it.

"Because she was squandering everything my father worked so hard for. She was going to change her will, leave everything to that loser. I couldn't let that happen." He grinned, baring his teeth in what looked more like a grimace. "Now it's all mine. And dear old Aunty is no longer in control."

Shocked he'd admitted that much, Gia racked her brain for what else to ask. "Did you put the belladonna plant at Jeremy's too?"

"Yeah, the fool invited me to the house, gave me the perfect opportunity to get rid of him, so he could show me the copy of the will my mother wrote just before she died. Fortunately for me, he chose to reach out to me rather than go through the proper legal channels, the poor crooked dupe. Look where that got him."

Hmm, so Jeremy really had forged the will to try to get Robyn's inheritance from Isaac after the fact. "So why plant the belladonna? Were you going to frame him for your mother's murder?"

"I shouldn't have had to frame him!" Spit sprayed from his mouth, illuminated by the light from the full moon. "Your dumb boyfriend should have arrested him. He was the most likely suspect, had a history of killing off his wives. So this time I beat him to it. So what?"

Gia held her hands up in front of her for protection. "Isaac, calm dow—"

He took three long strides to reach her, the shovel hefted high over his shoulder.

Gia dove over the split rail fence and rolled, slamming her knee against the concrete.

"Freeze!"

Gia stopped where she was. She couldn't have gotten up in that moment if she'd tried thanks to the pain radiating from her knee all the way to her hip and toes.

A figure emerged from behind the bushes lining the front of the house, gun pointed straight at Isaac. "Hands in the air."

"Hey?" Hunt knelt beside Gia and lowered her arms. "He didn't mean you, honey. You okay?"

"Keep them where I can see them, Isaac." Leo crept toward him.

A second officer approached Isaac from the other side.

"Hey." Hunt wrapped an arm around her shoulders. "Gia, babe, you okay? Are you hurt?"

Heat crept through her and she plopped, not very daintily onto her butt on the sidewalk. "Yeah, I'm okay, but dancing tomorrow might be off the table."

He laughed, shakier than she'd have expected, and pulled her close, then dropped a kiss on her head.

She wrapped her arms around him, and the line of sweat pouring down his back gave him away. He could play it as cool as he wanted, but he'd been terrified. She didn't blame him; so had she. "How did you... Savannah."

"Uh huh."

"She was able to get away to call?"

"Nope." He kept her in his arms, his chin resting on her head as they sat together and watched Leo arrest Isaac. "She texted Leo."

"Oh, wow. I never thought of texting."

Hunt laughed, it started off as a chuckle, then got deeper and louder. He shook his head. When he got himself back under control, he sighed. "Oh, Gia, what am I going to do with you?"

She grinned and sat back. "Well, I have an idea or two."

His expression turned serious. "So do I."

"Oh? You first, then, what's your idea?"

"Nope. You first."

She leaned up toward him and captured his lips with hers, then fell into his arms to snuggle against his warm chest. The night had turned chilly, but there in Hunt's arms, she didn't mind it so much. It was actually beginning to feel a lot like Christmas. Except for the bum knee. That would put a damper on things. "So, what's your idea?"

He tapped a finger against her nose. "I'm not telling you yet."

"When are you going to tell me?"

"Tomorrow night, maybe, after the wedding. It's a Christmas present."

"Fine, then, I'll wait until midnight, but not a minute longer."

Hunt helped her to her feet and guided her to where Savannah waited beside her car, filing a nail.

She gripped her hands to stop her filing and pressed her forehead against Savannah's. "Thank you, Savannah."

"No problem." She stayed there a moment, then stepped back. "Thank you."

"Me? For what? Getting you in trouble with Hunt and Leo, putting you at risk?"

"Nope." She grinned. "Thank you for getting to the bottom of this case. Leo would have set it aside to go on our honeymoon, but his head would still have been partly up here with the case. Now, he can let it go, and we can just enjoy ourselves."

"Oh, is that how you're spinning this?" Gia laughed. Only Savannah could get away with that.

"You bet it is, and you'd better have my back on this."

"Every time, Savannah."

Chapter Twenty-Four

Gia smoothed Savannah's train behind her, then stood and checked to make sure everything was perfect. She hadn't seen Hunt since last night, but he and Leo had rushed in just in time to get dressed and take their places for the wedding. "You look amazing, Savannah. You are the perfect bride."

Savannah gripped Gia's hand and squeezed. "And you're the perfect maid of honor."

Tears pooled in Gia's eyes and threatened to spill over.

"Hey, you promised, no crying before the wedding." Savannah sniffed and laughed. "I can't walk down the aisle looking like a racoon."

Gia laughed and hugged her. "Wouldn't that make for some great wedding pictures."

One of the French doors in front of them opened a crack, and Trevor stuck his head out. "Are you ready?"

"Oh, man." Savannah sucked in a deep, shaky breath.

Butterflies swarmed in Gia's stomach.

"Okay." Savannah looked at Gia and nodded. "I'm ready."

Savannah's father slipped through the crack Trevor allowed and kissed her cheek, then let out a low whistle. "Well, I'll be. I ain't never seen a prettier bride."

"Thank you, Pa." She threw her arms around his neck.

"You ready, baby girl?" He hooked her arm through his elbow and patted her hand.

She fluttered her lashes a few times to keep any tears from tracking through her make-up and nodded. "I am."

"You got this." Gia squeezed her free hand, then turned and took her place in line in front of Savannah.

An organ started to play, and Trevor threw open the doors with a flourish, then stepped aside.

A winter wonderland lay beyond the doors. He'd had the entire courtyard covered in snow. Snowflakes fell in soft, lazy flurries from somewhere above them. An archway that looked like something from an ice castle stood at the end of the aisle. Even the evergreens surrounding the courtyard bore snowy limbs and Christmas lights.

Rows and rows of guests stood on either side, some snapping pictures, some crying, some staring in awe at the beautiful bride.

Gia took her time walking down the aisle, careful not to limp. She wanted everything to be perfect for Savannah.

Cole, Earl, and Cybil all stood together, with all of Earl's children and grandchildren. Skyla stood with Willow, who stood arm in arm with a young boy, her head resting against his shoulder, her grin wide. She waved to Gia, and Gia smiled back.

Four of Savannah's brothers and their families took up the front row. Her younger brother, Joey, was part of the wedding party.

Trevor hurried around the side aisle and took his place next to Zoe, his date for the evening. If Gia wasn't mistake, that might be the next wedding she'd attend. That made her smile even more. She loved the two of them together.

Two seats stood apart from the others, set off to the side near a path that led around the house. Harley Anderson, the homeless man Gia had befriended, who'd saved her more than once, stood with his old flame, Donna Mae Parker. He wore a suit and tie, his long graying blond hair tied neatly back into a ponytail at his nape.

And the tears she'd tried so hard to contain spilled over. Ah, well, she'd tried.

Then her gaze fell on Hunt, in his tuxedo, and her heart flipped over.

Hunt kept eye contact with her as she walked toward where he stood beside Leo. She hadn't seen him before the wedding, since he'd been caught up at the station, and she'd been with Savannah getting ready and keeping her from going too crazy.

He smiled, and the butterflies in Gia's stomach went crazy. Heat rushed to her cheeks, and for the first time, she could imagine she was walking toward a future with him.

Savannah and Leo said their I dos and pledged to love and honor each other beneath a perfectly clear sky with a full moon and millions of stars twinkling like Christmas lights. It was the perfect Christmas Eve wedding, a bond it seemed the entire community had come to share with them.

The wedding and reception flew by in a haze of perfection and joy, until the guests who would return to their homes began to leave.

Alyssa and Carlos were heading out, since they had to be back early in the day to cater Christmas dinner, which they'd also join them for.

"Thank you for everything, Alyssa. It was perfect." Gia kissed her cheek.

"Are you sure you don't want us to stay and finish cleaning up?" She slid her hand into Carlos's.

He smiled down at her.

"Nah, I've got it. There's not that much left. You guys go ahead and enjoy your Christmas morning." It wouldn't take long to quick load up the dishwasher with the dishes left from dessert. Alyssa and Carlos had already done the bulk of the work.

"Thank you, again, and Merry Christmas," Alyssa said.

"Merry Christmas."

Klondike hopped onto the counter, and Gia scooped her up and put her back on the floor beside Thor. "None of that, now. You stay off the counters."

She stretched and lay on the floor as if that had been her intention all along.

Thor scooted closer to Gia's feet.

She petted his head. "I know, it's late. We'll head off to bed soon, I promise."

He dropped his chin onto his front paws. He hadn't been getting enough attention lately. Monday, she'd take him for a nice long walk. Maybe in one of the trails he enjoyed so much.

Gia turned on the water and started washing the few platters that wouldn't fit in the dishwasher.

"Hey there." Hunt grabbed a towel to dry. "Savannah seems happy."

"Yes, she does. I don't think I've ever seen her so happy."

Hunt looked toward the doorway. "Me neither."

Gia lay a platter on a towel for Hunt to dry.

"Oh, hey, Merry Christmas."

"Merry Christmas. Is it midnight already?"

Hunt shrugged. "Close enough."

With all the people surrounding them throughout the wedding, they hadn't had any time alone to talk about what had happened with Isaac. "I assume Isaac will be spending the holiday behind bars?"

"Oh, yeah. Isaac will probably be spending the next twenty or so holidays behind bars."

She handed Hunt the last platter and started loading the dishwasher. "Did he confess to killing his mother?"

"No, he tried to worm his way out of it, but he doesn't have a chance. Not only is he going away for his mother's murder, but his father's as well."

"Really?" Gia hadn't seen that coming. Isaac had seemed truly broken up over his father's death.

"Seems the heart medication he gave us was also laced with poison, poison he wanted us to find so we'd blame his father's death on Jeremy as well." He sighed and shook his head. "He was so bent on framing Jeremy for the murders, he didn't bother cleaning up after himself at his own house. We found traces of belladonna, plus the hole he dug the bush out of to plant at Mallory's."

"How is Mallory taking all of this?"

Hunt shrugged. "She didn't seem all that surprised, to be honest."

Gia finished loading and started the dishwasher, then started to wipe down the counters. "How about Ethan? Did you find him?"

"He got pulled over heading up I-95 into Georgia."

"Was he arrested?"

Hunt searched through cabinets to find places for the platters he'd dried. "No. Not yet, anyway. We don't have any evidence he did anything wrong, so we have no reason to hold him. We were able to get a partial print off the pot with the belladonna plant in it at Jeremy's, and it belonged to Isaac. And we found Isaac's prints all over the wills you found at Jeremy's, both of which were forged, by the way, and the paper he was practicing her signature on. We suspect he planted both after he killed Jeremy."

"So Robyn didn't change her will?"

"Nope."

"And it was Isaac who forged the will to make Jeremy look guilty?"

Hunt nodded. "He knew it wouldn't hurt his chances of collecting the inheritance, since the signature wasn't notarized, and he figured it would point to Jeremy's guilt."

"Would it have if I hadn't come across Isaac in Mallory's yard?"

"Who knows?" Hunt shrugged. "Probably not, since Jeremy's prints weren't on the pages and Isaac's were, but you never know."

"If he was trying to frame Jeremy for his mother's murder, why kill him?"

"We don't know, but he told us the Christmas card you found from Ethan was sent to Jeremy not him, and Ethan told the police officers in Georgia he'd only gone to Jeremy's house the day he was killed because Isaac called and said he was going over there to take care of some business and asked Ethan to come act as referee." Hunt hung his damp towel over the oven handle. "The way we figure it, and we should be able to prove it, is that

Isaac planned to frame Jeremy and Ethan for Robyn's death and Ethan for Jeremy's death, and then walk away with all of the money for himself."

"What about Mallory? Wasn't she in control of the money his father left him?"

"No. He made that up. His father didn't actually leave him anything. It was all left to Robyn, who in turn left if to him, but she'd planned to change that right after the wedding. If Robyn had died after the wedding, Jeremy would have inherited everything." Hunt pulled her into his arms. "I have to run. I promised Savannah I'd be right back."

"Go ahead. I'll be there in a couple of minutes."

Gia started wrapping the leftover food. It made her sad to think that whole family had been destroyed by greed. But at least Isaac would pay for what he'd done, and he wouldn't be able to hurt anyone else.

As the clock struck midnight, Savannah bounced into the kitchen and gripped Gia's hand. "Come on."

"Where to?"

"It's Christmas! Time to open presents."

She dragged Gia into the living room, with Thor and Klondike on their heels, to where all of their closest friends sat around the tree. She bounced up and down, clapping her hands together like a child on Christmas morning, and for the first time, Gia knew what it was to be part of a family for the holidays. She lowered her head so no one would see the emotions choking her, as she stood beside Savannah with her hand resting on Thor's head.

"Hunt, you go first," Savannah called out.

"Okay, here you go, cous." He held a red and gold package out to her. Savannah took the package and punched his arm, then shot a finger in the air. "Hey, wait a minute."

He frowned. "For what?"

"Just wait." Savannah disappeared out the door. When she returned a moment later, Christmas music played from the surround sound speakers. She winked at Hunt and grinned. "Mood music."

He laughed and breathed in deeply. He blew the breath out slowly and took Gia's hand. He studied her for a moment, his gazes boring into hers, then kept her hand in his as he lowered himself to one knee.

Gia froze. No way.

Savannah grinned widely, hands clasped beneath her chin, tears streaming down her cheeks.

"Gia." Hunt kissed the back of her hand. "Over the past year, I've become closer to you than I've ever been to anyone else. You make me smile, bring me joy, drive me crazy..."

Quiet laughter slid through the room.

"You are my everything, my world, the love of my life, and I can't imagine ever being without you." He looked deep into her eyes, seeming to search for something within her. "I want to spend the rest of my life with you and Thor and Klondike. Please, say you'll marry me?"

"Oh, Hunt." She had no hope of holding back the tears. A year ago, she'd never have even thought of getting married again. The thought of trusting a man was so foreign to her, she thought it was something she'd never again experience. But Hunt had changed all of that. He'd stood by her side, given her space when she needed it, picked up the pieces when she fell apart, shared her joy. He was her world. "Yes. I'd love to marry you."

He slid a heart shaped diamond ring onto her finger, the Christmas lights from the massive tree reflecting from its surface, then stood and took her into his arms. "I love you, Gia, with every last bit of my heart."

"I love you too, Hunt."

"Woo Hoo!" Savannah hooted, and a cheer erupted from all of those gathered. A champagne cork popped. "Merry Christmas!"

Thor barked and nudged his head beneath her hand.

In that moment, Gia's life couldn't have been more perfect.

Recipes from the All-Day Breakfast Café

Gia's Vanilla French Toast

Ingredients:

3 eggs
1/2 cup 2% milk
1 tbsp pure vanilla extract
1 tbsp butter
6 slices Italian or French bread (each about 1 inch thick)
1/4 cup powdered sugar
*optional – sliced strawberries, blueberries, raspberries

Directions:
Whisk eggs, milk and vanilla in a medium bowl.
Melt butter in a skillet over medium heat.
Dip slices of bread in egg mixture, make sure to dip both sides.
Brown each side of bread in skillet.
Sprinkle powdered sugar over top, add berries if desired, and serve.

Cinnamon French Toast

Ingredients:

    4 eggs
    2 tbsp cinnamon
    1 tbsp butter
    6 slices bread
    Maple syrup

Directions:
Whisk eggs and cinnamon in a medium bowl.
Melt butter in skillet over medium heat.
Dip bread in egg mixture, be sure to dip both sides.
Brown each side in skillet.
Add butter (if desired) and syrup to taste and serve.

Keep reading for a special excerpt!

WHOLE LATTE MURDER
An All-Day Breakfast Café Mystery

Ex-New Yorker and local diner owner Gia Morelli is still getting used to the sweltering Florida sun. But this summer she'll have to deal with a more dangerous kind of heat—when she's hot on the trail of another murderer…

Summer in Boggy Creek has arrived, and Gia's best friend, successful real estate agent Savannah, is getting hitched. Now she's enlisted Gia's sleuthing talents in a desperate search for the perfect wedding dress. But when Savannah mysteriously vanishes after showing a mansion to a bigwig client, Gia investigates the house Savannah was trying to sell. The first clue she finds is Savannah's car in the driveway. Inside the house, they stumble on Savannah's potential buyer—dead. Someone had apparently closed the deal—with a two-by-four full of nails to the client's head. Soon afterward, a woman's body is fished from the lake near the same house. The townsfolk are now sweating bullets over the murders, and the heat comes down on poor Gia to find her missing friend, and track down the killer…

Turn the page!

Chapter One

"I can't believe people actually torture themselves like this. On purpose." Savannah Mills tapped one long salmon-colored nail against the top offender in a heaping stack of bridal magazines piled on the All-Day Breakfast Café's counter. Light reflected off the rhinestone heart on the tip of her nail. "I think it would be easier to elope."

"Oh, stop." Gia Morelli slid one of the magazines out from the middle of the pile. "You're not eloping."

"Well, what am I supposed to do? I don't want to have to start cutting people off the invitation list, but we can't afford what it would cost to invite everyone to one of these venues." Savannah rested her elbow on the counter, propped her chin on her hand, and sulked. "I don't understand why planning a wedding is so difficult. It shouldn't be. Right?"

Gia didn't know what to tell her. When she'd gotten married, the entire affair had been arranged by the company her ex had hired to create an event that would boost his status in the financial community. She just showed up the day of, stood where they told her, and smiled at his guests. She should have realized then where that marriage was headed.

"Hey? Earth to Gia." Savannah waved a hand in front of her face. "Did you hear a word I said?"

"Um…"

"Ugh." She threw her hands up and flopped against the back of the stool. "What kind of maid of honor zones out while the bride is on a rant?"

"I'm sorry. I'm trying to think of something that will work without it costing a fortune." But Savannah was right. The cost of a wedding venue was excessive, and she and Leo didn't have that kind of money. Gia had been saving to try to help them out, but it was slow going. And Savannah refused help from her father, saying he had a hard enough time just keeping up with the bills.

Easing the death grip she held on the magazine, Gia opened it to a random page and set it on the counter. If she hadn't known how badly Savannah had always wanted a big wedding, with her extended family and an abundance of friends there to celebrate with her, Gia would have whole heartedly encouraged the elopement idea.

An image caught her eye. A laughing bride and groom, still clad in their formal wedding attire, playfully splashing in the surf. "Have you considered a destination wedding? You don't have to go somewhere far away; I'm sure Florida is full of beautiful locations. Maybe the Keys?"

Savannah's gaze bored through her.

"What? It was just a suggestion."

Cole, a good friend who often manned the grill despite the fact he claimed to be retired, tapped the page she had opened. "They do look awfully happy."

Gia shot him a grateful look, then braced herself to earn Savannah's wrath.

"But that puts the cost of attending on my guests, and I already know some of them won't be able to afford to attend."

She couldn't argue that. The cost of traveling, hotel rooms, food, plus missing time from work would make it difficult, if not impossible, for some people to attend—Gia included, since it would mean closing the café for a few days, at least. "I know you want a big wedding, but is it really worth the stress you're putting yourself under?"

"Maybe you're right." Seemingly defeated, Savannah folded her arms on the counter and rested her head on them. "Maybe I should just give up trying to plan the perfect wedding."

Guilt nudged Gia. "Oh, stop. Come on. This can't be all that difficult. What are the most important things to you?"

Savannah shrugged and continued sulking, an unusual look for someone who was usually filled with energy and almost always saw the positive in any situation.

Cole handed Gia a notepad and pen.

"Thanks." She tapped the pen against the counter. "Come on, Savannah. Help me out here. What do you want most out of your wedding?"

She sat up with a sigh. "Mostly, I just want somewhere all of my family and friends can gather to celebrate with us without it costing an arm and a leg."

A seemingly legitimate request, and yet… Gia set the pad and pen aside and flipped through page after page of advertised venues, not that they hadn't gone through them all already.

"I have an idea." Earl, the elderly gentleman who'd been her first customer and had since become a good friend, took a sip of his coffee, then set it aside and grabbed a magazine off the pile. "Instead of looking for venues that won't cost a fortune, why not see about having the reception on the beach or in a park?"

Savannah sat up straighter. "You think that would work?"

Oh, thank you, Earl!

"I don't see why not." He flipped through page after page without stopping. "You'd have to set up a tent of some sort, in case the weather was bad, but other than that, I think it would be beautiful."

Savannah shook her head. She still looked semi-interested, but skepticism was creeping back in. "What about food?"

Cole grabbed the pad Gia had discarded. "What kind of food do you want? We could cater it, I'm sure."

Savannah frowned. "I don't want you guys to have to cater it. I want you to have fun."

Willow, the All-Day Breakfast Café's only full-time waitress, though that might change later if the woman Gia was scheduled to interview turned out to be any good, stopped to chime in. "What if we all pitched in to make the food ahead of time, then I could get a few of my friends to serve the day of?"

"I don't know." Savannah chewed on her lower lip. "Where would we keep the food? It's not like there are refrigerators in a park. And even if we did a buffet, the food would still have to be heated up. How would we keep it warm?"

An idea started to form. Gia glanced at the clock over the cut-out to the kitchen. Their late morning lull would be ending soon, and she wouldn't be able to do anything about her brainstorm until later on when Trevor opened Storm Scoopers, the ice cream parlor down the road, and she could talk to him. "If I can work out the logistics, would you be happy with an outdoor wedding, somewhere pretty that wouldn't cost too much, even if we had to have it catered?"

"Are you kidding me? I'd be thrilled." She tossed the magazine she'd been looking through back onto the pile. "I really only care that everyone can come and have a good time."

"Great, then leave it to me." Gia added her own magazine and Earl's back onto the stack, then shoved the whole pile on a shelf beneath the counter.

Savannah's already big blue eyes widened. "Seriously?"

"Yup, I have something in mind I think might make you really happy." At least, she hoped it would. Savannah was her best friend in the world. She'd been there for Gia more times than she could count. The least she could do was help her plan a wedding that would make her day as special as she was.

She took her phone out of her pocket and shot Trevor a quick text asking him to stop in on his way to work. "Now. Are we still on for this afternoon?"

"Yup. Two o'clock. I'll pick you up here so we can start gown shopping." Savannah grabbed a muffin from one of the cake dishes on the counter. "Hopefully, a gown will be easier to find than a venue."

"Well, it can't be much harder. At least, chances are, it'll cost less." Gia set a plate on the counter in front of Savannah, along with a can of Diet Pepsi. "Do you want a real breakfast?"

"Nah." Savannah waved her off. "Thanks, anyway, but my client is meeting me here any minute. We can have lunch afterward if you want, before we go shopping."

"That works." Gia offered Willow and Cole something to eat. Earl had already finished his breakfast, so she offered to top off his coffee. When they all declined, she set a plate on the counter for herself and put a banana chocolate chip muffin on it.

May as well eat a little something before she had to interview the potential waitress, a chore she dreaded. Hmm…maybe Cole wanted to interview the waitress while Gia manned the grill.

"Oh, wow, I gotta run." Earl stood and grabbed his fisherman's cap from the stool next to him. "I'll catch up with you guys later. I promised my daughter I'd pick up my grandson from soccer practice this morning."

"I'll see you later." Gia sat next to Savannah and broke off a piece of her muffin. She paused with it halfway to her mouth. A fruit cup would probably be a better choice, given that she was trying on maid of honor gowns that afternoon too.

Savannah glanced at her watch. "I hope Buster gets here soon. If not, it's going to cut into our shopping time."

Earl stopped partway to the door and turned back toward her. "Buster?" With her mouth full of muffin, Savannah nodded. "Mm-hm."

Reversing direction, Earl yanked his cap off and headed back to the counter. "Buster Clarke?"

"Yeah, why?" Savannah wiped her mouth and spun her stool in his direction. "Do you know him?"

Earl propped one foot on the bottom bar of a stool and leaned an elbow on the counter next to Gia. "Yeah, I've heard of him. Guy's bad news."

Savannah frowned. "What do you mean?"

"He's a two-bit hood and a loan shark. I know a guy who got in a little over his head with that man and wound up in the hospital with two broken legs."

Savannah gasped.

Cole leaned on the counter on the other side of Savannah, caging her and Gia between them. "How'd you get mixed up with him?"

Savannah shoved her plate aside with her muffin only half eaten. "He came into the office and sought me out. He's looking at an expensive house, the old Oakley Manor House."

"That's the one out by the fairgrounds, isn't it?" Cole asked.

"Yes. It's a seven thousand square foot house on five acres of property. It was a bed and breakfast at one time, but it sold a while back, and the owner never opened it again. He never kept up with it either, and it fell into disrepair, but now it's in the process of being restored as a private home. It'll go for over a million dollars once finished."

Earl scowled. "Guess crime is profitable, if Buster can afford a house like that."

Savannah ignored him. "If I can sell it before construction is complete, I get a bonus. A nice bonus that would not only help us pay for our wedding, but would also put me ahead of Ward Bennett for sales."

Earl looked at Cole, then shifted his gaze back to Savannah. "Let Ward Bennett sell him the house."

Savannah bristled. "Look, I've already invested a lot of time in this, and Ward will get a share of the commission as it is, since the Oakley Manor House is his listing. Trust me, I'll be careful, but there's no way I'm giving up this sale to that weasel Ward."

Earl scratched his head and put his cap back on.

From what Gia knew of Earl—which was a lot considering he came in for breakfast every morning and spent at least half an hour chatting with her, some days hanging out all morning long—he wasn't easily ruffled. If he feared for Savannah's safety, it was with good reason. "Maybe you should consider giving up the sale. I have an idea that will make the whole wedding cost a ton less, and it's better to be safe—"

"Enough." Savannah stood, lifted her tote sized, teal purse off the stool back, and slung it over her shoulder. "I'm not giving up this sale. And stop talking about him; he's meeting me here any minute, and I don't want him to walk in and overhear."

Earl glanced over his shoulder toward the door and pitched his voice low. "Why is he meeting you here?"

"So we can drive out to the house together."

He lowered his gaze and shook his head. "Would you consider doing me a favor?"

Done with the topic, Savannah fished her sunglasses out of her bag and propped them on top of her head. "What's that?"

"Take your own car, and let him take his."

She started to argue, but Earl held up a hand. "Look, Savannah, you and Gia are like daughters to me, and I'm only giving you the same advice I'd give any of my own girls. If you insist on doing business with that man, at least take precautions. Tell him it's getting late, and you have to meet up with someone right after the showing, so you've decided to take your own car."

Savannah caught her bottom lip between her teeth.

"It's not even like that's not true." Gia didn't know Buster Clarke, but for Earl to be so worked up over it, the man must be bad news. And Savannah heading out to a deserted house in an area even more remote than Gia's community with a man she didn't know but whose reputation preceded him, did not sit well. The thought of calling her boyfriend, Savannah's cousin, Captain Hunter Quinn, shot through her mind at warp speed.

Savannah pointed a finger at Gia. "Don't even think about it."

"What?" The innocent look she aimed for was probably ruined by the *'you caught me'* expression she was most certainly wearing. Sometimes, having Savannah's thoughts run so similar to her own had its down side.

"Listen, guys." She kissed Earl's cheek and patted Cole's hand. "Thank you for worrying about me. I really do appreciate it, but this is my job. I don't have a choice but to do it, even if it's not always comfortable."

"Are you sure, Savannah?" Cole leaned closer to her. "I'm covering grill, and I'm sure Gia wouldn't mind rescheduling her interview so she could go with you."

A pang of hope shot through Gia.

"Aww…sweetie, thank you." She kissed his cheek as well. "You guys are the best, but I'm okay. Buster hasn't done anything inappropriate either of the times I've met with him so far, and once was at the office after everyone else had left. He's been nothing but professional, no matter what he does in his personal life."

Gia stepped forward, a sinking feeling in her gut that she shouldn't let Savannah go alone. "Savannah…"

Savannah's gaze shifted past Gia's shoulder and out the front window. "Shh. He's here. You guys behave now. Please."

The front door opened, and a middle-aged man strutted in, his mostly black but peppered with gray hair slicked back with more grease than Gia scraped off the grill after cooking five pounds of bacon. His perfectly tailored suit hugged the solid build of someone who spent a good chunk of his day in the gym. He reached a hand out to Savannah. "Savannah, dear. So good to see you. I'm sorry I'm late."

"Um…" She glanced at Earl, Cole, and Gia grouped together beside the counter. "No problem, Buster, but would you mind if we take separate cars out to the Oakley Manor House? I have a meeting right afterward, and I'll need to head straight there once we're done."

He shifted his gaze to the trio beside the bar, looked them up and down, and then dismissed them to look at Savannah. "Of course, dear. That's fine."

"Thank you."

Buster turned and headed for the door without acknowledging any of them.

Savannah shot them a wink, then followed.

Earl whirled on Gia. "I'm not comfortable with this. Sloan was hurt really bad by that guy."

"Did he press charges?"

"Nah, Buster's slick. He had a couple of his goons take care of Sloan when he couldn't repay the loan he'd taken, then threatened to come back for his wife and kids if he went to the police."

Bile burned its way up Gia's throat. "What ended up happening?"

"Sloan learned a hard lesson about the dangers of gambling. He paid back every dime, including the astronomical interest, and was grateful to be done with the whole thing. Once he finished rehabilitation, he went back to work, though he still walks with a limp."

Gia's gut cramped. "You said Buster had Sloan's legs broken because he couldn't pay him back. Where'd he come up with the money to satisfy the loan?"

Red blotches crept up Earl's cheeks. "A friend loaned it to him."

"Did he pay it back?"

Earl shook his head. "Sloan's a truck driver with a pack of kids and a wife who doesn't believe in working. He has a hard enough time keeping food on the table without having to pay back that kind of money. That's how he ended up in trouble in the first place, just tryin' to make ends meet."

Gia hugged him. "You're a good man, Earl, and a good friend."

He blushed even deeper, then turned to stare out the front window in the direction Savannah had gone. "Then why do I feel like I failed Savannah?"

"She'll be all right, Earl. She does have to earn a living, and showing houses is part of that. Besides, growing up with five brothers and a pack of male cousins made her tougher than she looks." She hooked an arm though his and nudged his side. "And, I happen to know she carries a can of mace somewhere in that massive purse, and she's not afraid to use it."

Gia glanced at the clock. Three hours before Savannah was supposed to meet her back there to go shopping. She had a feeling it was going to be a long three hours.

Chapter Two

Gia wiped her sweaty palms on her apron, then tossed it into the hamper. This was ridiculous. She was the interviewer not the interviewee; what did she have to be nervous about? It's not like she had to hire the woman. If she didn't seem like she'd work out, she wouldn't hire her. But that was the problem. Gia's track record for choosing which employees would work out was less than stellar.

Although, Willow and Cole had worked out perfectly.

Besides, she could always fire someone if they didn't do the right thing. Of course, firing trumped interviewing on her most dreaded business owner responsibilities list. She sighed and took a detour into her office.

Coward.

A quick glance at the clock on her phone told her she wouldn't have to return to work before heading out with Savannah, so she took a moment to freshen up. She ran a brush through her long dark curls, taming them as best she could between the humidity and two and a half hours spent standing over the hot grill with Cole. She used a wet wipe to clean the dark circles from beneath her eyes, courtesy of the eyeliner and mascara that had run while she'd stood over the steam all morning, then reapplied a fresh coat of each.

And with that, she promptly ran out of stalling options. Ugh…She'd already left the woman standing out front waiting for the better part of ten minutes. It was time to—in Savannah's words—pull up her big girl pants and get this done.

With a new burst of confidence, she strode through the doors to the dining room and stopped short. Sweat trickled down her back. Only one customer sat alone, a woman at the counter sipping a cup of coffee.

She appeared to be in her late twenties, early thirties, mid-length brown hair pulled back into a neat pony tail. Her capris and tunic style shirt were neatly pressed. She watched Willow like a hawk as she finished up with the few customers still remaining in the shop after the lunch rush. Nothing about her screamed don't hire me, and yet…

Gia approached slowly. "Excuse me, are you Marie Winston?"

"Yes, I am." She smiled, stood, and held out a hand. "Gia Morelli, I presume?"

"Yes." Forcing a smile of her own, Gia shook her hand. "It's a pleasure to meet you. I'm sorry to have kept you waiting."

"Oh, no problem. Willow was kind enough to give me a cup of coffee." She gestured toward the cup on the counter. "To be honest, I'm not sure the caffeine was such a great idea. I'm already nervous, and it just made me more jittery."

She seemed friendly enough. And honest about her feelings. Which was good. She supposed. "Sit, please. There's no reason to be nervous."

Marie sat, and Gia moved to stand behind the counter opposite her. Then she paused. Maybe she should have taken a stool and sat. That might better convey the cozy, homey feeling she encouraged in the café.

She resisted the urge to roll her eyes, barely. This whole interview process was lost on her. She should have let Savannah or Cole do the interviews. Or even Willow. "So, do you have any waitressing experience?"

The woman twisted an engagement ring with a small round diamond around her finger. "Well, not really. I have worked retail for ten years, though, and I'm a fast learner. I'm good with customers, enjoy working with people, and I can provide several references."

Her disappointment at Marie's lack of experience came as a surprise. Had she really expected she wouldn't have to train someone? That they'd fit right in as if they belonged there already. That's exactly what she was hoping, since it had happened that way with both Willow and Cole. She reminded herself the most rewarding things in life were those you worked the hardest for. "Why do you want to leave retail?"

"Actually..." Marie hesitated. "I don't want to leave my full-time job; I just want to add hours. I was hoping I could work here part time on my days off, or the early shift, before my shift at the mall starts. My fiancé and I are saving up for our wedding next year."

"Oh, congratulations." She bit back her first instinct to ask if they'd chosen a venue. If she'd picked any of the ones Savannah had discarded, she might need more than one part-time job.

"Thank you."

Hmm...part-time might be a good way to start. Then, if she didn't work out, Gia could simply reduce her hours until she left. Of course, Marie probably didn't plan to work two jobs indefinitely. And her full-time retail job most likely provided her benefits. So, was it worth training her to have her only work part-time and then most likely leave after she got married?

She checked the time. Savannah would be there in a few minutes. Time to wrap things up. She shot the woman a few more questions for the sake of appearing like she knew what she was doing.

She liked Marie. Her answers were short and to the point, honest from what Gia could tell, and seemed to jibe with what Gia was looking for.

Even the part-time hours could work out okay. But she really hoped to find someone with at least some waitressing experience. "How are you with multitasking?"

A warm smile spread across her face. "I am a multitasking genius."

Okay, that might trump experience. Gia nodded. "I would definitely consider hiring a part-time waitress who is a multitasking genius, and I don't even mind offering training, but I do have a few more interviews scheduled. I plan to finish interviewing within the next few days and make a decision by the end of the week, say Friday. I will contact you either way, though, so you don't have to sit around wondering what's going on."

"Thank you." Marie stood. "I appreciate that. I do hope to hear from you. I think I'd enjoy working here."

Gia thanked her and said good-bye.

Cole passed behind Gia and hefted a bus pan full of dirty dishes from beneath the counter. "How'd it go?"

Gia shrugged, checking the time on the clock above the cut-out to the kitchen. Five after two. Savannah was late. She checked her phone for text messages, missed calls, new voicemails. Nothing. "Not as bad as I expected. I actually kind of like the woman, but she only wants part-time hours, and she has no waitressing experience. Plus, she's looking to earn extra money for her wedding, so she'll probably leave once she's married next year."

"Hmm…"

"That's it? Hmm?" She'd been hoping he'd offer at least a few words of wisdom.

He scooted behind her with the dishes to load into the dishwasher, which meant he'd already cleaned up in the kitchen from the lunch rush. "I figure you'll decide what's best, but it's not that hard to train the right person, so I'd say go with your gut, and pick someone who will work well with your current staff. It's not like you won't have help training her. Willow's very patient. And a year is a long time. You never know what will change within a year."

"That's true enough." A year before her move to Boggy Creek, Gia would never in a million years have anticipated Bradley's deceit, the destruction of her marriage, the trial, the death threats. Nor could she have foreseen her move to Florida, or the joy she'd feel each time she walked into her very own home and the café she'd dreamed of for so long. All feats she'd never have been able to accomplish without Savannah's help.

She flipped her phone over and over, checking the clock each time it came around.

Cole paused on his way to the kitchen. "Something wrong?"

"Savannah's late." She could call, but she didn't want to interrupt if she was in the middle of a sales pitch. Maybe she'd shoot her a text.

The front door opened, and she breathed a sigh of relief. It didn't last long.

"Hey there, Gia." Trevor Barnes waved as he crossed the room.

"Please, let me know as soon as you hear from her." Cole glanced at the clock as he resumed his trek toward the kitchen, his concern clearly mirroring her own.

Trevor pulled a stool out from the counter and sat. "What's up?"

"Not much. What's going on?" Distracted, she shot off a quick text message to Savannah, asking how much longer she'd be. She had gotten a late start, after all, so it wasn't surprising she might run a few minutes late.

"I don't know. You texted me and asked me to stop by. So, here I am." A shock of his too long in the front brown hair fell across his eye, and he shook it back. "Did you want something?"

"Oh, Trevor. I'm sorry." How could she have forgotten that? She needed to get her head back in the game. "I'm just a little distracted today."

"No worries." He grinned his boyish grin. "So, what's up?"

Gia's gut unknotted the slightest bit, and some of her former excitement returned. "I was thinking about something, and I wanted to run it by you and see how you'd feel about it."

"Sure thing."

She poured him an iced chocolate macadamia nut latte, a new recipe she was trying as part of her summer specials menu, and set it in front of him. "Tell me what you think of it while we talk."

She rounded the counter and sat on the stool next to him.

He sipped his latte. "Oh, man, this is delicious. My new favorite."

"Thanks." Gia laughed.

Trevor was a great boost to her ego, since he greeted each new recipe with the same level of enthusiasm.

She had to wonder if he'd ever admit he didn't like something. She had a feeling he wouldn't. Trevor was too sweet for his own good and had a hard time saying no to anyone, especially a friend. She hesitated. Maybe asking him to host Savannah's wedding at his house wasn't a good idea. She didn't want to put him on the spot, and he didn't often, or ever, invite people to his home.

If it was for anyone other than Savannah, she'd refrain. But the memory of Savannah's earlier disappointment prodded her forward. "This was just an idea, a brilliant one, mind you, but just one idea, so please don't feel obligated to agree. You can totally say no."

Trevor's expression turned serious as he swiveled his seat to face her. "O-kay."

"You know we've been working on planning Savannah's wedding."

He nodded.

"And she's been trying to find the perfect venue, but with her extensive guest list, everything is turning out to be too expensive. So, Earl suggested having the reception at a beach or a park, but that would limit what we could do for food."

Trevor's eyes widened. A slow grin inched in to replace his somber expression.

"And I was thinking..." When she'd first seen Trevor's house, she'd been both shocked and amazed at the beauty of the grounds and the size of the mansion. Even now, all these months later, she couldn't fathom boy-next-door Trevor living there. "Your house and grounds are absolutely gorgeous, more beautiful than any park, and—"

"Yes."

"And I thought maybe...Wait. What?"

He nodded enthusiastically, bouncing a little in his seat. "Yes, I'd be thrilled to have Savannah's reception at my house. I can even give her and Leo and the bridal party all rooms for the night before the wedding. We'll have a big dinner, and everyone can hang out together, maybe have dessert in the great room by the fireplace. It will be perfect. And everyone can stay the night of the wedding too, if they want, so no one has to worry about driving home."

"Wow." She didn't know what to say. She'd been hoping she could talk him into having the wedding there, and even had her arguments in favor of all ready, but she'd never expected him to so fully embrace the idea. "That's awesome, Trevor. Thank you so much."

"Of course. Savannah's a good friend, and so is Leo. I'd love to share my home with them." A blush crept up his cheeks. "It's not often I have company out there and, truth be told, it'll be nice to have a house full of guests for a change."

She jumped up off the stool and flung her arms around his neck. "Thank you so much, Trevor. You're the best."

He hugged her, then sat back, blushing all the way to his hairline. He waggled his eyebrows. "Hey, does that mean you'll dump the cop and go out with me?"

She laughed. Though she and Trevor had become very close friends, there was no romantic spark between them, on either end. "Not right now, but I'll keep you in mind just in case things don't work out."

He swallowed hard and pulled at the neck of his t-shirt, then looked around and stage-whispered, "Just don't let Hunt hear you say that. And don't tell him I asked. I've been on that man's bad side, and I am not going there again. Ever. He's scary."

She couldn't argue that fact, even though, despite a rocky period of time between them, Trevor and Hunt got along well enough. She pulled an imaginary zipper across her lips. "No worries. My lips are sealed."

Now that Trevor had agreed to host the reception, at least she had a direction to move in. "Okay, then, I'll need to figure out what to do about food."

"No problem. I have a fully stocked kitchen with a commercial stove, two ovens, and an industrial-size refrigerator. And I know a great catering company if you're interested. They even have servers for during the event, and their prices are very reasonable, and they clean up afterward."

Gia's mouth fell open. She promptly snapped it closed and kissed Trevor's cheek. "You never cease to amaze me, Mr. Barnes."

"Hey, what's going on out here?" Cole carried a clean bus pan behind the counter and slid it underneath.

"Trevor has agreed to let us have Savannah's wedding at his house. He's even giving the bridal party rooms for the night before and the night of."

"That's great, man. Savannah's going to be thrilled." Cole frowned. "Speaking of, have you heard from her?"

Gia checked her text messages. Still nothing. And it was two-thirty already. Could be she hadn't answered the text because she was driving.

She dialed Savannah's number.

After four rings, her voicemail picked up.

"Hey, Savannah, it's me. I just wanted to check in with you since it's getting kind of late. Give me a call."

Picking up on the tension, Trevor frowned. "Is something wrong?"

Cole answered before Gia had a chance. "Savannah was taking Buster Clarke out to look at the Oakley Manor House, and everyone was a little uncomfortable about her going out there alone with him. He doesn't have the greatest reputation."

"She was supposed to be back at two, and it's already half past." Gia checked her phone for messages. Still nothing.

Cole pointed toward the clock. "Maybe you oughta give Hunt or Leo a call and let them go take a look."

"Are you kidding me? Do you know what Savannah would do to me if I sic those two on her when she's in the middle of selling a house? Especially that house." But she had to do something. It wasn't like Savannah to run late without calling, even if she was working.

"Do you want to take a ride out there? At least drive past and see if her car is still there?" Trevor finished off his latte and stood. "I'll go with you if you want."

Gia glanced at Cole.

He was already nodding. "Go ahead. If she shows up, I'll let her know you guys went out to the house to look for her and tell her to wait here."

"You'll call me the minute she walks in?" Gia was torn between waiting for Savannah to get there and going to check up on her. If she did get back and Gia wasn't there, they might not still have time to go shopping.

"I will," Cole said.

"All right. Come on." Gia grabbed her bag, fished her keys out, and headed for the door with Trevor. "I'm sure everything's okay, but I didn't have a good feeling about her going out there after Earl was so worked up about it this morning, and my anxiety level is through the roof now that she's running so late."

Look for WHOLE LATTE MURDER, on sale now!

Printed in the United States
by Baker & Taylor Publisher Services